MISLEADING LADIES

Cynthia Smith

BERKLEY PRIME CRIME, NEW YORK

MISLEADING LADIES

A Berkley Prime Crime Book/published by arrangement with the author

PRINTING HISTORY
Berkley Prime Crime edition/December 1997

The Putnam Berkley World Wide Web site address is
http://www.berkley.com

ISBN: 0-425-16112-9

Berkley Prime Crime Books are published
by The Berkley Publishing Group,
a member of Penguin Putnam Inc.,
200 Madison Avenue, New York, NY 10016.
The name BERKLEY PRIME CRIME and the BERKLEY PRIME CRIME
design are trademarks belonging to Berkley Publishing Corporation.

PRINTED IN THE UNITED STATES OF AMERICA

10 9 8 7 6 5 4 3 2 1

THE INTERVIEW . . .

"Mother, this is Emma Rhodes. She wants to interview you for a book she's writing."

Alicia arose at once and came toward me with one of those neon smiles that you get from people who really don't know how.

"My dear, how nice to meet you." All of a sudden I'm worth getting up for. Here's her shot at fame and immortality. The writer gambit gets 'em every time. "How can I help you?" Suddenly the Midlands left her voice and was replaced by diction that was her version of the Queen bestowing a knighthood.

Don't miss others in the series:
Noblesse Oblige and *Impolite Society*,
featuring Private Resolver Emma Rhodes!

MORE MYSTERIES FROM THE
BERKLEY PUBLISHING GROUP...

CHINA BAYLES MYSTERIES: She left the big city to run an herb shop in Pecan Springs, Texas. But murder can happen anywhere... "A wonderful character!" —*Mostly Murder*

by Susan Wittig Albert

THYME OF DEATH	WITCHES' BANE
HANGMAN'S ROOT	ROSEMARY REMEMBERED
RUEFUL DEATH	

KATE JASPER MYSTERIES: Even in sunny California, there are cold-blooded killers..."This series is a treasure!" —Carolyn G. Hart

by Jaqueline Girdner

ADJUSTED TO DEATH	MURDER MOST MELLOW
THE LAST RESORT	FAT-FREE AND FATAL
TEA-TOTALLY DEAD	A STIFF CRITIQUE
MOST LIKELY TO DIE	A CRY FOR SELF-HELP

BONNIE INDERMILL MYSTERIES: Temp work can be murder, but solving crime is a full-time job... "One of detective fiction's most appealing protagonists!" —*Publishers Weekly*

by Carole Berry

THE DEATH OF A DIFFICULT WOMAN	GOOD NIGHT, SWEET PRINCE
THE LETTER OF THE LAW	THE DEATH OF A DANCING FOOL
THE YEAR OF THE MONKEY	DEATH OF A DIMPLED DARLING

MARGO SIMON MYSTERIES: She's a reporter for San Diego's public radio station. But her penchant for crime solving means she has to dig up the most private of secrets...

by Janice Steinberg

DEATH OF A POSTMODERNIST	DEATH CROSSES THE BORDER
DEATH-FIRES DANCE	THE DEAD MAN AND THE SEA

EMMA RHODES MYSTERIES: She's a "Private Resolver," a person the rich and famous can turn to when a problem needs to be resolved quickly and quietly. All it takes is $20,000 and two weeks for Emma to prove her worth... "Fast...clever...charming." —*Publishers Weekly*

by Cynthia Smith

NOBLESSE OBLIGE	IMPOLITE SOCIETY
MISLEADING LADIES	

To Edith Goldman, friend
and fellow mystery maven.

ACKNOWLEDGMENT

My thanks to Dr. Richard J. Brauer for his help in guiding me through the medical details in this book.

MISLEADING LADIES

I

I WAS ON my way to a few days R&R after a rather emotionally draining case that resulted in my voluntarily giving up the chance to be a duchess. Since I was responsible for the arrest of my aristocratic lover's uncle for murder and drug-running, thus causing the venerable family name to be spread across the infamous smut-'n-scandal British press, I presume I was not regarded as ideal daughter-in-law material by his noble family. That's their side of the story. From my point of view, although my mother would dearly love to punctuate her conversations with references to her daughter the duchess, as you get to know me better, you'll understand how difficult it would be to picture me spending my life pouring tea, opening bazaars, and having my panty hose peeled off nightly by a lady's maid.

At the moment, I was just looking forward to spending a small part of the $20,000 gratuity gift I had just earned. (I hate to use the crass term of "fee." For one thing, it's undignified. Secondly, the tax people react unpleasantly to the word.) I had booked myself into bed-and-breakfast at

Jeake's House on Mermaid Street in the medieval coastal town of Rye and was looking forward to roaming the marshes and walking its ancient cobbled streets.

When I entered the first-class compartment of the Charing Cross-to-Hastings train, a solitary young woman with an old-fashioned, maroon crushed velvet hat over long dark hair and the equine features of the British upper class was in the middle of the going-forward trio of seats. Piled on the window seat next to her were two Harrod's boxes and three Peter Jones' bags. She glanced up through horn-rimmed glasses and with a look of instant dismissal went back to writing furiously on a yellow legal pad. I sighed inwardly. I had carefully chosen a mid-morning train that would be more likely to have an empty window seat so that I could enjoy the sheep-dotted lush green fields of Kent. What I hadn't figured into my equation was that an off-peak hour train would have only two first-class compartments. I had already noted that the other one had a mother and two small children, one of whom was in the process of projectile vomiting. Unfortunately, I cannot ride backwards without getting queasy. So I broke my usually inflexible rule to never engage in conversation with anyone on a public means of transportation. (The only place I lift that proscription is when I fly on the Concorde, where the risk of being trapped by a garrulous chicken parts salesman is minimal.)

"May I help you to move your things to another seat so that I can sit at the window?" I asked.

She regarded me with that frosty unflinching look with which the English upper class usually preface some devastatingly rude remark to their perceived inferiors.

"I will take the window seat," she said in predictably purse-mouthed public school diction and then proceeded to move her belongings and herself. It was just that sort of aristocratic sense of entitlement that had contributed to my rejecting marriage to my handsome future duke.

So much for my careful planning for a pleasant, relaxing trip through the English countryside.

I had spent a good deal extra for a first-class ticket to insure that I could sit back and enjoy the beauty of Sussex. Now here I was stuck for hours in a compartment with a member of the western world's most arrogant, insensitive, and ill-mannered genus, the British Upper Class. I settled back morosely and got a flash of optimism. Maybe she'll be getting off shortly.

"Are you going far?" I asked hopefully.

"Tunbridge Wells," she answered without even looking up.

I didn't have a clue where that was and how long I'd be treated to her prickly presence.

"Well," I said brightly, and rather shrewdly I thought, "that should give you plenty of time to get your work done."

She looked up. "That is only one half hour from here, and I am not doing work." She hesitated for a moment and examined me closely. I felt like a horse at auction. She was apparently deciding whether I was worth conversing with any further. I guess I passed the test.

"I am getting a divorce."

Uh-oh. Here we go again. I sensed another one of those instant confidante situations coming on. People tell me things. I must project some sort of simpatica that makes perfect strangers reveal to me the most intimate details of their lives, often within minutes of our meeting. I have learned that even seemingly tight-lipped, tight-assed types are prone to pour out to me the sort of personal specifics that would make a bartender blush. My first instinct was to step through the private door she had opened. After all, that is how I make my lavish living. The second thought was to ignore the invitation. I really was not ready to become involved again.

"Don't make the mistake of being too soft," I said before I could stop myself. "The worst thing you can do in a divorce is to allow pity or guilt to affect your judgment when you make up your list of entitlements.''

Score one point for instinct, curiosity, and my insatiable Ms. Fixit complex.

She rested the pad and pen on her lap and turned full circle to face me, her entire demeanor now warm and friendly.

"That's just what my solicitor keeps saying," she said with a smile.

She jumped up and moved to a going-backwards seat. "Please, take the window," she said warmly. "I didn't realize you are probably on holiday and would so enjoy the passing landscape. Kent is actually quite lovely, especially at this time of year."

There are definite perks to becoming personal with people. If you happen to press the right button, you might even turn a potentially disastrous encounter into a rather pleasant one. Even a pit bull becomes friendly if you toss him a sirloin. I settled happily into my coveted seat but felt I owed her a little more conversation for my quid pro quo.

"It sounds like you have a good lawyer," I said. "But aren't there enough excellent matrimonial attorneys in London? Why are you headed for Tunbridge Wells?" I eyed her maroon, big plaid Jaeger suit which made her look like the sofa in a men's club, silk shirt, and handmade boots. The hat, held in place by two jewel-topped hat pins, looked bizarre but expensive. She was an example of that unfortunately not uncommon combination of poor taste and rich pockets.

"You don't strike me as someone who has the need to pinch her pence."

She laughed and her entire face changed. This might end up to be not too bad a trip after all.

"This solicitor handled Daddy's divorces when he was practicing in London. He semiretired to Tunbridge Wells last year, and I felt he was worth the trip."

I wondered who Daddy was. She held out her hand.

"I'm Juliet Bishop—that's my maiden name." She turned sad and hesitated for a moment. "I guess I'll be returning to it after the divorce."

Now I knew Daddy. Even if you weren't interested in the antics of the aristocracy, this duke's messy marital history would be familiar since it had been chronicled constantly in full prurient detail by the English press. He was a flake with a title—perfect material for the excessive front pages of the evening papers. Of course, when you're of the nobility, they never call you crazy—you're referred to respectfully as "eccentric."

I now regarded my traveling companion with interest. Titles don't impress me but money does. Before you begin to regard me as some superficial twit whose values run to bimbo-basic, let me give you a bit of my history. Like many mothers, mine reared me on the aphorism "It's just as easy to fall in love with someone rich rather than someone poor." My anti-parent rebellion took the form of dating a series of intellectuals and radicals whose I.Q.'s were higher than their weekly incomes. By the time I reached my late twenties, grunge had begun to lose its appeal. I found I didn't mind eating at dreary diners and cheap Chinese restaurants, but only if I wanted to and not because I had to. My epiphany came about when my untenured college instructor lover took me on his idea of a romantic weekend to a rustic cabin he had rented in a state park. He spoke passionately of Thoreau and the glories of back-to-nature simplicity, but the need to nurture my poetic soul was unfortunately outweighed by the discomfort caused by the lack of indoor plumbing and limitless supply of swarms of black flies. So call me shallow—I then and there decided that Mom was right. From then on, I began to look with great favor upon the well-heeled and have managed to make them the basis of my social and business lives. Look into your deepest heart—wouldn't you find it pleasanter to go by limo than by bus? And wouldn't you prefer dinner parties where you're served caviar and duck cassoulet rather than salsa and chicken nuggets? And don't tell me you wouldn't give up a week of heart-shaped tubs in the Poconos for a cruise in the Caribbean. Since my business and personal lives overlap (my clients almost always come from social involvements), I work for only the rich and famous. After all, they're just as needful of my services and they do show their appreciation so much better than those in less fortunate financial positions. I'm not a snob, I'm a realist.

I shook her proffered hand. "I'm Emma Rhodes," I said with an answering smile.

"Have you ever been divorced?" she asked.

"No."

I saw her glance at my ringless left hand, which meant I had to talk fast to head off the personal inquisition. I didn't want to hear the usual "But how come such a pretty, smart, etc. girl like you isn't married?" I'm weary of the assumption that no woman can be single by choice, tired of having to defend my opting for independence and my preference for lovers rather than husbands. My life is my business, but her life was mine. I was in it this far with her, I might as well press for more details.

"Why are you getting this divorce?" I asked. "Obviously it's you who wants it." Implicit in that statement, of course, was the assumption that no man in his right mind would willingly give up such a prize. A bit of flattery always works wonders. Only in this case, it was more than a bit. Which is why I was so startled by her next remark.

"I just cannot stand his insane jealousy a moment longer," she said with trembling lower lip.

"He was after my money," or "He was unfaithful." That's what I expected. But jealousy?

Juliet Bishop had the classic look of the British royals, which means a long face, slightly underslung jaw, and the long thin nose that they consider aquiline and I consider correctable. Juliet's tweedy bottom took up far more of the seat than any woman of her age should. And then there was the brown hair that just hung dead straight. The hat looked like something she had picked up from the Queen Mother's dustbin, and why was she wearing the weird object altogether? Often hopelessly unattractive women accept their limitations and wisely opt for giving themselves style and character. If so, her goal was commendable but her taste was not. She came off as the archetypical 1940s movie heroine who appears dreadfully plain at the beginning of the film and then whips off her glasses in the second reel to emerge as a stunning beauty. Only in Juliet's case, all that would happen if she removed her glasses would be to reveal small, uninteresting blue eyes. I don't believe that physical perfection is the sole requisite for attractiveness, sexual or otherwise. Some of the most charismatic people I know possess none of the elements of conventional good looks. And many of the men and women I have met who were born with perfect physical beauty are crashing bores, perhaps because they felt they didn't have to do anything more than present themselves to get instant admiration and never got around to working on their personae. But Juliet was not appealing, she was not adorable, she was dull.

"Your husband is jealous? That's not surprising," I said with a professional smile. "The assumption that other men find you alluring reinforces his belief in his own excellent judgment in picking you."

Lord, I'm good. She looked pleased. And then a shadow passed over her face.

"But you cannot know how impossible it is to live with. He's accused me of sleeping with my voice teacher—good heavens, the man is sixty-eight years old—and he's *Polish*."

Obviously one of the ethnic groups suitable only for musical interludes.

"And he insists on being there when my fitness instructor comes."

Now that's a little more understandable. Those chaps are heavily into exercise of all kinds.

"It is driving me mad. Even the hostler who takes care of my horses. Why, I've known Redmond since I was a little girl. He taught me to ride. Oh, he's quite attractive, I grant you, in a rather crude rough way. But how could Sidney think I could ever have an affair with a *stableman*?"

She had to be kidding. Half the ladyships I know are boinking their chauffeurs, and the other half are having it on with their gardeners. A touch of dirt under the fingernails titillates rather than turns off. The upper-class women I know look upon their employees as purveyors of services—and that means all kinds. Lady Chatterley may have been a fictional character, but she was based on real people.

"He follows me, he checks up on me. He disbelieves me. It's demeaning and often embarrassing. Now he's gotten it into his head that I'm having an affair with Geoffrey Fraser, a man I was with at university. Just because I went to hear him lecture at the Courtauld on Bloomsbury. Actually Geoffrey's a dreadful bore and I went simply as an obligation. Sidney came with me and was certain Geoffrey was sending me sly, intimate glances. The idiot, Geoffrey cannot see two feet in front of him, he's blind as a bat. But Sidney went into a rage when we got home. Perhaps it's because he is fifteen years older than I, which I keep telling him makes no difference at all to me. I simply cannot bear it a moment longer."

I've seen it many times, where an older man marries a younger woman and spends the rest of his life in delighted wonder that this glorious young thing agreed to have him. Never mind that she's a hopelessly unattractive forty-year-old who regards him as her last desperate hope for marriage in a youth-oriented society where men of her age are trolling for twenty- and thirty-year-olds. He never gets over how her clear eyes and comparatively firm skin are willing to accept his cataracts and love handles.

"What does Sidney do—for a living I mean?"

"He's an actor, and a very fine one," she said proudly.

"What's his name?"

"Sidney Bailey," she answered.

I recalled a sandy-haired man who played supporting roles, the kind of actor who has a familiar face but no name. He must be up in his late fifties now. Come to think of it, I haven't seen him on the screen for some years.

"Didn't I see him in *The Ipcress File* with Michael Caine?" That's one of those good old movies that come up on TV every now and then.

"Yes," she said with shining eyes. "Wasn't he wonderful in that?"

If that was Sidney's last paying job, he wouldn't be jumping handsprings about her wanting out of the marriage.

"I assume he's fighting the divorce."

She shook her head. "No—he told me he only wants me to be happy."

Right.

"How much is he demanding of your community property?"

"Nothing," she answered. "He even insists I keep the house."

"What house?"

"The one he bought for me in Kensington, right off the High Street."

Wait a minute here. I know the area and those places go for from 800,000 to a million pounds.

"*He* bought it? You did say he was an actor."

"Oh, yes, but he also has rather large real estate holdings. He owns buildings all over London."

Going back to my old man-young wife theory, if he's that rich, why did he ever marry *her*?

"He's a brilliant businessman, which his father was not," she said. "He grew up very poor, in the East End. The family business was almost in ruins, and Sidney was forced to leave his acting career and take over. It turned out he had a real genius for real estate, and he has built it into a virtual empire,'' she said with proprietary wifely pride.

Aha. The mystery is solved. Poor boy meets baronet's daughter. The British reverence for nobility is chronic. Humble Sidney will probably be forever dazzled by the fact that a member of the aristocracy is willing to talk to him, let alone marry him. When he looks at her, he doesn't see the plain exterior—he sees the awesome blue blood interior.

''Where did you two meet?''

The likelihood of them running into each other socially seemed remote, since they would hardly move in the same circles. Sidney is not famous enough or rich enough to break through the barriers erected by the English highborn.

''In hospital,'' she answered. ''Sidney was having some minor surgery done at St. Albans.'' She noticed that I looked puzzled. ''I'm an aide there. You see, I adored biology and science in school. But my scores weren't high enough to be accepted by a proper medical school, and Daddy and Mummy wouldn't hear of me becoming a nurse. So I volunteered my services to St. Albans; I've been working there for almost ten years. I'm even allowed to assist one of the neurosurgeons now in the surgical theater,'' she said proudly.

''So you met over a bedpan,'' I said.

She laughed. ''It was mostly the sponge baths that built the friendship. He was shy at first, most men are. What I tell them at first to put them at their ease is, 'I will wash down as far as possible, then I will wash up as far as possible. You wash possible.' He was my favorite patient. I can't say it was love at first sight for me—he looked godawful of course—but I grew very fond of him.''

I sat back and looked at her. ''You're still very much in love with him, aren't you?''

Her eyes filled with tears. ''Yes.''

''Then why are you divorcing him?''

She looked miserable. ''I really have no choice. I've tried

everything to convince him that I love him, that I'm not interested in any other men. Believe me, being brought up by parents such as mine, I long ago swore that when I married, I would never be unfaithful. Nor would I ever divorce. Now here I am,'' and she took out a linen handkerchief to wipe away the now flowing tears.

I really did not want to take on another case at this point, but this one had my name on it. The chance meeting offered the promise of the kind of trouble which I am ideally suited to settle to the pleasure and profit of all those involved, including me. Actually, it was just this sort of encounter that got me started in my unique profession.

I am a P.R.—a Private Resolver. Please don't confuse this occupation with P.I.'s, those heroic seedy loners who spend their lives tracking down malefactors, living in mobile homes with beer-filled fridges and vintage collections of McDonald's and Dunkin' Donuts cartons. I have three homes: an apartment on New York City's Fifth Avenue, a flat in Chelsea in London, and a house in the Portuguese Algarve. Like Kinsey Milhone and V.I. Warshawski, I wear turtlenecks, jeans, and sweats, but the balance of my wardrobe contains gowns by Givenchy, suits by Donna Karan, shoes by Manolo Blahnik, and bags by Prada. Unlike the earnest but underpaid sleuths so beloved of mystery book writers, I never get stiffed by a client, because I deal only with people who can easily afford my high tariff and like my terms, which appeal to the gambler and bargain-hunter traits so prevalent among the rich. I only charge for success. I either settle or solve the situation within two weeks or I'm out of there and no one's out a nickel. No up-front money, no daily rate, no expenses. It's a straight deal—I produce and only then does the client produce $20,000 or the equivalent thereof in any hard currency.

Why do I limit myself to two weeks? That's simple. I have a very low threshold of boredom and a very high I.Q., which means that's all the time I need and if it required more, I'd lose interest. That combination of little patience

and big I.Q. used to drive my schoolteachers to distraction.
I never saw the point in wasting my time and brain on
anything that I considered uninteresting or useless, which
resulted in constant admonishment for not working up to
my potential. Until finally, to get them off my backs, I
announced I was suffering from Minimal Focal Faculty.
Everyone being so hot on respecting learning disabilities,
and most being too insecure to admit their own ignorance
of this diagnostic term (which I made up), they instantly
accepted my behavioral aberration and thenceforth gave me
compassion instead of censure.

My 100% success rate is based on the fact that I only
take cases that interest me and that I believe I can solve
quickly. (If that isn't a sign of a high I.Q., then what is?)
I got started in my unique profession quite by accident. On
a Scandinavian trip I had been sent on by the Wall Street
law firm who employed me as an attorney, I met a woman
in trouble. During that memorable hydrofoil trip from Co-
penhagen to Malmö, I heard the sordid details of her life,
featuring a potential personal scandal that could have
wrecked her and her very wealthy and respected English
family. I figured out a solution within ten minutes, which
I didn't tell her, of course. People never respect fast answers—they're only impressed if they think you've worked
on the problem for weeks. I offered to resolve the matter
and gave her my terms, which I made up on the spur of
the moment. Two weeks later, she was ecstatically grateful
and I was $20,000 richer. One of the shining moments of
my life was when I handed in my resignation, telling the
stunned senior partner that I no longer wished to submit to
his law firm's indentured servitude of sixty-five billable
hours per week demanded of junior law associates so that
he and the eighty-six other partners could spend their days
golfing at Winged Foot. I had a new career that not only
paid better but gave me the time and freedom to enjoy my
earnings.

"Maybe I can help you," I said to Juliet.

"You?" She looked at me with incredulity. "How?"

People always regard me dubiously when I make this offer. You can't blame them. What they see is a 5'6" woman with a size 8 figure, long dark brown hair and huge brown eyes. I've always ignored the fact that I'm beautiful but have to forever deal with the reality that others cannot. It usually takes a bit of talking before they can get past that and realize I have a mind.

I explained what I did for a living and what I could do for her. I could see her eyeing my Burberry raincoat and cashmere scarf and trying to reconcile the image with Columbo.

"You mean you think you could stop my husband from being jealous and paranoid?"

"Not necessarily. But I could find a way that would enable you both to live with it."

She looked hopeful, but doubtful. "You say you've done this sort of thing before? Can you give me some sort of references?"

"I can't give you a list of satisfied clients because one of the things I guarantee, besides success, is total discretion. But I've worked out problems for people whose names you would instantly recognize."

That very satisfied lady from the Malmö boat continues to recommend me enthusiastically to all her friends. It's amazing how much concupiscence, cupidity, and stupidity is rampant among the rich.

"What do you have to lose, Juliet? All you need do is delay your divorce negotiations for two weeks. If at the end of that time I haven't alleviated your problem and you still find marriage untenable, it will have cost you nothing."

"And what will it cost me if you are successful?" she asked, obviously very much intrigued.

"The minimum I expect from my grateful clients is the equivalent of $20,000, in any hard currency, which is about 12,500 pounds."

She didn't blink an eye. I knew she wouldn't. In her

circles, that's the monthly American Express bill.

"Minimum? You mean they sometimes give you more?"

I smiled. "Frequently."

She eyed me narrowly. "You mean they're that pleased with your services?"

"I once received a Picasso painting from someone who told me what I had achieved for her family was priceless. Who can you go to to help you through a difficulty like this? A lawyer charges for every hour he expends on you, even if his efforts result in total failure. A shrink charges for every forty-five-minute hour and does nothing except ask how you feel about your problem. I charge only if the goal is achieved."

She looked at me speculatively. "You must be rather certain of your ability to succeed."

I smiled. "I won't take on a case unless I am."

She sat up straight, thought for a few seconds, and then held out her hand with a wide smile. "Done."

For the next half hour, I sat with the legal pad taking notes. She told me that Sidney had moved out of the house but they saw each other constantly. She gave me his current address and phone number plus a list of his friends, many of whom I knew casually or well. She got off at Tunbridge Wells to tell her solicitor to hold off, and we said good-bye with the assurance that I would be in touch with her in two weeks.

"Not before?" she asked in surprise. "You mean I won't know what you're doing until then?"

"No."

I find that little word one of the handiest in the English language, and I marvel at how little advantage is taken of its valuable properties. I could have told her that since she wasn't paying me per diem I owed her squat in the explanation department. And that I regard progress reports a time-wasting nuisance demanded only by deskbound bureaucrats or controlling clients, both of whom I abhor and avoid. Now should I have told her all this? She'd have only gotten pissed and then I'd have had to deal with her annoyance. It's easier to just say, "No."

I cut my planned five-day stay in Rye down to one, which just gave me time to visit Hilder's Cliff, from which you can see fifty-three parishes over Romney Marsh, and take my usual walk through cobbled streets that have not changed appreciably since the fourteenth century. I love peeking in the mullioned windows of the tiny, oak-beamed, crushed together houses that are a delight to look at but must be hell to live in. Whenever I see these types of pre-served dwellings I marvel at the British tolerance for abject discomfort. But then, this is a country where you'll see two Bentleys in the driveway of a stately home whose occu-pants walk around in custom-made clothing over woolen underwear because there's no central heating. In the winter, British upper-class noses run as much indoors as outdoors since both temperatures are the same, and unless you station yourself within three feet of a fireplace, your lips will turn blue (thus the term "stiff upper lip").

I enjoy antiquity but I'm not one of those romantics who sighs longingly for the simplicity and tranquility of "olden days." The frequent sackings and burnings by Danish in-vaders and the Normans, the bloody battling among various kings and queens for control of this strategically placed town made life in those "olden days" sound no less risky than a midnight walk through Hyde Park. And if you think that living in a quaint seaside village makes you impervious to big city crime, just check the local newspaper for all the ads for home security systems. I guess the answer is that there's just no place to hide from human nature. But I never failed to get a charge out of genteelly sipping tea in the Mermaid Inn, knowing that hundreds of years ago smug-glers and highwaymen used to haul their contraband into the cellars and cutthroat buccaneers were carousing right where I was sitting.

However, I did not forget my new case. That evening,

after having freshly caught grilled sole with a large mug of cider at a waterside pub, I made a few calls to friends in London. By the time I got back the next day to my flat on the King's Road in Chelsea, I had arranged an encounter with Sidney Bailey.

II

YOU'D LOVE MY flat in London. Everyone does; I lend it to friends when I'm not in residence. It's not opulent, but it's comfortable, spacious, and wonderfully located. Each one of my three homes reflects its function as well as the mood of its owner. The New York apartment, located on the tenth floor overlooking Central Park, is furnished with elegant antiques. It has two bedrooms, a study, three bathrooms, large kitchen with butler's pantry, and maid's room. When I come to New York, I get formal, and the wood-paneled dining room has been the site of many marvelous dinner parties. My casa in Portugal is a vacation house in a sunny climate and is furnished in Iberian Casual. I also have visiting privileges at the house where I grew up in Rye, New York, named after the village in England by emigrants who settled in our town in the early 1700's. My parents are there when they're not in their Florida condo. Or traveling. They are the ones who taught me the value of money; I don't mean having it, I mean spending it.

My London home is a pied-à-terre, a base for running around London, England, and all of Europe. The flat is part

of a block atop four floors of offices on the corner of the
King's Road directly opposite the Chelsea Town Hall and
Library. It boasts a huge terrace where I sit on Sunday
reading the *Times*. I've tried to grow flowers and plants,
but I'm not in residence for predictable periods, and things
seem to turn brown when I'm there and bloom when I'm
not. There are bus stops on both corners and taxis constantly passing by. Waitrose, an upscale supermarket pur-
veying a myriad of superbly prepared foods ready for the
microwave, is but a few doors down. It's known as a singles spot because the neighborhood is filled with single men
and women, and at six any evening when the after-work
crowd pours in there's more action in the aisles than at the
checkout. One can frequently pick up dinner along with
someone to share it with. They also offer a selection of
nonvintage *vins de pays* that suit my peasant palate. My
years in Portugal where I lived on Dao and other simple,
delicious native wines have made me scorn the cork-
sniffers who have to pass judgment on every bottle with
the portentous gravity of a magistrate deliberating the pris-
oner's fate. A laundry that offers two-hour delivery is right
next door. You can get a pretty fair ploughman's lunch at
the pub around the corner, and I'm only three blocks from
the Chelsea Kitchen that offers a crusty beef-and-kidney
pie surrounded by a mass of crisp veggies and chips for
just six pounds. It's the perfect place for solo dining. I have
many women friends who wouldn't be caught dead alone
at a restaurant for fear everyone would regard them as pit-
eous social undesirables who can't find a dining companion. There are those maître d's who send a lone woman off
to a table in Siberia, which means next to the kitchen or
toilets. To put a positive spin on their behavior, perhaps
they feel the pathetic reject would be more comfortable
hiding from public view. I adore eating alone. I set up my
handy-dandy folding book rack and quietly read, savor my
food, and enjoy observing the behavior of other diners. But
then, that anyone would think I was dining alone out of

anything but choice is to me unimaginable. I was never much concerned with "how things look," although I grew up with a mother who very much did. Oh, the innumerable times I heard, "But what will *they* say!" or "Is that what *they* are wearing?" Being a very logical child, my constant query, "Who are *they*?" finally put a stop to her articulating but never her concern with public opinion. Me, I don't give a damn.

I met Sidney Bailey on Sunday at a concert at Wigmore Hall. He was there with my friend Alisdair Twombley. I didn't believe the name either, but he is an Honorable from a very old illustrious family. Alisdair is an actor manqué who is involved in the theater and knows everyone in it. I figured he would know Sidney, and when I asked for an introduction, he told me it would be easy since Sidney was taking him to a concert and wouldn't I join them. Sunday morning concerts at Wigmore Hall are a unique London tradition. They take place at the odd hour of 11:30 a.m. There is no intermission, but ticket holders are served free sherry or coffee in the lobby afterward. And then off to that marvelous English tradition of Sunday lunch. Wigmore Hall audiences are attentive and devoted; most have been coming for years and are very proper and quietly respectful. Considering the damp English climate, I found the minimal amount of coughing a stunning tribute to both the performer and the famed British stiff-upper-lip control. The hall is small and acoustically suited to intimate performances. The whole thing was charming and civilized but unfortunately was one of the kinds of activities for which I never seem to find time. I was delighted to go.

I "ran into" Alisdair in the lobby beforehand, as planned.

"Emma, what a delicious surprise to see you!"

He put on his best happy-chance-encounter-of-old-friends performance.

"You look marvelous, as usual." After we kissed, he introduced me.

I was wearing my Carolina Herrera cream pants suit with black-and-red silk Liberty print shirt. Sidney regarded me with the usual admiring appraisal I expect from men but nothing more. Score one for Sidney—he's not a womanizer.

"Why don't you join us for lunch afterward?" Alisdair asked. "They just reopened the restaurant downstairs and I hear it's quite decent. We have a reservation for two, but I'm sure they can squeeze in another chair."

Since our tickets were not together, we arranged to meet in the lobby afterward. I lost myself in Alfred Brendel's playing and mentally kicked myself for having missed out on this pleasure for so long. After three encores demanded by an appreciative audience, I sought out Alisdair and Sidney in the smoky crowded lobby and wondered again about the British unconcern about carcinogens.

They both held cigarettes in their hands but no glasses.

"No coffee or sherry?" I asked.

"The coffee is instant and the sherry is piss," said Sidney in a sonorous Shakespearean voice that indicated repertory training. "Let us have lunch."

I liked him at once. Lunch was a performance. Sidney regaled us with amusing episodes of his career. His conversation in no way indicated that he was anything but totally active in theater at that moment. I've noticed that permanent identification with members of that profession. An actor could have given up acting twenty years ago in order to make a living selling cars, but he will forever consider himself an actor. Sidney maintained a steady chatter that was as nonstop as his smoking and drinking. I had two glasses of wine, my limit, and Alisdair had three. Sidney grandly ordered a third bottle of what I recognized to be a very costly vintage. What the hell, I thought, the guy's loaded—in more ways than one. Then Alisdair, following our prearranged scenario, announced:

"Children, I don't want to break up the party but I must pop in on Mother right about now. The old dear hasn't been well this week, and I promised to stop by. So why don't you two just muddle along without me?"

After Alisdair's departure, Sidney seemed to relax. The gesturing bravura and theatrical articulation cooled down and I realized that the performance had been for Alisdair, not me. Apparently Sidney was in his own way auditioning for whatever role he thought Alisdair might have influence in obtaining for him. If I hadn't known he was a millionaire real estate tycoon, I'd have taken him for an actor hungry for a job.

That urge never leaves their bloodstreams—I think if a dying actor was given the choice between life-saving surgery and a shot at playing Hamlet, he would opt for the latter.

He lit up yet another cigarette and leaned back. We were in a quiet corner and were in that lovely postprandial state of comfortable well-being after a pleasant meal of grilled plaice, new potatoes, and the ubiquitous sprouts. I always order plain grilled fish in restaurants that dress their staff in ruffled white aprons and matching caps. Such garb indicates a tearoom mentality that makes me avoid the fancy French dishes on the menu that the waitress can't pronounce and the chef can't cook.

"I'm separated. My wife is divorcing me."

Did I ask him? Did I in any way hint that I was interested in his marital or personal affairs? No. It's just as I told you—people just tell me things. It's a gift and at this moment, a very useful one. I was quiet. I long ago learned the interviewer's trick of silence.

"I truly love Juliet and I thought she loved me. She's a lovely woman—daughter of a baronet. Way out of my league, but we always got on. Had wonderful times together. There's a bit of an age difference, too, but that never seemed to matter. I've always tried to do everything I can to make her happy. Now she wants a divorce."

He ground out his cigarette, although it wasn't finished, and lit up another. "Do you know I always shaved before going to bed so as not to possibly irritate her face when we cuddled in bed at night?"

Next I was expecting him to tell me he never forgot to put down the toilet seat.

"My first two wives divorced me, too, you know."

No. I didn't know. I wondered why Juliet had forgotten to mention that little detail.

"They're wonderful women, my wives. I take care of them, financially, and I always will."

"You mean the court awarded both of them alimony?"

"No," he said, taking another long sip of wine. "It's something I feel I must do. I owe it to them."

"Why? Didn't you say they divorced you?"

"Yes. My first wife left me for a starving mathematician. When they married, the only things he had was a slide rule and the unpronounceable name of Lechwandowski."

He seemed proud of the fact. I guess it has more cachet when your wife deserts you for an educated mathematician rather than a man who siphons septic tanks.

"Then why do you feel it your responsibility? At the risk of sounding Victorian, what do you owe to a woman who broke her marriage vows?"

"We were married for eight years and she took care of me for all those years."

I was puzzled. "Were you ill?"

"No. But she took care of my home, cooked for me, shared my bed. She was my companion and wife. For that, I shall be forever grateful."

"How grateful?" I asked.

"She regularly receives in the neighborhood of four thousand pounds a month."

"That's a pretty nice neighborhood. Her mathematician benefits handsomely from your gratitude. With that kind of income, it's handy to have a husband who's good at numbers."

"I know that he'll never make a proper living and I don't want her living in penury. I believe they had a daughter. I feel it behooves me to enable her to maintain the style of living to which I accustomed her. I can afford it.''

The man's either a saint or a schmuck.

''No resentment that she abandoned you for another man?''

He shook his head emphatically. ''No. She fell in love. That's an act of God.''

It sounded like the script from a play that closed in out-of-town tryouts or a television Movie of the Week. I looked for signs of sarcasm. Good Lord, he's totally serious.

''How about your second wife?''

''We were married for sixteen years. We have two children.''

Aha. Another little oversight on Juliet's part. A lot of women are loath to mention a spouse's previous marriages. If she tells you at all, it's usually with some offhand comment about how he was only twelve years old when it happened or the former wife was a psychopath who threatened a secondary circumcision if he refused to marry her. The real story is she's ashamed because (1) she obviously wasn't sufficiently attractive to rack up a similar multi-marital history, (2) people might think all she could get is used merchandise, and (3) his lousy track record indicates he's not exactly a winner in the marriage department, which could be due to his lack of selectivity or performance.

''What happened to your second marriage?''

''She left me for a bearded musician who conducts chorales, a calling that keeps him running hither and yon seven days a week and produces barely enough to cover his beard dye, which he apparently does himself since he obviously hasn't seen a barber in twenty years.''

''And thus you must support them in the style to which you accustomed her,'' I added.

''I owe her a great deal, too. She is the mother of my children, she made us a family.''

''How much obligation do you feel to her?''

''She gets six thousand pounds a month.'' He saw my

look of stunned disbelief. "I do not feel that her adulterous behavior after sixteen years cancels out my debt for those early years. I am not from the current 'what have you done for me lately' school."

I've run into various convoluted codes of personal morality, but most of them lean heavily toward self-interest. This guy leans so far the other way that either he's bucking for Mother Teresa's job or he has some psychological quirk that makes him endow all women with inviolate perfection.

I shook my head in wonder. "You mean you sit at your desk every month and write checks for each one of these defecting ladies? Doesn't it ever, as they say in Soho vernacular, burn your ass just a tad to be diverting income to such undeserving objects?"

"The term 'undeserving' is yours, not mine," he answered. "Besides, I don't send them checks. I established a trust fund from which they alone derive the income in perpetuity. That way the funds continue to come to them even after I die, but the principal remains with me and within my estate."

"I assume the payments cease when they die," I said.

"Oh, yes indeed. It's not transferable to heirs."

"So you have made them into valuable golden geese to their spouses. Did you do that to insure the permanence of their marriages?"

"Yes, I wanted them to have stability. And to reinforce their sense of solid dependability, it's an irrevocable trust, which means not I or my heirs can abrogate it at any time. The mathematician died last year, and Alicia remarried some boulevardier-type who was probably attracted to her income. She has a daughter. Celia, my second wife, is still happily married to her musician. He seems to be a nice man, and my children are very fond of him."

This was said without a trace of irritation or jealousy. This man has the most inverted set of emotional responses I've ever encountered. Yet he does not convey passive or phlegmatic qualities. In fact, I get the feeling that there's a volcano bubbling below. I wonder what would evoke an eruption—and I don't think I'd like to be around when it blew.

He had finished a third bottle of wine and his speech wasn't even slightly slurred. The waitress had already replaced the ashtray four times. I wondered why Juliet was bothering to divorce him. At this rate, she'll be a widow in three years.

"Where did you grow up, Sidney?" I asked.

"In London, W5, near Dorset Road. And lots of other places in London, depending on the state of my father's business at the time. One year we would be well-off, and the next year we could be on the dole. We moved so many times that I went to eleven schools. I was a good student, too. I loved biology—I wanted desperately to be a doctor. But I never had a chance to get to university." He smiled bitterly. "I am probably the only Jewish boy in the world whose father didn't give a damn about education."

No wonder the guy's such an insecure neurotic with Juliet. Poor, uneducated, and Jewish—he probably still feels he has to enter her father's stately home through the service entrance.

"The lack of schooling doesn't seem to have harmed your education," I said. "Your diction and vocabulary are marvelous, and I've heard you make classical references that would be appropriate for a first at Oxford."

I may have been laying it on a bit thick, but not excessively. During the lunch, he had quoted from a number of esoteric tomes and displayed an almost encyclopedic knowledge of history. He demonstrated the frequent superiority of the self-educated who pursue knowledge by their own choice rather than that of their parents. However, I've always noted sadly that these admirably self-motivated and self-taught individuals suffer forever from a sense of inferiority for not having the conventional credentials. Now I understood Sidney's willingness to support the mathematician and the bearded musician. It's the unschooled individual's overinflated awe of formal education.

The dining room was emptying but there were still some other lingerers. We were on a roll here and I did not want it to end.

"May I have some coffee?" I asked.

"Good Lord, I am sorry—of course," and he summoned the waitress. I asked for a double espresso in the hope that Sidney would do the same; people usually follow the lead of the one at the table who orders first. I wanted the strong coffee, but he needed it.

"Make that two," he said.

"So your father was an up-and-down money type. What did he do?"

"Anything that would net him a quid," he answered with a snort. "Father was what you would call an entrepreneur. He looked for opportunities, and sometimes they came along and sometimes they didn't. Sometimes they turned out great and sometimes they bombed. Toward the end of his life, he turned to property speculation."

"Did he leave you a going business?"

"Oh, it was going, all right, going straight down the toilet. Properties all over London, riddled with debts. I had to step in and take over for the sake of the family. There I was, an actor, doing what I loved and just starting to make a name for myself—did you know I was in *The Ipcress File*? I had to give it all up. Although I still dabble here and there—you know, once an actor always an actor."

"You seem to have done well with the business. You must have talent for business as well as theater."

He sat back and looked rather smug. "I must say, I've done rather brilliantly."

So his father was not a role model. Someone had to account for his bizarre overprotective attitude toward women.

"Your mother must be very proud of you."

His face lit up. "My mother was a saint. She died five years ago. Even when we were at our worst, almost nothing to eat for my brother and me, she'd manage. We would come home from school and she'd be there with some treat for tea. I don't know how she did it. And no matter what hovel we lived in at the time, she would keep it clean and cheerful. Sometimes my father wouldn't come home for days at a time, doing god-knows-what, she'd never say a word. She was a wonderful woman. I saw to it that she was well cared for until the day she died.''

Was this where the need to take care of women started?

Now, you might reasonably expect that at some point in this litany of his life, Sidney would turn to me to ask, ''And what about *you*?''

Forget it. Men adore talking about themselves to an attentive female. If I were to break in with some facts about me, he'd look politely interested for three minutes and then instant MEGO, which is the journalistic acronym for ''Mine Eyes Glaze Over.'' Sidney was a lucky man today. He had not the usual merely dutiful female listener who patiently serves her time, but one who was sincerely interested. And don't think he didn't know it. Not just a man, but an actor with a live captivated audience? The guy was in pig heaven. You would think he might wonder why I was so interested in hearing all about him, but for sure the question never entered his head because the answer to him was obvious: he was utterly fascinating.

''So there were just the four of you in the family? How about aunts, uncles, cousins?''

He sat back and smiled. ''Oh, we had a great bunch of those. My uncles were in business with my father, so we saw a lot of them. I'm still close to them. I'm their big hero because not only did I save the business but I made them all rich.''

''How about grandparents?'' I might as well track down the entire tribe.

''Would you like more coffee, or dessert?'' he asked solicitously.

''More coffee would be lovely,'' I answered. ''I'll skip dessert, thank you.''

"I don't see why," he said playfully. "With your figure a bit of that gorgeous trifle I saw on the dessert trolley wouldn't hurt."

"This figure stays that way from avoiding dessert trolleys," I said, wondering why he had taken the unprecedented step of shifting the subject to me. The last query about grandparents?

I rubbed lemon peel on the rim of my cup and said casually, "Most children adore their grandparents. You know, love and indulgence without discipline, it can't be beat." He said nothing. "Did you see yours often?"

He was silent for a minute and fiddled with opening yet another pack of cigarettes. "My grandfather was a sad, bitter man. His wife ran off to America with their boarder and left him with small children to bring up by himself. He never got over it. And the family has never heard from her from that day."

No wonder he didn't want to talk about it. A quick change of theme was in order before he got too sad. There's nothing worse than a morose drinker to kill all productive conversation.

"Hey, you haven't said a word about your children. Where are they and what do they do?"

I hit the jackpot. His face lit up.

"Alexandra is an architect. She's married to an architect and they live in Salzburg. I bought them a house there. I fly over to see them often—they're both too busy to get away. She's just been chosen to design an addition to the university—the first woman to ever get such a commission there," he said proudly.

"And your son?"

He made a face. "Andre is a bum. He calls himself a composer, but I've never heard anything he's written. I doubt anyone has or ever will. Whenever I phone him at eleven in the morning, I've usually woken him up. My daughter is a workaholic and my son is a bumaholic," he said with disgust.

"Does he live in Salzburg, too?"

"No, he has to live in Amsterdam. For his music, he says. I think it's for the drugs."

I noticed the waitresses were looking pointedly at our table. We were about the last ones in the restaurant.

"Sidney, I'm going to Amsterdam on business next week. I don't know anyone there. It would be nice for me if I could maybe take Andre out for a meal."

"That would be wonderful," he said. "You'd probably be the smartest and best-looking woman he's dined with in years."

Notice not a word questioning what my business was. I knew I needn't worry about making up some cover story because an actor rarely evinces interest in anyone else's occupation unless it involves himself. I shouldn't criticize his behavior since how much different am I? My profession requires playing different roles in order to elicit information, which was just what I was doing right now. I'd been portraying the charmed female who was dying to know all the details of his emotions and life when actually I'd been putting him through an interrogation. Did I feel guilty for this dissembling? Not a whit. He had the pleasure of doing what he loved best—talking about himself—and I had the benefit of learning facts that should ultimately benefit him. The way I saw it, it was a win-win situation.

"I've met some of his friends—they look like the scruffy bunch that hangs around Trafalgar Square. But don't you dare pay for dinner. I send him enough money every month for him to afford to take you out. Here's his number," and he proceeded to write the address on a page he tore out of a small Liberty leather notebook. He looked up with a smile. "And while I'm writing his number for you, how about giving yours to me?"

We exchanged phone numbers just in time for the waitress to place the check on our table. With barely a look, Sidney dumped a wad of bills on the table and left a very happy bowing waitress. With that kind of insouciant spreading of largess, he must be surrounded by happy bowing waiters wherever he goes.

We walked out and opened our umbrellas automatically in the British reflex action upon exiting a building, exchanged friendly cheek kisses, got into taxis with Sidney's "I'll ring you" and my "Yes, please do" and went our separate ways.

AS I PUT my key in the door, I heard the phone ringing.

"Hello, Emma."

I smiled as I sank down cozily into the deeply down-filled couch and kicked my shoes off.

"Hi. How did you know I was in town?" I asked.

"My dear, you are speaking to a Detective Chief Superintendent of Scotland Yard." I heard a small chuckle. "Actually, one of my sergeants saw you at Wigmore Hall this morning."

"A police sergeant who likes Chopin?" I said incredulously.

"We're not all Philistines, you know," he said. "However, the sergeant was on duty—we've had complaints about a wave of pocket-picking there. It seems that when you music lovers crowd into the lobby for your post-performance sherry, you're too transported by appreciative euphoria to guard your personal effects."

Pretty high-flown language for a cop, you might think—but Caleb Franklin is not your ordinary policeman. A graduate of Cambridge, he rose to his high position within a fairly short time in spite of the Yard's unspoken antipathy to the elitely educated and to blacks. His nearly unbroken record for solving murders has made him a star in the department as well as a darling of the press. He's smart, he's great-looking, and he's my lover.

"Did you catch the blackguard?" I asked.

"Not this time—but we will. However, the police presence did act as a deterrent and there were no incidents today."

"Did the sergeant enjoy the performance?"

"She said she found it amazing."

"That's wonderful. Maybe you've expanded her horizons."

"You haven't heard why she was amazed. She couldn't believe all those people would sit still for that long listening to one chap banging away at a piano without even backup drums and an amplifier. So I think that puts paid to my Pygmalion career. How about dinner tonight?"

"You're on."

"Pick you up at seven."

Caleb Franklin was the descendant of a slave Benjamin Franklin brought with him to England in the 1700's. After teaching him to read and write, Franklin freed him, and he married an English schoolteacher and begat generations of educators. Caleb was the first in his family to enter law enforcement. What drew him to that improbable field was a John Wayne sense of right and wrong and a strong desire to improve the quality of life for his fellowman. To his surprise, he discovered a talent for deductive logic and an ability to persuade and lead that led to rapid recognition and promotion.

When I opened the door that evening, he was carrying flowers and two bottles of Veuve Cliquot champagne which he dropped to the floor and took me into his arms.

"You taste and smell wonderful," he murmured into my hair after emerging from a long, passionate kiss.

"Um," I said, "don't talk," as we kissed again.

He lifted his head and sniffed. "Mmm—something else smells pretty good."

"I cooked."

"I figured. That's why I brought the champagne."

"How did you know?" I asked.

We walked into the kitchen as he put the champagne in the fridge and I went about arranging the flowers in a crystal vase.

"It was the same reasoning that made you wear that

lovely simple gown with the single back zipper instead of a complex outfit that requires time-consuming removal,'' and he picked me up and carried me into the bedroom. ''Why would we want to go out when everything we want is in?''

He was a wonderful lover. The act of making love displays the essence of a man. I've had lovers who were skilled and physically satisfying. But to me, sex involves emotional as well as physical pleasure, and men who perform well but without heart are a turnoff. Caleb was caring and considerate as well as powerfully passionate. I knew that his concern with pleasing me was not as a macho measure of his sexual ability but as evidence of loving tenderness. We remained entwined in each other for a while.

''I'm hungry,'' I said.

''I assume you made some sort of casserole that awaits our pleasure in the oven,'' he said, kissing my shoulder.

As we sat at the candlelit dinner table, I watched him open the champagne. He had the kind of looks that were admired by men and women alike. Well over six feet tall, with a powerful body that owed its origin to genes but its maintenance to daily workouts, he had the coffee-colored skin and strong regular features that made you wonder why anyone could find fault with miscegenation.

He poured into the iced flute glasses and we lifted our glasses.

''To your new case,'' he said, smiling.

''How do you know I'm on one?''

He sipped his champagne and sat back. ''There's an air of electricity about you that isn't there when you're at rest. Remember, I've seen you both ways.''

I sighed. ''Having a Scotland Yard lover is worse than sleeping with a shrink. You lose your right to privacy.''

''Well, why don't we not talk about it until after dinner,'' he said, refilling our glasses. ''Let's not spoil this delicious food. You are a marvel, Emma—what is this superb concoction?''

"You may call it Danish Fisherman's Pie. Actually, it's Emma's Seafood Jumble—I made up the recipe."

"Which means, like all Emma's creations," he said, "it's fast and comparatively easy to make."

"Right. I love to cook but I don't have the patience to make a career of it. My specifications for a dish are a small list of ingredients and short time for preparation. What we have here are merely potatoes, onions, fresh seafood—this time shrimp and halibut—and a mustard cream sauce. You slice the potatoes and onions very thin—I use four cups of potatoes to one cup of onions—precook the potatoes for ten minutes, then alternately layer potatoes, fish, and onions in a greased two-quart casserole, salted and peppered to taste, pour the sauce over and bake for forty-five minutes in a 350-degree oven."

"What's in the sauce?"

"It's just a plain white sauce of three tablespoons of butter, one quarter cup of flour, and two cups of milk blended on top of a double boiler, then add two tablespoons of mustard and one half cup of dry white wine."

I piled some more on his plate. "It may not be as good as the food at The canteen, but it'll do."

"You mean Michael Caine's posh restaurant at Chelsea Harbor. Since the only canteen I can afford is the one at the Yard that dishes out only fry-ups and indigestion, I fear I have very little basis of comparison."

"Do you remember him in *The Ipcress File*?"

"Of course. I liked that picture."

"Do you remember an actor in that named Sidney Bailey?"

Caleb leaned back in his chair and eyed me with a canny little smile.

"Should I?"

"Sort of stocky, blond man—he'd been around for a while in small parts." I took more salad. "I met him today."

He walked over to his jacket and took out a pad and

pencil, then came back to the table and started writing.

"What are you doing?" I asked.

"Getting ready to take notes about your new client, darling. You're about as subtle as a British politician."

I was chagrined. "I thought that was a rather brilliant segue."

"Perhaps it was—for a plumber. But remember, I'm a detective. I assume you want information about Mr. Bailey. Do you suspect he absconded with the box office when they played *As You Like It* in East Uppingham?"

"It's not the actor side of him that concerns me. It's his other real-life role, the one that bought him a house on Allen Street this past year."

Caleb's face turned serious. "Now that had to set him back a quid or two. You want me to find out what else does he do to support that lifestyle?"

"London real estate and Isle of Jersey corporations," I said.

He sighed. "Another of Mrs. Thatcher's offshore millionaires. It's all legal, you know."

"I know. I never could understand why you don't block that tax loophole. How can you allow people who earn millions to pay no taxes?"

"The same way your country gives a free ride to the oil industry and farmers. Actually with us it's a tradition, and you know how much we honor traditions."

"Exactly how does it work?" I asked.

"There are these little old ladies who on the Isle of Jersey, Sark, and a few other tax-exempt territories situated off our coast who on paper are among the wealthiest women in the world. You put your millions or properties into a corporation nominally run by these ladies and a bank. They get paid for doing nothing more than signing checks and papers placed under their unknowing noses by the bank from time to time."

"But how do you connect to the corporation?"

"You are listed as the financial adviser or manager, for

which you draw a nominal salary—on which you pay nominal taxes. It's all a bit dodgy but it's done.''

I thought for a moment. ''People who go through these machinations are those usually willing to walk a fine line with the law, I should think.''

''Quite so,'' said Caleb. ''We have a chap who deals with these sorts of matters. He works closely with the Inland Revenue and knows where the bodies are buried and who buried them—fiscal bodies, of course. The other bodies come to me. I'll have him check into Mr. Bailey.''

He sat back and looked at me. ''So now that you've accomplished the reason I've been so well taken care of this evening, must I leave?''

''Not until you've helped me load the dishwasher and we've finished the second bottle of champagne—in bed.''

He sighed. ''Madam, you drive a hard bargain.''

I got up and put my arms around him. '' 'I do then with my friends as I do with my books. I would have them where I can find them, but I seldom use them.' ''

''Is that from the sayings of Emma Rhodes?''

''Another American—Ralph Waldo Emerson.''

He pulled me down into his lap. ''Equally eloquent, but surely not as sexy.''

I sighed. ''O.K., we can load the dishwasher later.''

III

AFTER CALEB LEFT the next morning, I phoned Juliet Bishop. I really hate to talk to clients while I'm on their case, they're usually so demanding. But Juliet was a well-bred lady. She answered my questions politely but ventured no probing of her own. What I needed from her were the names and addresses of the ex-wives.

I could hear the shock in her voice. "But how did you know Sidney had been married before? I don't remember telling you that."

Sometimes silence answers a question better than words. I said nothing. After a few seconds, she got the message that I would not be forthcoming about my means or methods.

"Actually, both of them live abroad. I believe that has something to do with the conditions of the trust fund Sidney set up for them from which they derive their incomes."

"Trust fund?" I asked in a display of shocked ignorance.

"Yes," she said. "He put aside a rather large amount of money to generate substantial monthly sums that go directly to his two former wives." Her upper-class upbringing that trains one to hide true feelings couldn't mask the umbrage that came through. Who could blame her? I know it's supposed to be civilized to maintain cordial relations with former lovers and spouses, but I prefer the men I'm involved with to have completely severed relations with all my predecessors and if possible to detest them thoroughly. I don't consider that attitude mean-spirited, just normal garden-variety jealousy.

That had to be a hefty trust fund. I did some rapid mental figuring. I was slow in school arithmetic, but somehow I find I'm a whiz when dollar signs precede the numbers. If my math teachers had based their examples on percentages of discounts in Loehmann's, I probably would have gotten all A's instead of B's. Sidney's fund was generating 10,000 pounds per month, that's 120,000 per year. To kick off that amount at say 5% interest, the principal would have to be over two million pounds. That's a tidy sum to be able to tie up and not miss.

"He's a generous principled man," she said. "Even when he could really use that money for his business, he would never think of touching their trust fund."

There was no admiration in her voice, only bitterness.

"Perhaps he can't," I said. "The fund may be irrevocable, structured to permit the principal to return to him only after the deaths of the beneficiaries."

"I'm afraid I don't know about such things," she said, sounding a bit more cheerful. It's certainly preferable that your husband's continued kindness to previous spouses is forced rather than voluntary.

"Where do these fortunate ladies live, Juliet?"

"Alicia lives in Prague, and Celia lives in Salzburg."

This was like pulling teeth. "What are their full names and addresses?"

"You don't mean you're going to see them," she said.

Silence again. It works every time.

"I don't have their addresses, but Alicia just remarried again, someone named Rudolf Sykes. I believe the man she left Sidney for died last year. Celia, Sidney's second wife, is still married to a musician named Edward Ramsay.''

"Thanks," I said. I hung up.

My next call was to Israel.

"*Emma*—sweetheart!'' As always, Abba's ebullience requires that one hold the phone away from the ear for fear of causing temporary deafness. "Where are you calling from, *ahuvati*—if you crave my body again, I can hop a Concorde and be at your side within hours!''

I smiled. He was obviously surrounded by colleagues and was playing to the stands. Abba Levitar is my closest, most trusted friend, and just the thought of getting into bed with his 5-feet, 6-inch, 250-pound body makes me giggle.

"Thanks, Abba, but I'll manage to quell my hot passion. Two cold showers ought to do it. I'm in London, and at the moment it's your mental rather than physical faculties that I crave.''

"Feel free to use any part of me, *motek*. You know that my mind and body are always at your disposal.''

"Who do you know in Prague?''

"What level of society are you looking for? Criminal or legal? Politically correct or government pariahs?''

"Nothing that stratified. I'm looking for an introduction to the widow of a mathematician named Lechwandowski.''

"That sounds more Polish than Czech.''

"Actually, he and his widow are English.''

"Hold it, let me ask. You're in luck. Our Prague specialist is sitting at my desk.''

Abba is a high official in the Mossad, Israel's internationally respected secret service. How a nice Jewish boy, a Brooklyn College psychology major, rose to the top of this elite corps that deals only with the prime minister is a story I shall never know since its operation and workings are classified.

"He says he knows a Lechwandowski family—a mother and daughter—but it can't be the one because he says they're rich, and from what I know of mathematicians, they usually don't have a pot to piss in."

"Unless they're smart enough to marry rich women. This one gets 4,000 pounds a month from an ex-husband in England."

He whistled. "That can buy one helluva lot of *palacinkas*. You say the lady's a widow? I'm ready to retire. Tell me she's Jewish and the *shidach* is made."

"What am I, Yente the matchmaker? First place, she's probably in her late fifties or early sixties—too old for you."

"Good," he answered, "so I'll inherit sooner."

"Second, she's Church of England."

"So for a catch like me, maybe she'll convert."

"And third—she's already remarried."

"Well, nobody's perfect," and he guffawed loudly.

He then gave me the name of a contact in Prague who would get me to Grace Lechwandowski, the daughter.

I CHECKED IN at the Palace Praha Hotel, put on jeans, a beige cotton sweater, and Nikes, and began my stroll around Prague to reacquaint myself with one of the most enchanting and oldest cities in Europe.

Rodin called it "the Rome of the North," Chateaubriand called it "the celestial Jerusalem," others have called it "the Czech Athens." What perhaps had always made it a magnet for artists and writers was the presence of three totally separate cultures—Czech, German, and Jewish, which afforded the advantage of being in contact with a wide range of creativity. The three ethnic divisions were so defined that there were separate banks, theaters, schools, pools, parks, coffeehouses. Prague's German press would review a performance in far-off Vienna, but ignore the guest performances of the *Comedie Francaise* at the Czech National Theater. Czech newspapers retaliated by refusing to mention Enrico Caruso's performance at the German Theater. The role of the Jews was to act as cultural medi-

ators between the two warring factions. Prague has also
been a city of folklore and occult legend, The Golem being
the most famous. This manlike figure of clay was thought
to be brought to life at the will of its alleged creator, "High
Rabbi" Löw, in the sixteenth century. It is a tale that has
fascinated scholars, historians, and playwrights for centuries.

There's only one way to enjoy a city—walk it. I never
could understand how people think they are seeing a place
when they view it through the windows of a bus, or learn
about it from the canned spiels of tour guides, or see it only
through the small lens of a camera. A city has a character
and a soul, and the only way to appreciate it is not to see
it but feel it. That can only be achieved by meandering
through its streets, taking the time to look up so that you
don't miss some fascinating architectural details, stopping
to sit at a sidewalk cafe and people-watch, maybe strike up
a chat with someone at the next table, getting lost and
having a delightful conversation with a native who manages
to convey directions even if both of you speak different
languages. You cannot get the sense of a city when you
embark determinedly on daily scheduled missions to cover
specified sites that have been arbitrarily selected by the department of tourism, who feel they must offer up a quota
of sights of interest for the tour traveler to report on to the
folks back home. Most visitors seem to dash from one place
to another on a timed pace that prevents them from coming
upon small treasures that may offer details of historic sig-
nificance but were not deemed "grand" enough to enter
into the guidebooks. You see them rushing about deter-
mined to cram in all the "sights" in the shortest possible
time as though accumulating notches in their belts. What
they miss are those chance encounters that offer insights
into what life is like in the city and often are the most
interesting and illuminating highlights of the trip.

I love wandering around Prague. It may be the only capital city in Europe that remains architecturally as it was

hundreds of years ago. This timeless beauty may be the only benefit bestowed upon the city by Communism. The harsh Soviet system imposed on the country created such a poor economy that little new development took place, leaving the exquisite Gothic, Renaissance, and Baroque structures to stand alone. No glass monoliths, no huge modern structures destroy its skylines—yet. Unhappily for visitors but happily for residents, prosperity is not around the corner but is upon the country and signs of progress are becoming visible which could transform the city into just another glitzy metropolis. But right now, you can enjoy seeing it as it was centuries ago.

Fortunately, there are marvelous elements that must remain untouched. Prague is built on seven hills like Rome and is divided by the Vltava River (also known as the Moldau, celebrated in the wonderful music of Czech composer Bedrich Smetana), spanned by a series of enchanting, graceful bridges. It is a city for romantic imagining. As I stood in front of the Royal Palace, I could envision knights in full armor charging on plumed horses up the broad magnificent Riders' Steps to celebrate coronations. I stood on Charles Bridge and saw views that would be familiar to the fourteenth-century architect Peter Parler. As I sat in one of the boats that cruise along the river, the unchanged facades of the beautiful old buildings that line the shores made me forget for a while that the rooms inside those apartment houses now had televisions instead of harpsichords.

I couldn't visit Prague without visiting the Josefov, the Old Jewish Quarter. First place, it is fascinating. And secondly, Abba would never forgive me if I didn't. It is a testimonial to the heroic perseverance of a remarkable people who, despite centuries of constant persecution, hold positions of world leadership and offer, as a group, the most outstanding contributions to the arts and sciences. Cramped together in a comparatively small area are ancient synagogues and other buildings that make up an enclave created

in the twelfth century. In 1541 and 1744, the Jews were
suddenly banished from Bohemia but returned. Their ex-
clusion from political and economic life and their enforced
social isolation from the rest of the population conditioned
the development of a characteristic culture in this small
territory. I walked down U Starého Hřbitova to reach the
most remarkable monument in the Town, the Old Jewish
Cemetery. Since the area of the cemetery was strictly limited by city officials, which precluded horizontal expansion,
the ingenious Jewish Town fathers built upward and new
graves were piled atop existing ones. As a result, in a comparatively tiny area, 12,000 graves in tiers huddle under the
elder branches. Mossy stones bear the carved emblems of
the tribes they commemorate; grapes for Israel, a pitcher
for Levi, hands raised in benediction for Aaron. Emblems
on some stones symbolize the family names; a carp for
Karpeles, a lion for Löw whose most famous member was
Rabbi Jehuda ben Bezabel, who built the legendary Golem,
which it was said he could bring to life by opening its
mouth and inserting slips of paper bearing magic formulas.

I gasp with delight every time I gaze down on the Old
City. From above, it looks like a Baroque warren of splendid domed churches and spires, and a russet-scaled laby-
rinth of medieval rooftops that gleamed in the late
afternoon sun. I got a kick out of learning that the slants
of tiles open their rows of flat dormers as a ventilation
device to dry laundry. Walking through its cobbled streets,
you come upon houses with facades and gables decorated
with pediments, scrolls, and pargeted men and animals.
Streets rise abruptly, lanes turn into corners in fans of steps.
Walking offers the fun of coming upon the unexpected and
making your very own delightful discoveries. I remember
stumbling into a treasure trove of small shops that were a
community of French merchants in the twelfth century. In
the center of the small square is a jewel of a Renaissance
fountain. These structures may not be considered by the
Tourist Office to be as important to visit as the monumental

complex of Hradčany (Prague Castle), but to me they bring an insight into the everyday lives of ordinary people hundreds of years ago that gives me a far better feel of the country and its history than cathedrals and museums. Of course, I'm not suggesting you skip the conventional tourist attractions. I'm a sucker for the famous clock tower on Staroměstaké náměstí where I join the crowd that gathers regularly on the hour to watch the sixteenth-century horological masterpiece mechanism activate a procession of the Twelve Apostles, with the bell being tolled by the skeleton figure of Death. In Salisbury, England, I always visit Stonehenge. And in Vienna, I like to stop into Freud's home, where his apartment is kept just as though he still lives there. And of course, I've been to the top of the Eiffel Tower many times. But my fondest memories of visits to foreign places are of finding smaller unexpected and unheralded sites that I feel are my own personal discoveries.

The Czechs look back proudly to the reign of Charles IV (Karel IV) in the fourteenth century when Czechoslovakia became the seat of the Holy Roman Empire and virtually the capital of Europe. This was their golden age when Czech was the language of rulers and subjects, and the king founded the university in Prague. Then came Austrian domination under the Hapsburgs, followed by the Thirty Years' War, which devastated the country and reduced the population by one-half. Since there were now fewer people left to tax, the feudal lords' incomes were smaller. So what did they do? Increased taxes, of course, which finally pushed the peasants' buttons too hard and they revolted. Which only serves to prove that government stupidity remains unchanged throughout the ages. This is the same wisdom used by New York City officials who keep increasing subway fares to make up for the decreasing revenues caused by defecting passengers who find other means of transportation to avoid the higher fares. Feudalism finally died in the mid nineteenth century and the Czech Republic became reality in 1918. The country was doing fine until Hitler took a fancy to it, and then underwent years of repression and economic devastation under first the Nazis and then the Russians. It wasn't until 1989 that the nation emerged from the oppressive Soviet yoke to join the free countries of Europe.

Today, Prague has become one of the hippest cities in Europe. Its low prices and unspoiled beauty attracts the young from all over the world and has created colonies of expatriates from everywhere, much as Paris did in the 1930's. The youthful presence is apparent when you walk down Wenceslas Square, which is the Times Square of Prague, and see the blue-jeaned and bearded gathering in the sidewalk cafes. It's not really a square but a broad boulevard starting at the Národní Museum (National Museum) and the equestrian statue of St. Wenceslas. It's a great street for strolling and window-shopping. I tried to avoid the jewelry shop windows because I'm a pushover for fine garnets, which are abundant in Prague, and I already have three necklaces, two pins, and earrings from previous visits. I stopped at a shop to admire the collection of antique pieces and spotted an unusual garnet-tipped hat pin. I had to go in to find out its provenance. The salesperson told me it was a one-of-a-kind early nineteenth-century piece, and the top was a replica of one of the saint's heads from the Romanesque St. George's Church. The workmanship was exquisite and I was tempted to bring it back for Juliet as I would if I saw any object that might please a friend. But good sense and reason prevailed. Gifting a client could tilt the relationship balance the wrong way. Who's beholden to whom around here? Besides, even in low-cost Prague, the price would make a major dent in my personal exchequer.

It was about three o'clock, which gave me an hour before my appointment. I suddenly realized I was hungry—the last food I had was on the plane from London to Prague which, like all airline food, was indescribable and inedible. I headed down toward the bottom of the street where all the action is, stopping along the way at a stand to buy a hot dog (that's what they're called), which comes with a blob of mustard and a slice of marvelous heavy sour rye bread, and brought it to the table of one of the cafes.

"*Jedno pivo, prosím,*" I asked the pink-cheeked waitress.

I always learn something of the language of every country before I visit; at least enough to cover rudimentary needs. After all, I am on their turf and the least I can do is try to make myself understood to them rather than the other way around. It smacks of British colonialism to do otherwise.

She brought an ice-cold bottle of beer within minutes, totally unperturbed that I had brought my own food. I love the wonderful laissez-faire attitude prevalent in European sidewalk cafes. People at adjacent tables were reading newspapers and looked like they had been there since breakfast. Just like New York, right? I once arrived early for a date and sat at a New York sidewalk cafe with a glass of white wine reading a newspaper. Within ten minutes, the waiter advised me that this wasn't the Christian Science Reading Room and what else did I want to order. There used to be a chain of counter-style restaurants in New York where the seats were specially designed to become uncomfortable after fifteen minutes. Come to think of it, the chairs in McDonald's don't exactly lend themselves to long-term lounging. In European eating places, time is not a factor, only service is. At about four o'clock, I asked the waitress for my check and directions.

"*Kde jesou Radost Cafe?*"

The Radost was the expatriate hangout where I would meet Abba's referral, who would introduce me to Grace Lechwandowski. Besides the fact that I love the man dearly, Abba is an invaluable resource for me. The nature of his work connects him to an international network of contacts that provides access to anyone anywhere in the world. If I ever needed to reach a Yak driver in Katmandu, Abba could undoubtedly set up the meet within a day.

I walked down a few steps and into a smoke-filled room that hummed with conversation. Every table for four had at least eight people crowded around it, some writing earnestly in notebooks, presumably their short life histories, others talking enthusiastically and it seemed at once. I heard German, English, French, Spanish, and Japanese. I stood at the door waiting to be spotted.

"Miss Rhodes?" A tall young man with a brown beard was standing in front of me, smiling. "You are very much on time. I'm Jan Malecek."

"How did you recognize me?" I asked as I followed his weaving through the tables.

"Dov's description was simple—five six, long brown hair, great figure, and very beautiful."

I looked around. "I think many here would fill that bill."

"Ah yes, but I know all who do. You are a new face and body so I spotted you immediately. We're pretty much a bunch of regulars here, so newcomers stand out. Especially if they look like you."

His English was public school British with an overlay of Czech. He looked to be about twenty-five, and I wondered if he was an agent or one of the sayanim, the civilian volunteers all over the world who work for the Mossad. He led me to a table at which four young people were engaged in what looked like a friendly but intense conversation. I smiled to myself; when you're in your early twenties, everything is of vital importance; the world seems filled with injustice, inconsistency, and idiocy, and if your blood doesn't come to a boil at least once a day, you're a hopeless wuss.

"Meet Emma Rhodes," Jan said.

They looked up and greeted me with no curiosity about my provenance. Unlike older people who have learned to hoard time and want quick explanations so they can judge instantly what and who is worth spending it on, the young just let things happen.

"Emma's a writer. She's here doing research." That was the party line Abba and I had planned.

I always identify myself as a writer; it's the kind of profession that provides the excuse to ask questions and explains my free high-living existence with no visible means of support. Announcing that I am a Private Resolver requires clarification that is a time-consuming pain in the ass. It's not an occupation listed in the Yellow Pages, and people assume that I'm a Private Investigator, which immediately relegates me to the social status of a process server or a washroom attendant. I explain my unique profession only to my parents, to whom I felt I owed some explanation since they paid for my expensive education of four years in college and three years in law school and were somewhat puzzled when I walked out of the prestigious law firm that that was supposed to be the dream goal of every young lawyer, second only to being a John Grisham or Scott Turow. I pointed out that P.I.'s dig up facts for clients who need that information to help them out of whatever jam they're in. They're like shrinks; they find out what's bothering you, but you have to work out what to do about it. I deliver the whole completed package. I not only ascertain what's wrong, but I right it. My mom and dad accepted my new occupation with the equanimity with which they accepted all my decisions. But then, I have unusually great parents. They provided me with love, moral and ethical values, and an education, and then allowed me to take over the rest of my life.

"What are you writing?" asked one of the young women.

"Emma, this is Grace," said Jan.

I looked directly at her and felt a frisson of surprise. Good heavens, she's gorgeous, but why didn't I notice it before? Long blond hair, blue eyes that slanted slightly, indicating some Russian Georgian in her ancestry that added a touch of exoticism to her perfect features, and the kind of cheekbones women would kill for. She had the face of a high fashion model—but not the persona, which was why it was so easy to overlook her beauty. Her carriage, the way she sat sprawled in the seat, and her lack of animation conveyed none of the confident self-awareness that such stunning looks usually engender. Worse than that, she was graceless and seemingly uncomfortable in her own skin. Whoever did such a job on her? She looked to be about twenty. Someone had to work really hard to make her unable to appreciate her God-given assets. I can't wait to meet Mama.

"I'm writing a book about marriage—remarriages, exactly. I'm looking for women who have divorced and remarried and created new lives for themselves."

"Why come to Prague?" asked one of the young men, who was introduced to me as Leif and spoke with a Danish accent.

"I should think you'd have a field day in the U.S.," said the American named Keith. "The high school I went to in San Francisco, every kid came from a divorced home. Like when I first heard the term 'nuclear family' I thought it meant people who grew up in Hiroshima."

I was ready for that one. When you're creating a cover story you damned well better be prepared to deal with doubters.

"A frequent aftermath of marital breakups is the woman moves far away to change her life completely. That's the angle I'm pursuing now. Prague is a big town for expatriates, and I figured I'd find people to interview here."

"Like my mother," said Grace quietly. She spoke in that soft tentative voice of people who are afraid to speak up because of not being certain of the value of their contributions. I'm not a great proselytizer for psychiatry, but this young woman needed therapy big time.

"Your mom has remarried twice, hasn't she?" asked Jan.

"Yes," said Sarah, the young Englishwoman next to Keith, "and her new husband is real dishy."

Grace flushed. Her face registered an expression I couldn't identify. Embarrassment? Shame? Fear? Hate? It was a mélange I found extremely interesting. Now I really must visit that home.

"Oh, I would so appreciate the chance to interview your mother, Grace. It would be a great help to me." I looked at her brightly.

She was reluctant, but I thought her first reaction to any new thing would be negative.

"Why don't you take Emma home with you now, Grace?" asked Jan.

Grace looked distressed. She was not eager for Mom and me to meet. I got the feeling that she was not happy about bringing anyone home. The lady must be a real treat.

"You don't have to if she don't want to," said Leif, putting his arm around her. The protective gesture and the way he looked at her made it apparent that he was very much in love with her. It was nice that she had someone who cared; this young woman needed all the TLC she could get.

"Oh, go ahead, Gracie," said Keith. "Your mom would probably be thrilled. I know mine would love to be able to spill her guts in a book. I never met a divorced woman who didn't want the whole fucking world to hear her side," he said grimly. "If she was dumped, she wants to lay it on the fucker who shit on her. If she's the one who pulled out, she's a wonder woman for having stood that cocksucker's abuse for so long."

Keith's pungent vocabulary reminded me of my college days. I chose to live at home while attending college after deciding that dorm life may sound like one long jolly pajama party but in reality could be a drag. Being consigned to a monastic cell with another person and her wardrobe and stereo didn't do it for me. I had my own nice big room at home, and I was an only child, which meant no siblings to impinge on my privacy. And I had parents who believed in guiding but not interfering. It was just a twenty-minute drive to school in my red FIAT (which I sadly learned stood for "Feeble Italian Attempt at Transportation"). I've always felt that the distance from home of the college of your choice is in reverse ratio to happiness in your home situation. Kids who went from Rye, New York, to Reed College, Oregon, were sending a message.

In my second year at Sarah Lawrence, the two most actively used adjectives in my conversations were shitty and fuckin'. This finally got to my mother, who had been an English lit major and revered language.

"You may be gaining an education, but you're obviously losing your vocabulary," she said one day. "Let's make a house rule. From now on, every time you use shitty or fuckin', let's see if you can give me two possible adjectives you might have used."

It became a challenge and made me clean up my act. Too bad Keith didn't have my mother—but who else could be so lucky?

Grace arose awkwardly, unfolding her lovely willowy body, and said with no enthusiasm whatever, "O.K., why not?"

Leif loked concerned. "Are you sure?"

She nodded. "I'm sure."

The house was situated a short cab ride from the center of Prague. It was set in a lovely tree-lined neighborhood of large well-kept homes. We entered a gate and walked through an extensive flower-filled garden where a husky young man was kneeling and carefully deadheading blooms, which he dropped into a wheelbarrow. He jumped to his feet when he saw us, although his hungry eyes were only on Grace.

"*Dobrý den*," he said shyly as he wiped his hands on his worn pants.

I answered, "*Dobrý den*" but Grace just nodded and walked on.

She was either unaware or unconcerned about his obvious adoration, just as she seemed to react to Leif. It was odd. Women usually react in some way to male approval. Unless he pinches your bottom, which one responds to with a kick in the groin, or hurls crude sexual suggestions on the street, which one responds to in kind, such as commenting on his probable lack of suitable equipment, women usually enjoy being admired. This young woman had all the earmarks of an emotionally battered child whose self-confidence had been so eroded that she could not accept let alone believe approval.

It was a large impressive house of russet-colored stone and red tiled roof. Tall windows were framed in decorative ochre stone topped by stone carvings of nymphs, birds, and emblems. Grace opened the huge, carved, arched front door and led me inside. We walked through a vast foyer backed by a wide, soaring, curved staircase at the foot of which stood an urn filled with tall flowers. She led me into the salon, where a woman was sitting in front of a huge ornate stone fireplace. I stood still in shock. Instead of the period overstuffed furniture that I expected, the room was furnished in stark, sparse, and obviously authentic Bauhaus. The austere lines of the minimal chrome and black leather furniture were in striking contrast to the kitschy exterior.

"My father was a mathematician," said Grace, when she saw my expression. "He worshipped simplicity," she said proudly.

"At the expense of my comfort, of course," said a petulant voice. "What did he care? He never spent any time in this room anyway—all he did was lock himself up in the study and play with his stupid numbers." It was the woman in the chair speaking with an English accent that bore the stamp of the Midlands. She was sipping from a cut-glass crystal tumbler that was filled with a brown liquid that did not look like iced tea.

Grace flushed angrily but remained silent.

This is Alicia, Sidney's first love? Apparently beauty was never one of his prerequisites for a wife. She was in her late fifties, with very light golden blond hair that had been

teased and sprayed into the kind of immovable object one
sees on women of a certain age. She had a wide mouth that
seemed to have no upper lip, a broad rather flat nose, and
very small light blue eyes which she tried unsuccessfully
to enlarge with a profuse application of blue eye shadow.
A mask of pancake makeup, penciled eyebrows, and bright
red rouge and lipstick completed the picture of unsubtle
artifice. Why don't older women realize that heavily ap-
plied makeup is heavily aging and gives them the look of
old hookers rather than young lookers? What added to her
unattractiveness was a sulky expression that discouraged
friendly overtures. This is a woman who would have no
friends other than those she could use. Grace got her col-
oring from her mother but fortunately little else. Alicia was
wearing a navy blue gabardine coatdress with brass buttons,
gold loop earrings, and a Cartier watch. I tried to see what
Sidney could have seen in her. Granted that it was many
years ago; faces change, bodies change, but one's nature
doesn't.

"And who is this?" She looked at me with the sort of
thorough once-over that you know is a flaw-finding mission. I have an aunt like that whose piercing appraisals
causes men to check their flies and women to start licking
nonexistent lipstick off their teeth. The highest compliment
you can get from such people is total silence. I passed mus-
ter. I mentioned I was wearing jeans and a beige cotton
sweater, but I didn't tell you the jeans were custom-made
for me in Milan last year and the sweater was a hand-knit
number that set me back five-hundred dollars. Women like
Alicia make it their business to notice such things. She was
the kind of woman who knew the price of everything but
the value of nothing.

"For God's sake, Grace, stand up and stop slouching.
You'd never know I spent a fortune on ballet lessons to
teach this girl poise and grace." She made it sound like
"poison grace." She barked one of those mirthless mocking laughs that my married friends refer to as the "mother-

in-law laugh" that usually precedes a zinger. "Grace—I certainly went wrong the day I named you."

I would have moved to Irkutsk to get away from this virago, but Grace just assumed a stoic expression and said nothing. When I was a child, there was a thirteen-year-old boy named Darren living next door who got tired of being belted by his father. One night while Daddy slept, Darren took a big rope and lashed him to his bed. When he awoke the next morning, Darren told him if he ever touched him again, he could expect an even more severe fate while he slept. Dad never touched him again. Apparently Grace didn't have the stomach or strength to rebel and had allowed herself to be beaten down all her life. Pity. But why does she stay?

"Mother, this is Emma Rhodes. She wants to interview you for a book she's writing."

Alicia arose at once and came toward me with one of those neon smiles that you get from people who really don't know how.

"My dear, how nice to meet you." All of a sudden I'm worth getting up for. Here's her shot at fame and immortality. The writer gambit gets 'em every time. "How can I help you?" Suddenly the Midlands left her voice and was replaced by diction that was her version of the Queen bestowing a knighthood.

I explained the thrust of my project and asked if she would allow me to interview her. I knew she'd go for it. The term "interview" conveys a certain glamour that is seductive. They get visions of Barbara Walters and themselves as Cher or Hillary Rodham Clinton.

"Of course," she said, now the gracious hostess. "Grace, why don't you ask Alena to bring us some coffee?"

We moved over to the black leather Corbusier sofa that was flanked by two black leather-and-chrome chairs. I sat down cautiously. The Bauhaus bunch were notorious for superb design that totally ignored the needs of the human body. I placed my tape recorder on the glass-and-chrome table and took out my notebook and pen. I go in for total authenticity.

I started by asking her what made her marry her first husband.

"Oh, Sidney—Sidney Bailey was his name—was a sweet boy and madly in love with me. He swept me off my feet. I was very, very young when we married, you see."

Of course. Most older women claim to have been child brides.

Sidney was not poor when they married, but he was on his way to becoming a millionaire, she explained.

"That must have been pleasant."

"Not really," she said, crossing her legs neatly. "To talk to him, we were always down to our last quid. He was always telling me how much money he was losing—not that I cared or knew about business. I fancy he thought that would stop me from spending. He was always giving me aggro when I bought a few things—had the screaming hab-dabs, he did, when I paid fifty quid for a hat at Harrod's. But you couldn't fool me," she said with that smug look of the stupids who think they've outsmarted the world. "I knew he had a proper bundle. I saw to it that I had every-thing I wanted." And then I could swear her eyes misted over. "Everything except true love." Straight out of a Bar-bara Cartland novel.

"You mean he stopped caring for you?" I asked.

"Heavens, no," she said, as though the possibility was unthinkable. How could anyone fall out of love with a prize like her!

"Then what happened?"

She sighed. "It was the jealousy."

Bingo! The word I'd been waiting for.

"He was jealous? How did he show it?" I asked.

"When I'd be off for a day with a friend, he'd get all stroppy and ask if I weren't with a man. When I was

visiting Mum and Dad for a week, wouldn't he phone twice
a day to be sure I weren't off somewhere with a lover. At
me all the time, he was, never believing me, never trusting
me. Me who never lied in her life, as anyone who knows
me will tell you.''

Don't people who claim they never lie realize that very
statement disproves their allegation?

I asked her for details about her marriage only because
I had to indicate interest in order to establish my credibility.
I was forced to listen to the usual divorced person's litany
of fancied or real injustices and hardships suffered at the
hands of the monster who they had mistakenly married.

''What finally caused the breakup? I assume it was you
who asked for the divorce.''

She looked at me pityingly. ''But of course.''

How could I be so foolish? Who in his right mind would
ever want to leave such a paragon of goodness and beauty?

''How did your families feel about this?''

''Mum and Dad were happy about it. They never cared
for him because he was Jewish. I always had to visit them
alone.''

That must have been a plus for Sidney. Sharing an overdone Sunday joint and sprouts in the Midlands with the
kind of couple that would sire an Alicia would constitute
a violation of human rights to someone like Sidney.

''How about your husband's family?''

''I wouldn't know. I never met them.''

I was startled. ''Not once in eight years?''

She shrugged. ''Sidney never brought it up and I certainly didn't care. Who needs in-laws, and Jews at that?''

I've heard of love being blind, but Sidney had to have
been comatose to marry this woman. But then, I'm often
amazed at how even highly intelligent men can be taken in
by blatantly excessive acts of love and devotion simulated
by predatory women. Other women can spot phony female
pretenses in seconds—why can't men? Probably their egos
convince them that her behavior is a genuine reaction to

their adorable attractiveness, in which case they get what they deserve.

I guessed I wouldn't find out anything about Sidney's family from this charmer. Something in his background must have accounted for his choice and treatment of women.

"How did Sidney react to your request for a divorce?"

"He pleaded with me to stay. But I had met Sergei." Enter the bearded mathematician stage right.

"Where did you meet him?"

"I was taking a course at our local university. I've always believed one must improve oneself," she said with a self-satisfied smile.

I was impressed. "What kind of math did you study?" I asked.

"Math? Don't be ridiculous. What would I want with that useless gibberish?"

I'm glad Einstein and Euclid aren't listening.

"I studied flower arranging," she said proudly.

Well, that ought to make the world a better place.

"We met at the canteen. We shared a table one afternoon. Sergei taught mathematics at the school. We began to meet for tea every day. He was so sympathetic. I could tell him how Sidney was hounding me and he was so understanding. One thing led to another, and we fell in love."

"What else did Sergei do besides teach?" I looked around the room appraisingly. "Apparently he was able to provide for you quite handsomely."

She gave a little snort. "If we lived on what he brought home we would be in a bed-sitter in Aldershot. Sidney takes care of me."

I looked properly surprised.

"But alimony usually ceases when the recipient remarries."

She looked smug. "It is not alimony that I get. Sidney set up some sort of trust fund that pays me a nice income for the rest of my life."

"That's quite decent of him."

She looked surprised, as though that concept had never entered her head. "He just doesn't want to see me living like a dustman's wife."

"But why should he care?" I asked innocently. "It was you who left him."

"My dear, don't you understand? Sidney still loves me!" she said triumphantly.

As I said earlier, the man's either a saint or a schmuck.

"What made you move to Prague?" I asked.

"Well, the money comes from one of Sidney's businesses—I don't understand that sort of thing, but I must keep out of England in order to get it. We lived in Germany for many years but moved to Prague in 1989 because Sergei said our money would go much further here. He died last year." Her face lit up. "And then I met Rudy."

As though on cue, the door opened and in came a tall slim man right out of a Noel Coward drawing room. He was wearing a blue paisley silk dressing gown and an ascot, for God's sakes, and to top off the perfect picture of a 1920's sophisticate, was smoking a cigarette in a holder. He was quite handsome if you go for the oily, sleek continental type. I happened to glance over to Grace and was stunned by the transformation. Her usual blank phlegmatic expression was replaced by a look of ecstatic adoration. She looked at him so passionately and longingly that it was almost painful to witness. He glanced her way for a split second and the whole story became apparent. They were lovers. That's why she can't leave home to be free of that vicious harridan. The entire tawdry scenario was so apparent to me that I looked over at Alicia to see how she handled this bizarre situation. Nothing. Her face registered only total joy. The woman was too vain and stupid to see anyone else as a threat to her.

"Darling, are you feeling better?" She turned to me. "Poor Roly-Poly was so exhausted. He just got back from a business trip to Moscow and I insisted he have a bit of a lie-down.''

That accounts for the bedroom attire at four in the afternoon. Moscow would be the perfect business venue for Mr. Sykes. He looks like the type who would deal in anything that fell off the back of a truck that could be flogged for black market rubles.

''Darling, this is Emma Rhodes.'' She had walked over to him, and he put his arm around her. ''She's a writer and she's going to put me into her book.''

Are you wondering if my conscience should feel troubled by my deception? Forget it. First place, that there might never be such a book isn't a problem because everyone knows not all writers' manuscripts make it into publication. As for the possibility that this woman might feel betrayed and used if she knew the truth—terrific, she deserves a little hammering.

''This is my husband, Rudolf Sykes,'' she said proudly.

He looked to be about ten years younger than she, which would put him in the late forties. He came up to me with a broad smile, and I wondered who paid for those perfectly capped teeth. He took my hand and for a moment I thought he intended to kiss it.

''It is a pleasure to meet you, Miss Rhodes.''

I would guess he started life as Rastislav Shashlik or something like it. Slavic origins were in his accent, and the pseudo courtly manner indicated growing up in a poor country that only had very old movies on the telly. When he assumed a pose in front of the massively carved fireplace with a foot on the massive brass fender, Paul Henreid came to mind.

A white aproned woman entered carrying a silver tray bearing a coffee service. She set it down on the table between us.

''Darling,'' Alicia said lovingly to her husband. ''We're just having coffee. Won't you join us? That will be all, Alena,'' she said grandly. She was apparently attempting

the role of lady of the house, but her Wolverhampton background just couldn't quite carry it off. She poured too much
coffee in each cup to allow room for cream. Luckily I drink
it black. Then she dipped her own spoon in the sugar bowl
instead of using the proper serving piece. She genteelly
passed around the pastries, and then greedily attacked the
two apple tarts and cream cakes on her plate. When Grace
reached for a second tart, she said sharply, "You don't need
that, Grace. You'll get fat."

The woman is incredible. Grace looks like she could put
away the entire tray with no effect on her model's slender
body, while the brass buttons on Alicia's coatdress were
pulling so badly across her protruding stomach that I moved
out of the line of fire to avoid getting wounded when they
start popping off. You may be wondering why I haven't
interjected any counter comments when Mama made her
vile attacks on her daughter. Believe me, I was sorely
tempted. As you can probably figure by now, keeping my
mouth shut is very much out of character. But this is not a
social visit. I would dearly enjoy a bit of termagent-
trashing, but that would antagonize my subject and end our
interview. Insofar as defending Grace from that destructive
bitch, the pattern of their relationship was established long
before I came on the scene and unless Grace herself does
something to stop it, it will continue forever. Alicia is one
of those women who should never have become a parent.
She is too self-involved to give herself to the demands of
bringing up a child, and she views her daughter as a com-
petitor rather than a source of pride. That dumpy unattractive woman cannot bear to be overshadowed by her
beautiful daughter and has spent her life in a corrosive campaign to demean and destroy the girl. I must say I get a
little fiendish pleasure thinking how she will react when
she finds out that Grace's loveliness has caught the eye of
her husband and that her worst fears have been realized:
her daughter has stolen her man.

Grace was so used to her mother's haranguing that she

didn't even blink. I noticed that lover-boy gave her a small sympathetic smile and she glowed. Mama was too busy stuffing her face to notice.

"And what do you do, Mr. Sykes?" I asked.

"He's in finance," said Alicia proudly.

That could cover anything from loan-sharking to book-making.

"I handle investments for people," he said grandly.

I looked terribly impressed. "Could you give me some of their names?" I asked. "It adds authenticity when I describe the details of your business."

He didn't miss a beat. "My client list is confidential," he said.

Nonexistent would probably describe it better.

Both the women beamed at him. The guy has it made. He has two adoring women, one for support and one for sex. The old bag keeps him in the style to which he has apparently become quite accustomed; that silk dressing gown did not come from Marks and Spencer. It's a lot easier to pretend ardor with a fifty-eight-year-old body when a nubile one awaits you just down the hall.

I closed up my notebook and turned off my tape recorder. "I thank you very much, Mrs. Sykes. I think I have all I'll need. And thanks so much for the coffee." I got up to leave.

"Would you like me to phone a cab for you?" asked Rudy.

"Yes, please." I headed for the door. "I'll wait outside. I'd like to enjoy your garden."

"I'll come with you," said Grace.

We walked around the grounds for a few minutes.

"Where can it all end, Grace?" I asked.

I know I should keep my nose out of it, but I'm naturally drawn to situations where nice people can get hurt in the hope that I can somehow prevent it. I consider myself in one of the helping professions and there is no such thing as "off-duty."

She looked frightened. "What do you mean?"

"Come on, Grace. Your mother may be too dense and self-congratulatory to see it, but it's apparent that you and your stepfather are having an affair."

She stopped dead. "How did you know?"

I sighed. "Don't you realize that your whole body language and demeanor changed the minute he came in the room? And the little intimate looks you exchange give the whole game away. At some point she'll find out and then what will you do?"

"Then Rudy and I will leave," she said defiantly.

"Correction, my dear. You will leave."

"Rudy loves me. He'll want to go with me."

I'm fifteen years older than she, but I felt like fifty years older.

"Rudy may love you, but he loves security more. He'll go where the money is, Grace. You can bet on it."

"You're wrong," she said hotly.

She'll fight me tooth and nail, but some of what I am saying will sink in eventually. It always does. I've used this technique before to alert unwary people to the evils of others, and it's a thankless task. We may no longer kill the bearer of bad tidings, but we sure as hell would love to.

"Grace, what do you think attracted him to your mother in the first place? Her charm and sweet disposition? He's a man who likes good living, and he needs someone to give it to him. If it comes to a toss-up between her and you, you'll lose."

The cab arrived. As I got in, I turned back to her. "Be careful, Grace."

WHEN I GOT back to my hotel, I found a phone message from Jan Malecek.

"I just wanted to know how the interview went, if you got what you need," he said when I called him back. "And if you're staying in town, how about having dinner with me tonight?"

When I came down to the lobby at seven, I almost passed him by. In place of the scruffy student-looking type was a cool, well-dressed man in a handsomely cut, tan tweed jacket, brown turtleneck, and fawn gabardine slacks. I was glad I had decided to wear my Claude Montana pants suit. It's a dark taupe silk jacket with a plunging neckline that zips up front and fits clingingly over matching high-waisted narrow pants. It was one of those wild bargains that feeds the soul of every shopper. Bergdorf's original tag read $2,400, but I picked it up for half price because it was the only one left, and my size yet. I felt so lucky that day that I ran out and bought a lottery ticket. I lost. I enjoy the outfit because it has the kind of accessorizing versatility that works well for me. Tonight I went for simplicity, which meant no jewelry except for gold clip earrings with fauve pearl centers. Were I aiming at formality, I would have created a totally different effect with opera length pearls, a diamond pin, and earrings. My simple brown leather Coach bag and Gucci shoes completed the sporty look I wanted.

He approached me with a broad smile. "You were beautiful this afternoon. You are stunning tonight."

In the dimly lit Radost Cafe, I had taken him for a peer of his twenty-year friends. Now I could see he was closer to my age, more than likely in his thirties. He smiled when he noted my surprise.

"That's why your friend Abba likes me so much. I can pass for anywhere from twenty-two to forty-two. He calls me his *schlemileon.*"

"That's quite a talent," I said. "If you shaved off the beard, you might be able to pass for a teenager."

He led me to his car, a shiny new BMW.

"You surprise me again," I said. "I was expecting a ten-year-old VW or a Hugo. What do you do to afford those fine clothes and car?"

He shook his head and laughed. "You Americans are so direct. A European would at least wait until after dinner to ask such a personal question."

"That would be too late," I answered. "I have to find out before dinner so that I know if I can order the expensive specials."

He laughed aloud. He had a marvelous hearty laugh, and I began to feel that this might turn into a pretty great evening.

"Please," he said as we drove off. "Feel free to choose anything your heart desires. Does that tell you anything?"

"Yes. Either you make a lot of money or the restaurant doesn't."

"Let's say it's a bit of both. I'm a lawyer."

"Obviously a well-connected one. You're full of surprises. Here I thought you were some starving student. Now you'll tell me you're Václav Havel's brother-in-law."

He turned to give me a sharp glance and returned his eyes to the wheel. "No. His nephew."

I was stunned. "I was only kidding."

"Fortunately, I'm not. My mother is his sister."

"Do your friends at the Radost know you're related to the President of the Republic?"

"No. It's a fact I only use professionally but try to hide socially."

"Why?" I asked.

He shrugged. "It gets in the way of genuine relationships. I wouldn't have told you if you hadn't mentioned it."

"Don't worry," I said. "I won't ask you to fix any traffic tickets."

We stopped in front of what looked like a small, undistinguished neighborhood restaurant.

"I figured you would prefer Czech food and they make the best here."

This man is getting better and better. How did he know? You see, when I travel, I eat French food in France, Italian food in Italy, and refuse to dine on anything other than the native cuisine anywhere. Part of getting the full feel of a country is to sample their cooking, and to miss out on that experience because you may be wary of the unfamiliar is a major loss.

Parking is no problem in Prague. There are so few cars, since not many can yet afford them, that the streets are empty. Jan parked right in front. The inside of the restaurant looked like someone's great-grandmother's dining room with pale yellow stone walls covered with old-world paintings and tapestries, heavy mahogany tables, chairs, and sideboards, and large metal chandeliers with ten arms giving off the collective illumination power of a fifty-watt bulb.

Jan was greeted as a regular and we were shown to a cozy candlelit table in the corner that was set with starched napkins that stood up like pyramids and heavy old-fashioned silver. I sat down and tried to unfurl my napkin, but it continued to stand at attention.

"I may have to beat this into submission," I said.

"Try the soupspoon," he said. "That could flatten a rottweiler."

We both began to giggle so uncontrollably that the host came over looking concerned.

I let Jan order for me. Reading Czech is not one of my accomplishments, and since this was not one of the regular tourist places, there were no translations. When I fall into a situation like that on my own, I have one of those Esperanto-style discussions with the waiter if no one in the establishment speaks English, French, German, or Spanish, all of which I can manage. I no longer take the plunge of pointing to some indecipherable listing on the menu after my experience in China where I ended up with a half-live fish squirming on my plate.

We started with halusky to accompany our aperitif. These were delicious potato blobs mixed with bacon and goat cheese. Then came kulajda, a marvelous creamy soup with a touch of dill. For our main dish, we had svíčková, beef slices in cream sauce with a slight tang of lemon garnished with cranberries. Deciding we had enough potatoes, which are ubiquitous in Slavic restaurants, and that the alternative of dumplings would be too heavy, we opted for the third choice of rice. All was accompanied by red Czech wine. We ate slowly, we talked a lot, and dishes were served at a slow unhurried pace that prevented the overstuffed feeling that could destroy enjoyment of dessert. Of course, that must be *palačinky*, the delectable fruit-filled crepes which I consider a highlight of Czech cooking.

We didn't touch on Jan's affiliation with the Mossad. This connection must be secret or he could lose his effectiveness if not his life. He told me that his father was an English Jew who sent him to Eton, his own alma mater, and had taken him to Israel on a vacation when he was twelve years old.

"That visit changed my life. It seemed to strike some kind of seminal chord in my soul. So I decided to reclaim that side of my heritage and was bar mitzvahed the next year."

Then he took my hand. "And how did you become a writer?"

"I didn't."

He looked surprised.

"Actually, I'm a lawyer. That is, I was a lawyer."

Now he looked totally confused. So I told him my whole story, which seemed to fascinate and enchant him. Who says men don't like smart women?

"You're absolutely marvelous. You deal in human relations and actually help people. I deal in greed and merely help one business extort money from another." He looked rueful. "I wish I, too, could help people."

"Your golden opportunity may come soon. Your friend Grace is heading for trouble." I told him the entire story.

"The poor kid." He was visibly upset. "She is such an innocent. That unctuous son of a bitch must have found her an easy prey. What can we do to get her out of that snake pit?"

"I'm afraid nothing. At this point, she's so smitten and

dazzled by that con man that she won't listen to anything against him. Who can blame her? Growing up in a house with a domineering destructive mother and a wimp of a father who retreated into his work, she's ripe for love and attention at home. In walks this smooth professional charmer whose stock in trade is recognizing vulnerability, and you have all the ingredients for disaster.''

''But Grace is a bright and highly intelligent woman. What if we expose him to her as a charlatan?''

''You think that would bring her to her senses? If we found out that he had previous wives, and I'll bet he has a history of marrying rich older women, she'll feel he just hadn't yet met his true love—her. And if we proved he's a mountebank who hasn't earned an honest crown in years, she'll feel all he needs to make it on the straight and narrow is the help and love of the right woman—her.''

''But that's nonsense,'' protested Jan.

''Some things just won't go away,'' I said. ''Susan B. Anthony removed our self-doubts and made us feel we're qualified to vote; Betty Friedan removed our fears and made us realize we could function equally in a man's world. But no one can excise the nurturing instinct that makes us fool ourselves into believing we can change any man with love.''

''You're saying there's nothing we can do to help her?''

I nodded. ''You just have to wait for the inevitable fall and be around to help her pick up the pieces. That's what friends are for.''

He took both my hands and looked into my eyes. ''So wise and so beautiful. A winning combination.''

I could see where this was going and I wasn't willing to make the trip. I stifled a yawn and looked at my watch.

''I have an early plane to catch tomorrow morning, Jan. This has been lovely, but I must get packed and off to bed.''

I could see that he figured a place for him in that statement, but I'll deal with that misapprehension when it comes. It's not that I don't feel attracted to him, but I never did casual sex even before these danger days. I have always been monogamous in relationships and right now I'm spoken for. As things went, I had no need to go through the nuisance of explaining my position to him.

As I approached the desk in my hotel to pick up my key, two police persons appeared at my side.

"Miss Rhodes?"

"Yes."

"Please, we would like to talk to you. Will you come with us?"

Jan spoke to them in Czech. When they saw him, their eyes widened slightly and their demeanor became subdued and respectful. They answered him rapidly.

"What's this all about?" I asked.

Jan turned to me, stricken. "It's Grace. They are holding her for the murder of her mother, and you are needed as a material witness."

The young policewoman said something to him. I heard the words "*policejní stanice.*" He answered sharply and the two officers nodded.

"I gather they want me down at the police station," I said.

"Yes, but I'll take you in my car."

IV

❦

AS WE WALKED through the station house, I was conscious of heads turning in our direction.

"I guess they know you around here."

Jan laughed. "It's not me they're staring at, my dear Emma—it's you. Their usual customers are not such elegantly dressed beauties."

When they brought us to a room, we saw Grace slumped disconsolately at a table. When she saw us, she jumped up and threw her arms around me and began to cry.

"I didn't do anything. Why did they bring me here?" she sobbed.

I held her and spoke to her soothingly. A man entered the room, and the police couple moved respectfully to the back of the room.

"I am *Policejní* Rada Ludvik."

He spoke English with a heavy Czech accent. Tall and burly, he looked like Marlon Brando before he began to burgeon into a Paul Prud'Homme look-alike. I later learned his title translated into "Police Counselor" and was the highest in the department. His presence indicated the importance being assigned to this case.

He looked at Jan. "Are you here as *Slečna* Lechwandowski's attorney or as a friend, *Pane* Dr. Malacek?"

He addressed him with the respect policemen reserve for those who are politically connected or whose work they admire. In Jan's case, it was probably both.

Lawyers in Europe are addressed as doctors. Actually, they should be called that in the U.S., since attorneys now get the degree of Juris Doctor. Can you imagine how much they'd charge then? They would probably demand JD license plates entitling them to park anywhere in order to make emergency calls on sick corporations.

"Both," said Jan with a smile. He turned to Grace. "If that's all right with you, Grace."

"Oh, yes," she said gratefully.

The inspector turned to me. "And Miss Rhodes is also a friend, I see. But she has no need for a lawyer; we merely wish to talk to her."

"I understand that," said Jan. "However, since I am here, I would like to sit in on her questioning."

The inspector gestured expansively with a smile. "Of course. I have no problem with that."

I wondered if his geniality owed itself to his disposition or to the fact that he knew he was talking to his President's nephew. Whatever it is, it can't hurt.

"Now," said Jan, "I would like to be alone with my client for a while. I will call you when we're ready."

"Certainly, *Pane* Doctor," and he motioned to the two police persons, who followed him out of the room.

Jan sat Grace down, and he and I drew up chairs around the table.

"Now tell us everything, Grace," said Jan calmly. "Take your time."

"It all happened after you left, Emma. Oh, what an idiot I've been. You were so right and I was such a fool."

I felt a stab of apprehension. I sat up straight. "You didn't confront your mother, did you, Grace?" Could she have been that stupid?

She nodded in misery.

"You told her about you and Rudy being lovers?"

She nodded again.

"Why? What did you expect to gain?"

She looked at me, in abject misery. "I just wouldn't believe what you said about Rudy. I thought if I told her that he really loved me and not her, she would divorce him, and he and I could be together."

I groaned inwardly. Her understanding of human nature put her on a level with Forrest Gump.

"We had a big fight," she continued. "She told me she didn't believe me and that I was a lying slut." She was crying softly as she spoke. "She said I was making up terrible stories because I was jealous of her, because I could never get a man to love me. Then she called Rudy in and told him what I said."

She stopped and began to sob. Jan went to the door and asked the policeman to bring a glass of water. We waited until she had drunk some water, blown her nose, and got herself under control. My heart went out to her because I knew what was coming next.

"He laughed and told Mother that I was imagining things. That I was an impressionable and unstable young girl who probably misconstrued his casual affection." She stopped for a moment. "Then he walked over to Mother, kissed her, and told her she was his only true love. Then he told her he had to go to an important business meeting and walked out of the room without even a backward look at me."

The man should have his balls put in a vise. I think that con men and Casanovas have their consciences surgically removed at birth.

"Then what happened?"

"Mother screamed at me, told me I was an evil whore and to get out of the house forever. Then she slapped me."

"What did you do?" I asked.

She smiled. "I slapped her back." She smiled even

more. "That sure was a shock to her, and Alena."

"Alena? Where was she in all this?"

"Oh, she had just come in to pick up the coffee service."

"You mean she saw and heard the entire thing?"

Grace nodded. "Most of it, I guess."

I looked at Jan and his eyes rolled back.

"Then I went upstairs, packed my things, and left. I went to Leif's."

"You didn't go back into the room to say good-bye?" I asked.

She shook her head. "Why would I? She made it plain she never wanted to see me again. All I wanted to do was get out of there."

"That was it?" I pursued.

She nodded. "Until the police came there and told me my mother was dead." Her eyes filled with tears. "I hated her. I never could do anything that pleased her. Ever. My daddy loved me. But he couldn't stand up to her. She would lock me in my closet if I was bad. He always came to let me out—but he never stopped her from doing it. She used to make me wear funny long ugly dresses when I was little. I had to wear the same dress for weeks. The children always made fun of me. She said dresses were expensive." She added bitterly, "But she always had nice new things." Suddenly she started to sob. "Why couldn't she love me? I loved her. She was my mother."

I walked over and put my arms around her and let her cry.

"Did the police accuse you of anything?" asked Jan.

She shook her head. "They just wanted to know about our fight."

Jan went to the door and spoke to the policeman. A few minutes later, Inspector Ludvik returned. Jan asked him to describe the details of *Pani* Sykes' death.

"We received a call at eight from a woman named Alena who said she worked at the Sykes house and her mistress was dead. 'Killed' was the word she used. We arrived and

found *Paní* Sykes lying in front of the fireplace with the
back of her head bashed in. The woman Alena told us the
victim had had a big fight with her daughter, who she saw
hit her mother.''

"Did she see Mrs. Sykes fall?'' I asked.

He shook his head. "She left the room while they were
still arguing.''

"Did she hear Grace leave?''

"No. She was preparing dinner. The radio was on as was
the exhaust fan, and she says she would not have heard
anything. She was in the kitchen all the time except for the
moment when she went out to the herb garden, which is at
the corner of the house, to pick some dill. She saw no one
leave the front door except the seamstress, who had been
working upstairs in the sewing room. She did not go back
into the salon until almost two hours later to announce dinner. That is when she found her employer dead on the
floor.''

"Rigor mortis couldn't possibly have set in yet. How
long did the medical examiner say she had been dead?'' I
asked.

"The *Patalog* refuses to pinpoint the time exactly. But
the estimate was between thirty minutes and two hours.''

I shook my head impatiently. "He should be able to be
more accurate than that. The room was relatively cool, and
a body begins to lose heat at the rate of one and one half
degrees Fahrenheit per hour.''

The inspector's eyes narrowed. "You seem to know
quite a bit about dead bodies, Miss Rhodes.''

Jan cleared his throat. "She is a writer, Rada.''

His face cleared. "Ah, of course. Of mystery stories, I
assume.''

Silence becomes my assent, and prevents me from
having to produce an outright lie. In my line of work, as
you can see, I have to bend the truth a bit from time to
time, but always for a just cause. I know this sounds like
my own brand of self-justification, but I do have a personal

code of morality that dictates that dissembling is to be kept to an absolute minimum. In other words, I say as little as I have to. Now I was waiting for the usual reaction that would determine if he was a TV watcher or a reader.

"You are like Sue Grafton, then."

He was a reader, and of current mysteries. Some of the old-timers compare me to Agatha Christie. And the TV watchers call me Jessica Fletcher.

"I wish, Inspector," I said with a smile. There, that wasn't a lie. I like her books and I admire her bank account.

"Surely you haven't had time to do the autopsy yet. How do you know that she didn't die a natural death?" I asked.

He smiled patiently. "You did not see the wound in her head."

"She could have had a heart attack and then fallen against the metal fender of the fireplace."

"Ah, yes, you are familiar with the house."

"The way I see it, Rada, you have no basis now for charging anyone," said Jan. "You may ask both of these ladies whatever questions you wish, and then I will take them home."

The inspector didn't look too happy, but he of course agreed. I left the room while he spoke to Grace, which took under a half hour. Then she came out and I entered and sat down in the chair she had vacated next to Jan. I described my visit with the late Alicia Bailey Lechwandowski Sykes, omitting the mother-and-daughter details, of course.

"As a writer, Miss Rhodes, you surely must be a keen observer of people, yes?" asked the inspector.

"Yes, of course," I answered.

"How would you describe the relationship between *Paní* Sykes and her daughter? Would you say they got along well?"

It would have been foolish to paint a rosy picture of an idyllic mother-daughter relationship because Alena had probably given them the true story. Knowing the gossip-loving tendencies of household help—what else do they have to talk about—I figured she had probably laid it on heavily. What I could do was try to mitigate the damaging impression her tales had undoubtedly made.

I noticed the wedding band on his finger. "Do you have any children, Inspector?"

He nodded.

"Is one of them by chance a girl?"

"Yes. She is six years old."

"Does she argue with her mother?"

He smiled. "All the time."

"What to wear to school, why can't she have new jeans, when can she have her ears pierced? Right?"

He nodded. "True, they fight, but never to an extreme point."

"That's because she's only six. Wait until she hits the teens and the issues become heavier, like who she can't go out with and what time she must come home. Then you'll hear screaming that will send you to the nearest pub. Mothers and daughters argue, Inspector. If all such disagreements ended up in homicides, your department would need two hundred officers to handle the caseload."

"Was Mr. Sykes present?" he asked.

Aha, a different tack.

"For a short time, yes."

"What would you say his relationship with his step-daughter was?"

Now we were in dangerous territory. I didn't think he knew anything but was merely on a hunting expedition like any good interrogator.

I shrugged. "They seemed friendly."

Jan still kept a straight face. I could see why he was not only a good lawyer but an excellent agent for Abba.

"Have you spoken to Mr. Sykes yet?" I asked.

"He has not yet returned home. We have police there to break the news to him."

Wait until he finds out that his meal ticket has been punched.

"If that's all, Rada," said Jan, arising, "then I'm going to take my two ladies home."

"Very well. But I must insist that you keep *Slečna* Lechwandowski available. Miss Rhodes will be free to go once we have completed our questioning."

I told him I had an early flight the next day, but I would change it to a later one.

WE DROPPED GRACE off at Leif's, who took her into his arms immediately and showed the kind of concern and sympathy she needed desperately right now. He lived in a small flat one flight up in the Malá Strana that looked very much like student apartments everywhere. The parlor was large and bright, but there was one tiny bedroom, an even tinier bathroom that would require the tall Leif to take a bath with his knees up to his chin, and a kitchen with no counters. Jan took me back to my hotel and we went into the bar for a nightcap.

"She didn't do it, of course," I said as I sipped my brandy and soda.

"I'm an attorney," he said stiffly. "We do not consider the guilt or innocence of our clients. Everyone is entitled to a defense, no matter what."

"You know," I said, "in my lingerie drawer, right under the silk teddies, is a piece of paper that says I have a bona fide J.D. degree."

He blushed. "I'm sorry. That did sound a bit pompous. Of course, you as a lawyer know that. No, I don't believe she did it. But that, unfortunately, is an opinion based on emotion rather than fact. We'll need more than that to establish her innocence."

"No, Jan—the police will need more than they have to establish her guilt. I assume the Czech Republic has abandoned the law structure of the Soviet and now an individual is innocent until proven guilty. What the police have now is barely convincing. Grace had a fight with her mother. Big deal. Alicia fell and hit her head on the brass fender.

Why assume she was pushed? She may have been tippling too much with the cooking sherry. She may have had a heart attack or some condition that caused her to faint. We don't know her medical history. There are too many unknowns here to make a case—yet. We'll have to wait for the autopsy."

Jan smiled. "You must be very good at your work, Emma. You lay out the facts concisely."

"That's my legal training," I said. "But now let me give you my layman's insights. I believe that anyone given sufficient provocation could be driven to violence and Grace certainly had that in spades. One is not supposed to speak ill of the dead, but I don't believe in elevating someone to sainthood just because they passed on. The woman was a vicious bitch who, if she had four legs instead of two, would've been put down years ago. However, if Grace did kill her mother, either accidentally or deliberately, I can't see her denying it. She's so loaded with guilt and self-doubt that she would willingly take the blame for every wrongful death that occurred in the neighborhood since 1989."

"Then I assume you'll want to stay for the autopsy," Jan said.

"I'd really like to, but I'm on a case that has a scheduled time limit and I really can't allot more than another day," I said. "Do you think it could be done tomorrow, and could I be there?"

"Of course," he said with the confidence of the well-connected. "I'll see to it."

Now that I'd gotten all the possible information about the first Mrs. Bailey and it was a dead end, if you'll pardon the pun, I had to be off on phase two of my research mission. If you're wondering if this trip was necessary, let me point out how much had been accomplished here. Juliet Bishop's accusation of Sidney's jealousy had been substantiated and Sidney Bailey's account of his ex-wife support had been proven. Is it really necessary to check the validity of a client's allegations? You bet. You wouldn't believe the

number of times I've been given fancies instead of facts
and then asked to solve the situation. What I now had to
learn was whether the pattern continued with wife number
two, and what caused Sidney to pursue such aberrational
behavior. Then I'd figure out a way to break it.

AT TEN O'CLOCK the next morning, we were standing
in the outer room of the Prague morgue, Inspector Ludvik,
Jan, and I.

"Are you sure you wish to go in, Miss Rhodes?" asked
the inspector.

"Quite sure, Inspector. Not to worry, I won't faint. This
isn't my first autopsy."

Perhaps you're wondering why I even wanted to witness
such a procedure. I didn't want to, I had to. The purpose
of a medical-legal autopsy in the case of sudden and suspicious deaths, as opposed to an ordinary hospital autopsy,
is to provide sufficient evidence for either the defense or
the prosecution. What must be established is the time of
death, the instrument of death, the pathological condition
inside the body that resulted in the death (internal bleeding,
lacerated organs, heart damage), and the manner of death.
Sometimes fatalities occur without any external signs of
trauma, which cannot be found unless one knows specifically what to look for. All this requires a highly skilled
medical examiner and that's why I needed to oversee his
work.

It wasn't a he, it was a her. Standing over the metal table
on which the body lay was a short, sturdy woman in a
bloodstained white coat who was introduced as the *Patalog*,
Dr. Heyrovsky. (As you've probably gathered, *Patalog* is
the Czech term for medical examiner.). She looked at me
with total disinterest and went on with her work. I could
see the fluids in the body had already been drained, the
intermastoidal incision had been made over the top of the
skull, and the "Y" incision down the center of the body
had been completed. The efficiency with which she worked

gave me immediate confidence that her forensic opinion would be valid.

I have seen a number of autopsies, but I never get over the shock of seeing a human being reduced to something akin to the frog I had to dissect in biology class. The reaction was a little stronger because this was the first time it was someone I knew socially. I don't think I could have been as cool if it was someone I liked.

The coroner began to recite her findings in Czech to Inspector Ludvik, and Jan furnished an instant translation.

The victim had eaten within an hour of her death. The alcohol level in her blood was not significant. Her heart was normal. The urine showed no sign of drugs. Time of death was between thirty minutes and two hours before she first examined the body, as established yesterday. No injuries to internal organs were found. There were no signs of a struggle, no skin or fibers under the nails to indicate a violent struggle with an assailant. The *Patalog*'s conclusions were that the cause of death was a severely depressed fracture of the skull in the neighborhood of the parietal/occipital suture caused by impact with a sharp metal object. Death resulted from bleeding into the brain.

"Inspector, please ask the doctor if the blow could have been caused by a fall, or would she have had to have been thrown against the metal object?"

She listened patiently for his translation and then looked at me with what looked like a soupçon of respect.

Actually, she said, the deceased had what she described as an eggshell skull that was not as thick as a normal head. Ordinarily this sort of extensive skull damage would have required the victim to have been hurled with some degree of force. But in this case, a fall alone could have caused the death.

We left the grim room, and Jan suggested we three go to a nearby cafe to talk things over. My stomach hadn't settled to the point where I wanted anything more than coffee, but the inspector was made of sterner stuff and ordered herring salad and hard-boiled eggs. Czech style coffee is a muddy brew served in small cups; they don't believe in percolators and filter brew machines. Coffee is made like grandma used to make it, if your grandma came from Eastern Europe; ground coffee is thrown into a pot of boiling water and allowed to settle to the bottom, then poured into your cup, usually through a small strainer. If you don't mind the cloudy look, it tastes fine and makes one wonder about the elaborate hundred-dollar machines that you find in the pages of Bloomingdale's and Williams-Sonoma catalogs. Sugar is customarily offered, but requests for milk or cream gets you sweetened condensed milk—and it's extra.

"I don't see any basis for murder indictments here, Inspector," said Jan.

Inspector Ludvik said something that sounded like "*afectki.*"

"Manslaughter," repeated Jan.

"In the absence of any witness who saw Grace push her mother, you don't have anything," I pointed out.

"True," he said. "However, we do have method, we have means, and we most certainly have motive." He paused. "You see, we have spoken to Mr. Sykes."

He could have hit pay dirt, or he could be on a clever fishing expedition. But he was dealing with pros—Jan and I merely looked at him with polite interest.

He looked amused but ventured no further explanation.

"And where did Mr. Sykes claim to have been during the estimated time of death?" I asked.

He eyed me with interest. "The wording of your question makes you sound more like a lawyer rather than a writer, Miss Rhodes."

"In my country, one is frequently both."

"Ah, yes, I am a great fan of John Grisham," he said. "But you did not answer my question."

"I wasn't aware that you asked me one, Inspector," I said sweetly. "But I am an attorney."

He looked at me admiringly. "So then I must address you as Dr. Rhodes."

"You can only if you wish to, Inspector. The title is not customary in my country. Lawyers in America aren't regarded with the same kind of respect they get here."

He looked puzzled. "I have heard this and I wonder why. They are men—I beg your pardon—people who have been highly educated and deal in very important matters involving business, life, and death."

"Perhaps that's why. People resent those they depend upon and tend to judge them harshly. If the lawyer wins for you, or the doctor cures you—they're gods. But if they lose, they're scorned as inept money-grubbers. My generation grew up trusting no one and nothing. Today, we give all our idols clay feet, Inspector, which is sort of sad. A country needs heroes."

He shook his head. "This applies very much to my profession as well, Miss Rhodes. When I was a child, the *policista* was regarded with honor and respect. Today . . ." he made a gesture of futility, "the young look upon us as their enemy."

We all sighed collectively and then started to laugh. "We sound like our parents!" I said.

Jan nodded. "How many times have I heard my father complaining about my generation's lack of appreciation."

"And mine about our lack of respect," said Inspector Ludvik.

"And aren't you sick of hearing how great it was in the old days?" I asked.

We all smiled in the companionable contentment that comes to people who have enjoyed shared experiences. Jan summoned the waiter and asked for refills for our coffee cups.

"And now back to Mr. Sykes and his explanation for his whereabouts," said the inspector. "He has what the American TV shows call an airtight alibi. He was with someone, but was loath at first to give us any names."

"Let me guess," I said. "He was with a woman but was too much of a gentleman to compromise her good name. But after a very slight amount of pressure, he reluctantly divulged her identity."

The inspector looked at me in surprise.

"Yes, it was very much like that."

"She is a married woman, of course, and quite rich, right?"

He looked even more amazed. Then his expression turned stern.

"You are mocking me. You knew of this relationship."

"No, Inspector, I did not know—nor would I ever do anything so rude as to mock you. What I do know is the nature of the man—he's a philanderer. I'll wager that when you interview his paramour, she'll tell you indignantly how his wife never understood or appreciated him. I'll also bet she had to pry out of him that his wife is given to wild uncontrollable extravagances that force him to live in virtual penury. Of course, the sympathetic lady presses money upon him, which he accepts only with the greatest reluctance because of his incredibly wonderful manly pride. Being so smitten—and now knowing he's in the position to marry her—I wouldn't rely too heavily on her veracity about his alibi."

Jan looked at me with a twinkle in his eye. "Obviously being a writer has made you an astute student of human nature, Emma."

"You may be entirely correct, Miss Rhodes. And you can be assured that we will press her for the truth. But what Mr. Sykes told us of the cause of the fight between Grace and her mother is a very strong incentive for murder."

"May I ask what he told you?" I asked innocently.

"That the girl fancied he was in love with her even to the point of believing they had sexual encounters, which she told her mother. He claims the girl is emotionally unstable and highly immature and has always been a problem." He looked pointedly at Jan.

There was a short silence. "I think, Jan, the inspector is hinting that if Grace would be willing to confess to murder, you could go for an insanity plea. In other words, an innocent young woman should plead guilty in order to spend the rest of her life in a loony bin."

The inspector looked uncomfortable.

"Inspector," I asked, "why are you accepting Mr. Sykes' version of events? How do you know this love affair was all Grace's fantasy?"

"Why should he make such an allegation if it were not true?" he asked.

"Because it's in some way to his benefit for sure."

He smiled. "I think, Miss Rhodes, that your apparent distaste for this man has possibly clouded your objectivity."

"You forget, Inspector, that I have one piece of information in this situation that you don't have."

He sat upright. "What is that?"

"I saw the three of them together—Mrs. Sykes, Mr. Sykes, and Grace. That Grace adored her stepfather was unmistakable—just as certain that he was sexually involved with her."

"All this you got from an exchange of looks," he said laconically.

"Inspector Ludvik, your job, much as mine, involves being an observer of human behavior. The visible interaction among people is often far more reliable than their words. There's a certain intimacy and intensity that develops between two people who are in the throes of a sexual relationship. Usually it's so clearly evident they might as well be wearing signs. If you're experienced, you can spot it at once."

He tilted his head as if in homage. "I bow to your superior knowledge in this area, Miss Rhodes. I myself am not a very emotional or demonstrative type of person, as my wife keeps complaining. I'm afraid that if I witnessed the exchange of burning glances that you describe, I would attribute it to poor digestion.''

We all laughed. The inspector looked at his watch. "I'm afraid I must go.''

"I'm leaving on an evening plane," I said. "I don't know where I'll be. But you can reach me easily via my London phone. I check the machine constantly. Your sergeant has the number.''

WHEN I GOT back to my hotel, there was a message that Juliet Bishop had called. I had phoned her yesterday but was told she was out of town. I wanted her to inform Sidney about his ex-wife's demise so that the support checks would cease. Knowing how bureaucracy works, I thought it might take months before he got official word. When I told her the news, she gasped.

"Did she have an accident?" she asked.

"Sort of. The police are still investigating.''

She was silent for a moment. "Sidney will be sad. He's such a love, he still has a soft spot for both his ex-wives. Oh, dear, how will I tell him without revealing my source?''

"You might say that the police found his address in Alicia's book and called your home.''

"Of course, that's perfectly reasonable," she said happily. "Aren't you the clever one.''

That's why I get paid the big bucks, ma'am.

Right after she hung up, the phone rang again.

"So, *tsotskele*, you're rolling in corpses again, I hear. It seems people are just dying to meet you.'' It was Abba, and he roared with laughter at his own humor.

"I see you've been talking to Jan.''

"Yes, another Rhodes conquest, I gather. The guy has the hots for you, sweetheart. I could hear his testosterone pounding over the phone.''

"He's a very attractive guy, Abba. Interesting family, too.''

"He told you he's Havel's nephew? I'm surprised. Usually he keeps that tidbit under wraps. I think he's afraid people will ask him to help them get government contracts for big projects like erecting pissoirs all over Prague. So who's the stiff?"

"Number one ex-wife of my client's husband."

"That would make her too young to have died of old age. Did the butler do it?"

"No, but the authorities are leaning toward the daughter."

"That would be the Lechwandowski babe you wanted to meet."

Abba has a mind like a computer. Once data enters, it's saved forever.

"I gather you don't concur," he added.

"Nope—and you wouldn't either if you met her, and would you ever love to. She's just your type, Abba. Tall, blond, beautiful, shy, and naive."

"Impossible. How can she be shy and naive when men are chasing her ass all the time, which they must if she's gorgeous."

"You didn't meet her mother. She would've made Sharon Stone insecure about her looks."

"Then I take it we're all happy the old bag bought the farm," he said.

"I'm not sure about the current husband. She's given him a cushy life. Her income stops with her death, which means he may now have to depend upon his own resources, which I suspect are meager."

"Have you checked the will?"

"Not yet. I figured I'd wait until the inquest is over."

"Why wait? Maybe he chose not to. Cui bono—who benefits. If he's the big heir, he may have decided to get rid of the Lechwandowski curse."

He expected me to ask for a definition of the curse—which would be "Mrs. Lechwandowski"—but I wouldn't give him the satisfaction. Abba sees himself as a cross between Jerry Seinfeld and George Carlin. I keep telling him his wit comes closer to Henny Youngman.

"He couldn't have. He wasn't there at the time she bought it. He has a witness who claims he was elsewhere."

He snorted. "A witness! I could produce one of those in twenty minutes. It's a snap to find someone who will swear to anything provided the incentive is right. How did the victim meet her untimely demise?"

I described the circumstances of Alicia's death, and then told the entire story.

"Do you think we can get Joan Collins to play the mother? The thing sounds like a fucking soap opera, and I use the adjective accurately. You said this Sykes has meager resources? Honey, his equipment alone is worth a fortune. He services mother and daughter regularly, and I'll bet his 'witness' is another broad he's been *shtupping*—the son of a bitch has a golden schlong!"

"Do I detect sounds of admiration with a touch of envy, Abba?"

"Fuckin' A. Now if you tell me the cocksucker is eighty-two, I'll take the gaspipe."

"I'd say early fifties."

"Jesus Christ—I'm forty-two and in a good month I can count on twice a week."

"Don't compare yourself. With you, sex is a sideline. With Rudy, it's a career. And I don't mean to be your sexual scorekeeper, but last month while you were in my casa in Portugal, as I recall you had a rather stellar batting average with that six-foot Scandinavian sexpot."

I could hear his delight over the wires. "Oh, yeah—I was a plenty horny dude, wasn't I?"

"What is it with you men?" I asked. "Why do you measure your value by sexual performance? We women don't rate you that way."

"You sure as hell do," he said firmly. "It's one of the side effects of the fucking women's movement. Used to be you married a virgin and whatever you did was fine; what did she know? Now you sleep with a woman, she has a basis of comparison. We have what to worry. Does the expression 'Was it good for you?' ring a bell? Nowadays we're like actors playing Hamlet. The audience weighs our performance against every other actor who had the role. You better be Laurence Olivier or you'll never get booked in that house again.''

I started to laugh. ''That's why I love talking to you, Abba. You always manage to use such elegant frames of reference, no matter how tawdry the topic. But getting back to Alicia's death, you're right about the will. I'll check into it.''

''You told me the stiff hit her head on a metal fireplace fender. What makes it a homicide?'' he asked.

''Suspicion and circumstances,'' I answered. ''There was nothing to trip over and no medical reason for her to pass out. The assumption had to be she was pushed. Especially after the rip-roaring run-in she had with her daughter.''

''That's all bullshit. The Czech Republic now puts the burden of proof in the prosecutor's hands. There were no witnesses. You can assume anything you fuckin' well please, but you can't make a case out of assumptions. I can see them holding her for questioning, but I can't see even a basis for indictment.''

''I think you're right,'' I said. ''However, with Grace's shaky psyche, living with the unproven accusation of matricide hanging over her head will be rough.''

''If she inherits, she'll be O.K. It's amazing how rich people overlook transgressions when the transgressor has money and is, in effect, one of them. Remember the case in Long Island when that society woman killed her husband with a shotgun claiming she thought he was an intruder—which everyone knew was a crock of shit? They let her off, and she went right on being socially acceptable at hunt balls and polo matches even though everyone knew she was guilty as hell. If she'd lived in Brooklyn and stabbed her husband with a kosher meat knife claiming she thought he was a *gonif* who came to steal the hundred dollars she had hidden in the Breakstone's cream cheese box in the icebox, the grand jury may not have indicted her, but the neighborhood would have. Believe me, she'd have to move to Florida to find herself a canasta game. As my mother always said, money talks.''

''Words to live by, Abba. Thanks for your inspirational lecture. Now I have to catch a plane to Salzburg, and Jan is waiting downstairs to drive me to the airport. I'm off to meet the second Mrs. Bailey.''

''Watch yourself, *ahuvati*. Ex-wives may be injurious to your health. Part of my Mossad training was to never view any death as a single event.''

''Now I suppose you'll tell me to have a nice day,'' I said.

''Look, *motek*, when your work like mine sometimes involves violence, paranoia is a plus.''

JAN DROVE ME to the airport and waited with me in the lounge.

''I'll probably never see you again, Emma,'' he said sadly.

''Never is a word I never use,'' I said with a smile. ''The world, and certainly Europe, isn't very big anymore. Both of our professions require moving around—so who knows when I'll be in Prague or you'll come to London. We'll certainly be in touch. I won't be needed for the inquest, but I want to know the results.''

My plane was announced over the loudspeaker, we kissed good-bye, and I headed for Amsterdam.

V

―――――――――⦅⦆――――――――――

I STROLLED ALONG the banks of the Schinkel of Kostverlorenvaart Canal admiring the typical seventeenth- and eighteenth-century houses for which Amsterdam is famous. I was meeting Andre Bailey for lunch at one of the many waterfront restaurants, and I chose to walk from my hotel to enjoy the uniquely Dutch scenery. The houses were built by the rich merchants and important magistrates of the Golden Age, and they boast gabled carved facades, wrought-iron balconies, and splendid details that are not visible from the tourist-laden boats that ply the canals constantly. Modern offices have been installed in many of these houses, but I was charmed to see that they still have the old pulleys on the roof that have been used for centuries to haul furniture because the staircases are too narrow.

Suddenly I got that irresistible Dutch aroma, which meant I was approaching one of the herring stands that dot the landscape of Amsterdam streets. Bees may be drawn to honey, but give me herring any day, especially when I can dip it into chopped sweet raw onions, toss my head back, and chomp it down Dutch-style. I knew I was going to have lunch soon, but this would just be my first course.

I entered the canal-side restaurant Andre had designated when I'd phoned last night, spotted him immediately from his description, and wondered if he went for older women. He got up when I reached the table and stood at about six feet four. A full rust-colored beard and a head of curly hair with heavy dark eyebrows over fantastic green eyes, the guy was a knockout if you like the type and I do. Sidney had told me his son was twenty-seven—well, that's only eight years difference. The good thing about my work is that adages warning against mixing business with pleasure do not apply. I don't have health care but I get other dandy benefits, like meeting the kinds of interesting men you don't usually run into at church socials and bars.

Apparently the feeling was mutual, because he was looking at me in a way that held promise for the future.

"Emma Rhodes?" he asked hopefully.

I had dressed carefully for the meeting. In my business, first impressions are of vital importance—not just mine of him but him of me. It can determine the success of the interview and the ease or difficulty with which I extract needed information. When I stand in front of my closet, I evaluate my audience and what sort of effect I want to create. This was a young man who was a hip musician. If I wore a Donna Karan suit, he'd probably think I was a social worker or a narc. If I wore a Lagerfeld number, I'd look too unreachably stylish. The pastel St. John outfits I reserve for bankers and lawyers. I opted for my moss green leather Prada pants suit, and did I ever make the right decision.

I nodded and smiled. "Andre Bailey, I presume." We sat down.

"You're looking at me as though I just stepped off the *Starship Enterprise*," I said.

"I'm sorry if I seem surprised. I was expecting a somewhat, well, different type of woman."

Great voice, too. Deep, resonant. I'm big on voices. A

high squeaky voice would turn me off faster than an announcement that he was anti-abortion.

"Why?" I asked.

"You told me you're a friend of my father. His women friends tend to be, well, somewhat dowdy . . . and older." He smiled.

Great teeth. My God, I thought, his eyes crinkle when he smiles. I've always been a sucker for crinklers.

"Believe me, I am not complaining," he said.

We looked at each other happily, both pleased at what we saw, until the waiter approached. We scanned the menu quickly. I always eat fish in Holland or anywhere that I know it's fresh out of the water. He ordered grilled turbot and beer for both of us.

"Your father tells me you're a composer."

He grimaced. "My father told you I was a bum. Since he's never heard my music, and probably would not appreciate it when he did, he figures I'm a lazy dilettante who hates work and is contented to live off him."

"Well, he did tell me that when he phones at eleven in the morning, you're usually just getting up."

"That's because most performances are in the evening and I usually don't get home until quite late."

"You perform?" I asked.

He sighed patiently. "Look, I'm a serious composer of minimalist music. It's not Bach or Handel, it's more the kind of music created by Phillip Glass and Steve Reich. I have a group of six musicians who perform my work with me."

"Why on earth doesn't your father accept it?"

"First place, he cannot understand it. His taste stops at Chopin and Beethoven. But the real problem is that I refused to go to university. I was accepted at Cambridge, and it nearly killed him when I turned it down. But I'm a musician and the academic world offers nothing for me. I refused to go to school to live out my father's dream." He paused. "I have my own dreams."

"It's harder with sons," I said. "Fathers expect much more from them than from daughters. And thanks to the women's movement, women are working in professions previously populated only by men, so their achievements seem greater."

"Don't I know it. He probably boasted to you about my hardworking architect sister. What he probably didn't tell you is that he supports her and her husband just as he does me. And when Alexandra gets her thousand pounds a month and the Austrian shilling-pound rate of exchange is less favorable, she rings dear old Dad for an addition to compensate for the difference."

"Your sister lives in Austria?"

"Yes—in Salzburg, near our mother. She uses my mother for dining privileges and my father for support. And they view her as an independent woman," he said in disgust.

Ah, sibling rivalry. As an only child, I found it nice to hear that sometimes there's a price to pay for having had a live-in playmate while growing up.

"I assume your mother is English," I said. "What made her move to Salzburg? It's a beautiful city, but most expatriates select places with higher temperatures and lower costs of living."

"It's her husband. He was offered the position as director of the Salzburg Chorale Society. Which was perfect since I believe my father's off-shore trust fund arrangements required that the recipients live abroad." He smiled ruefully. "My father's financial machinations are usually rather convoluted. I don't really understand them too well, but I believe he set aside a rather large sum from which my mother and ex-wife number one derive handsome incomes."

Suspicion is a built-in in my business. This guy's a sweetheart, but I trust no one. I was curious as to how much he really knew about the terms of the trust.

"What happens to the fund after they die? Does it pass on to their heirs?"

He shook his head. "Oh, no. I believe all of it goes right back to dear old Dad. It's theirs for their lifetimes only."

"Well, not really," I said. "He could undoubtedly dissolve the fund any time he wishes."

He mocked surprise. "Surely you jest. My father reneging on his sworn forever support of his former wives? Never. His commitment to women who have mistreated him is an all-consuming neurotic compulsion. It's funny how people develop their own warped moral codes. He'll engage in the most devious practices to avoid taxes and is bloody brilliant at walking the finest line possible to keep on just this side of legality in dealing with the Inland Revenue. But a promise made to women is a sacred irrevocable trust."

"Your father supports you, your sister, and two ex-wives. He's practically a growth industry."

"I always felt the wives were de trop. Not that Alexandra and I are so deserving, but we are his children." He paused. "And we never betrayed him. My mother is a wonderful woman, but her actions didn't entitle her to lifetime maintenance. And that other one is nothing but a worthless bloodsucker."

Not anymore, sonny boy.

He looked disgusted. "My father is used to being abused by women. He seems to thrive on it. Now I hear his current wife is showing signs of imminent departure." He shook his head. "The old boy may be a huge success in business, but he sure as hell is a disaster in marriage."

"Don't worry," I said, "I'm sure it's not genetic."

He smiled. "He's really a good guy. He's dependable as the Rock of Gibraltar, he's generous, and he is loving. But when it comes to women, he's what my uncle would call a total *shmatte*."

"Andre, I'd love to interview your mother for my current book project."

I had given him my cover story about being a writer. I went on to explain my need for speaking to divorced women who have rebuilt their lives. I had been trying to figure out a way to meet wife number two without bothering Abba again. Here it was, right in my lap.

He smiled broadly. "She'll be delighted to talk to you, I'm sure. I'll call her and tell her you're coming." He stopped and looked at me with what Danielle Steele describes as a "meaningful look." "When are you planning to go to Salzburg? Not today, I hope."

I can see future plans forming in his mind. And we haven't even eaten lunch yet. I'll deal with that later. A change of subject is called for.

"Doesn't your father support his brother, too?"

"Oh, no. Uncle Dennis split from the business years ago. He never really enjoyed the process of making money the way my father does. He just enjoys spending it. He sold out his share and raises rare fish in a little village near Paris aptly named Plaisir."

"Did Dennis help your father take care of their mother or did Sidney do it alone?"

He shrugged. "I wouldn't know. She died before I was born."

I had just taken a sip of beer. Luckily it wasn't food or I would have required the Heimlich maneuver. Sidney had told me his mother had died five years ago.

Why had Sidney lied? Conflicting statements set off bells in my head. Very often they are the small hanging threads that you pull to unravel the whole matter.

The waiter served our food and we spent the next half hour enjoying the beautifully grilled fish and boiled new potatoes that had been dipped in fresh dill. I never talk business when I eat fish. It's hard to keep alert for conversational nuances and fish bones at the same time, and a misstep in either pursuit could be disastrous.

The waiter cleared the table and brought coffee.

"Has your father ever heard anything you composed?"

He shook his head ruefully. "No. And he probably wouldn't like it if he did. I think he doesn't consider it serious because the sound is so alien to him. It's a generational thing. Older people are locked into liking what they know, melodies they can walk out humming, rigid tonal structures. Atonal music is not high on their music appreciation list. My father will barely tolerate Benjamin Britten and Samuel Barber.''

''Maybe because he hasn't heard it played by so-called respectable conductors. Most people are afraid to trust their own tastes in art or music, so they wait for it to get the seal of approval by experts.''

Andre smiled one of his crinkly specials. I had to actively resist the urge to pinch his cheek. Any of them.

''Well, he can now. We've been invited to perform next month with the Amsterdam Concertgebouw Orchestra.''

I was so delighted, I leaned over and kissed him full on the mouth.

''But that's marvelous. They're one of the finest orchestras in the world. That means you've been fully accepted by the Establishment. Andre, your father will positively dance with delight.''

He ran his tongue over his lips. ''Mmm, I think I like your manifestation of pleasure better.'' He looked at me.

''Where are you staying?'' he asked.

''The Amstel.''

He signaled for the check. ''That's a venerable, luxurious, and very conservative place.''

''Where do you live?'' I asked.

''On Beethovenstraat.''

''That figures. Is it far from here?''

''Nothing in Amsterdam is far from anything else in Amsterdam.''

''Can we go on foot? I love walking.''

He dropped bills on the table—like father like son—grasped my arm, and looked down at me. ''We could, but we won't. It takes too long.''

I didn't ask too long for what.

I know I've told you my rule on monogamous relationships. But have you ever heard of the exception that proves the rule (a saying I never quite understood but it comes in handy here). Well, this is it. Andre was adorable and irresistible and my instant gut decision (or wherever part of the anatomy governs such decisions) was to go for it.

He had a lovely flower-decked terrace outside his bedroom, which made me ashamed of the ash-covered plateau I had off mine. Since neither of us smoked, there were no postcoital cigarettes. We just sat quietly, smiling at each other in perfect contentment. I hoped he wasn't one of those men who feel they have to ring you in the morning. First place, I'm not one of those women who goes all emotional if the usual "I'll call you" sign-off doesn't happen within twenty-four hours. And second place, I wouldn't be there anyway because, in about an hour, I'd be at Schiphol Airport on my way to Salzburg.

AS I SAT back in my seat on the plane, I wondered about the discrepant dates of Sidney's mother's death. Why would he claim to have cared for her up to a year ago, when Andre said she died over twenty-seven years ago, before he was born? Alicia couldn't have straightened out this enigma since she'd never met any member of the family, another odd fact. It's those little inconsistencies that often have big effects on the outcome of cases. Seeking solutions to a situation or a murder involves the amassing of myriad details, some of which may seem niggling and unimportant. But experience has taught me that a seemingly minor detail may be the basis of total resolution of the case and nothing should ever be regarded as insignificant. As I pick up these bits of data, they get tossed onto the back burner of my brain where they sit until I come upon information that makes a fit, like putting together a jigsaw puzzle. It would be a waste of time now to try to figure out Sidney's motivation for pouring out that whole tale of his saintly mother. I had no doubt that his reasons would become apparent to me in time.

VI

I WAS STANDING on my favorite Salzburg spot, the footbridge across the rushing Salzach River. The whole of Salzburg, virtually as it was centuries ago, was gloriously visible from that vantage point. The day was crystal clear, allowing the cluster of ancient churches, including the Salzburg Cathedral, to stand out against cloudless blue skies. Behind them loomed the brooding Festung Hohensalzburg, the largest preserved medieval fortress in central Europe, that was erected in 1077 and boasts all the modern conveniences of its day such as sumptuous private and state rooms, dungeons, and the last word in fully equipped torture chambers. All this against a background of gleaming white snowcapped Alps. I swung around and saw small, picturesque houses that looked like dollhouses lining the riverbanks. In fact, all Salzburg has the look of a stage set, and I expected Miss Piggy and/or Cookie Monster to appear at any minute.

I walked across the bridge to the old city on the left bank until I came to St. Peter's Church. The square in front of the building is rimmed by two-story buildings that were built during Mozart's time, and you look up and fully expect Constantia Mozart to pop her head out of the window and holler for Wolfgang to come upstairs for dinner.

Then I took the usual tourist stroll along the Getreidegasse, which is lined with shops selling everything from lederhosen to Tyrolean hats, with colorful gold-and-red-and-green signs that portrayed the nature of the shop for the benefit of customers of hundreds of years ago when large segments of the population could not read. The streets are so narrow that one could reach out from the window on one side of the street to touch a window on the facing side. What I find so enchanting is the fact that the streets seem to have been planned so that at each end is a framed view of an aspect of a church, or a garden, or a charming shop.

It was time to stop for coffee *mit schlag* (pure heavy sweet cream), a treat no one should miss. If you are coming from the United States, the land of the fat-free frenzy, you may go into shock when you first dine in Austria. There should be a sign posted at all border points that reads: "Calorie and Cholesterol Counters—Do Not Enter." If you're a strict nutrition maven, you run the risk of dropping dead from either stress caused by trying to find or starvation caused by being unable to find healthful food. Fish is virtually nonexistent, pasta is strictly a side dish and is usually gravy-covered noodles that accompany *Stelze* (roast knuckle of pork) or *Schinkenfleckerl*, a baked dish of noodles and ham. Vegetables are cabbage and potatoes. The *Wiener schnitzel* (veal cutlet) can be delicious if fried only lightly. Roasted meats are stuffed with pork and chicken livers. A popular appetizer is chicken livers with cheese. Just reading the menus makes you feel your arteries are hardening. And don't be surprised when your ankles swell up to the width of your calves; they don't know from low sodium here, and the salt content of everything is incredible. Everywhere you go, there are hot dog stands and delis that display more variations of sliced meats than you were aware existed. Some of the leading Viennese chefs decided to introduce nouvelle cuisine a number of years ago in the interest of improving nutrition, and the protests of the citizenry almost reached insurrection proportions. As you walk the streets of Austrian cities and towns, the passing parade of bulging guts and flared hips are a testimonial to the national lack of concern for dieting. Weight-Watchers would undoubtedly file for bankruptcy within a month here.

As I entered the cafe, I stopped at the rack near the door where dozens of newspapers hang from wooden bars for the convenience of patrons. I took an English-language paper and headed for the pastry case to point out my choice of kuchen, which the waitress brought over to my table with coffee. The place was filled with newspaper-reading people who looked like they had been there all day. There's either a very large leisure class in Salzburg or a vast corps of unemployed, in which case it sure beats waiting around for the movies to open when you're in between job interviews. I lingered for a while over my coffee and then walked back to my hotel.

As I entered my room, the phone was ringing. I hoped it wasn't Andre's mother calling to change the date we had arranged for later this afternoon. It wasn't.

"Hello, darling, we haven't spoken to you for ages. How are you?"

I smiled with pleasure. "Hi, Mom—how did you find me?"

"You're not the only detective in the family. I called Abba and he told me you were in Salzburg. The rest was easy. I knew you'd be at the Goldener Hirsch. You always adored the place when we used to stay there. Are the buildings still pink and blue?"

I'm crazy about my mom and dad. I know it's not P.C. to appreciate one's parents; it's far more stylish to attribute all one's neuroses to their Freudian foulups in raising you. I think most people love their parents, but I enjoy the added benefit of liking mine as well.

"Yes, Mom. Everything looks just the same with the wonderful antiques in every room. They've added a newer building across the Getreidegasse."

"You're not staying there!" she said in horror.

"Of course not. If I wanted modern, I'd go to the Sheraton."

"That's my girl." I heard a male voice.

"Hi, Daddy." I heard the echoing sound of a conference call. I envisioned them both sitting in the den talking at the phone.

"What are you doing in Salzburg, Emmy Lou?"

My dread secret is out. I was named after my father's favorite aunt, a lady I never met but grew to hate as I was forced to carry a name that might have been highly suitable for a delicate southern lady or a country western singer but was an embarrassment to a girl child who preferred batting softballs to pouring tea and playing lacrosse rather than the piano. I changed my name after seeing Diana Rigg play Emma Peel on the English TV series *The Avengers* and deciding she was my kind of woman. My mom understood and accepted the name change instantly, but Daddy continues to cling to the original in the vain hope that someday he'll see me in a big organza hat serving lemonade on the veranda.

"I'm on a case, Daddy."

"What's the body count to date?" he asked with a chuckle.

"That's not funny, dear," said my mother fiercely. "I do hope there are no murders, Emma."

That's as much as she would ever say to let me know how she feels about my bizarre profession. One of my favorite qualities in my parents is their "Yes we care but" laissez-faire attitude. I know they worry about my somewhat unconventional life, but they never burden me with their concerns. Mom and I have had lunch at the Carlyle Hotel in New York many times and not once has she mentioned stopping into Vera Wang for a look at wedding gowns. It may sound like our familial relationship resembles a stereotypical WASP noninvolvement policy, but it isn't. Throughout my life, I have always gone to my parents with any problem, emotional or practical, in the comfortable certainty that they will do whatever they can to help. And they haven't given me a cutoff date. My father once told me that parenthood is the only job in the world from which you can never be fired or quit.

"I'm just trying to prevent a divorce between an actor and a baronet's daughter," I said, knowing that noble titles would distract my mother from the danger possibilities of my work. It's not that she's a snob but that mention of British royalty will make it a more titillating topic when she talks proudly about her daughter's career over the bridge table.

"What's the baronet's name?" she asked.

"Mom, you know I can't divulge that information."

"Well," she said, slightly miffed. "I just thought I might know him."

"Honey," my dad said. "The only lord I've ever heard you mention is Lord and Taylor."

I could hear my mother taking a deep breath in preparation for zinging him with a snappy response.

I've always enjoyed their fond badgering relationship and resulting bon mots at home, but not on an international phone call.

"Look, my dears," I said, "can I call you tomorrow? I have to shower and change for an appointment now, so I really don't have time to chat."

"What will you wear?" My mom always has to have the complete picture. She used to ask me what I was wearing whenever she phoned because she liked to envision me as we spoke. I broke her of that habit when for the fourth time I answered "nothing"—I often walk around the house starkers. I remember how startled she was by this revelation.

"You mean you're totally naked? You never did that

when you were home,'' she said in horror, as though my morals had obviously sunk to unspeakable levels of depravity since I left her stabilizing influence.

I reminded her that the presence of my father would have made that unacceptable, but I'm alone now and freeing oneself from the constriction of clothes can be very pleasant. Somehow the totally alien concept of anyone going about her business in the nude intrigued her and she began to picture all the possibilities.

''Do you ever eat that way?''

''No, Mom, the risk of a breast falling into the hot soup or some steaming Mussels Mariniere landing in my bare crotch is too great.''

That finally stopped her.

''I plan to wear my navy blue Donna Karan jumpsuit,'' I said now.

''Very good,'' she said approvingly. ''Stylish enough to be impressive, but not so drop-dead fashionable as to be intimidating.''

Now you can see where I get my awareness of the Psychology of Dressing.

CELIA BAILEY RAMSAY lived on what used to be the unfashionable side of the Salzach River in a section that had been home only to tradespeople and nowadays has become a marvelous mixture of artists' studios, trendy nightclubs, and fashionable houses, much like SoHo in New York City. The house was a tall three stories of pale yellow stone with a red tile roof not far from the Steintor Gate on a narrow street that looked unchanged from the Middle Ages. I rang the bell at exactly three o'clock. I'm always dead on time. Unless there's a damned valid reason, I see lateness as the ultimate and unforgivable rudeness because it conveys the latecomer's implicit message that her time is obviously more valuable than yours. I waited for minutes until I was about to leave, when the door was opened by a tall, slim, redheaded woman on crutches with her leg in a cast and her neck in a brace. She smiled and held out her hand.

"Miss Rhodes? Sorry for the delay in answering the door, but as you can see, my movements tend to be a bit slower these days. Please come in."

I followed her into a small foyer that led into a warm, sunny room with glass doors overlooking a garden ablaze with spring flowers. She noticed my look of delight as I viewed the hundreds of tulips and daffodils massed against a background of forsythia bushes.

"I know, it would be lovely to sit outside, but I'm afraid it's a bit cool today for me. You see, we're archetypically British when it comes to gardening, but not when it comes to temperatures. Unlike our countrymen who seem to pride themselves on ignoring damp and chill, Edward and I love warm and cozy."

She had a rich low voice and spoke in an educated English accent with just a hint of Yorkshire slipping in every now and then. She wore jeans and a cotton turtleneck sweater that matched her startling green eyes. A necklace of amber beads set off her rust-colored hair. If I didn't know how that little ovum has to get fertilized, I would have sworn this one made it on its own because Andre and his mother looked so alike that the presence of any other genes seemed questionable. There was no sign of Sidney anywhere. She motioned for me to sit facing the garden, and she sank down into the adjacent chair.

The room had the inviting warmth of an accumulated decor rather than a deliberately designed one. Some chairs were covered in slightly worn brocade, some in cheerful chintz. The modern couch was the nubby white Egyptian cotton lawson style that the Habitat stores featured a few years ago. Authentic Oriental rugs were scattered about, and the walls were covered with a pleasing hodgepodge of lithographs and paintings that denoted the enjoyer rather than the collector. The large coffee table was glass and brass, but lamps and silver-framed family photographs rested on small elegant wooden tables throughout the room. It was an eclectic mix but it worked.

We regarded each other silently for the initial sizing up. My opinion of Sidney's taste in women moved up ten notches from the nadir it had sunken to after meeting the unlovely harridan who was number one on his spouse parade. This woman was lovely looking, intelligent, and most important, she exuded niceness—a quality that, as Supreme Court Justice Potter Stewart said about pornography, "I cannot define it but I know it when I see it." No wonder she turned out such a winner son.

She moved very gingerly, which indicated her injuries were recent. I know it's impolite to pry, but to sit there looking at someone who looks like The Spirit of '76 and pretend not to notice is unnatural—for me, anyway.

"What happened?"

She said simply, "I fell off my horse yesterday."

I awarded her more points. Most of the riders I know would say, "My horse threw me," thereby placing blame on the animal rather than on their own equestrian ineptitude. She took full responsibility for the spill. This was a solid lady. Too bad Sidney lost her. But I'd find out about that later.

"How?" I asked.

She made a face. "I don't really understand how it happened. I take my horse on the same route every day. We were galloping along and suddenly I felt myself hurled forward and I was on the ground. Broken leg, broken collarbone. It's just lucky we hadn't reached the quarry yet."

"Or you would be dead," said a male voice. "I've told you over and over to please change your itinerary; that stone quarry is too hazardous. Why is a husband the last person a woman will listen to?"

"Edward, darling—come in and meet Emma Rhodes. She's a friend of Andre's and wants to interview me for a book on divorced women. Isn't that a lark?"

He was what I call an "ish." Everything about him was

ishy—his hair was brownish, which is an indeterminate
shade without sufficient solid tone to be called brown. It
was longish but without enough bulk to rest on his shoulders and thus be termed long. He was slimmish, but the
little potbelly that made him look like a hard-boiled egg on
stilts prevented him from being regarded as slim. He had a
wispy mustache and somewhat scraggly beard, and wore
pink tortoise-framed glasses. He would be called tallish
since he didn't stand up straight enough to be considered
tall. He wore an old tweed jacket and black turtleneck over
jeans, and looked like a man who every morning would put
on the clothes that he had slung over the chair the night
before until his wife replaced the outfit. I made a quick bet
with myself that he wore white socks with black shoes and
I won. He carried a large stuffed shoulder bag that was
overflowing with papers that turned out to be music. He
looked sweet and kindly, but having dealt with chorale di-
rectors many times, I know that put a baton in his hand and
he would instantly become a Marine drill sergeant.

"Edward looks like the absentminded professor, Miss
Rhodes—but don't let that fool you. Ask him for Fauré's
Cantique De Jean Racine and he'll reach into that traveling
file cabinet he wears at all times and put his hands on it in
seconds."

"Please call me Emma," I said.

She nodded with a smile. "And you must call me Celia."

Edward Ramsay smiled, displaying National Health irregular teeth. Then his face turned serious. "Speaking of
Mozart—you're quite sure you can't sing with us
tomorrow, darling? Three of my other altos have the flu,
which leaves me with only two. And without your strong
voice to lead them, they'll surely be lost." He looked distraught.

"I'd love to be in the concert, Edward—you know that.
But I can't possibly stand for one and a half hours. My leg
and neck would protest severely."

"Yes, of course, darling," he said sympathetically. "It was rotten of me to even suggest it."

"Which Mozart are you doing?" I asked.

"*Vesperae Solennes De Confessore*," he answered with the polite tone of one who expects his audience to be totally ignorant and then turned to Celia to continue his conversation.

"*Dixit, dominus, domino meo sede*," I sang quietly.

His eyes opened wide. "You know it?"

I nodded. "I've sung it many times. Our chorale group just did the *Vesperae* last month."

"What voice do you sing?" he asked.

Ever the master of suspense, I was silent for a moment and then smiled. "Alto."

I know, I've never told you about this area of my multifaceted life. Given my frequent allusions to my accomplishments and talents, you may find it hard to believe that I'm really not one of those vainglorious *fanfarons* who must proclaim her superiority constantly. Right, you're thinking. I can almost see the skeptical smirk on your face. Not that I'm going to do a number professing excessive humility, heaven forfend. But I'd like to explain that the only reason for references to my special abilities has not been to brag unbecomingly but merely to explain my specific actions and behavior of the moment. Up to now, there had been no reason to tell you that I studied voice from the age of seventeen on and have been singing in chorale groups since college. Believe me, Kiri Te Kanawa has nothing to fear. I do not have a great voice, but I thoroughly enjoy singing, and chorales are ideal because you have the joy of performing without the responsibility; errors are noted only by the conductor and the singers on either side of you. You may want to ask why I took singing lessons if I showed no specific talent. To answer a question with a question, how come your mother insisted you have lessons in piano, violin, clarinet, or whatever, even though the dog used to hide under the bed when you practiced? Because studying a musical instrument was considered part of your education and would be something that would bring you pleasure for the rest of your life. Then why not study voice? It's the most portable instrument you have and one you can take everywhere. Assuming you have a mildly pleasant voice, you can be taught to sing well enough to provide enjoyment to yourself and listeners. If you've ever heard records of Rex Harrison singing in *My Fair Lady* or Richard Burton in *Camelot* you would see what I mean.

Edward took me by the arm and led me over to the piano.

"My God, a Beckstein!" I said in delight. "I haven't seen one of these for years. My voice teacher had hers shipped to America from Germany."

He smiled proudly. "It's one of the finest instruments in the world. Now please sing for me. You can read the words and music over my shoulder."

"That won't be necessary," I said. "I know it by heart."

He looked dubious, but he didn't know as you do of my photographic memory. I sang the alto voice of the entire *Dixit* movement, all ten pages, except for the Gloria Patri's of the solo parts. When I finished, Celia applauded and Edward's face was suffused with joy. I don't have a great voice, but it's strong and on key.

"You will sing with us tomorrow morning, of course," he said with the positive assurance of a chorale director. He didn't ask if I had planned to stay overnight in Salzburg. My participation was a given as far as he was concerned. As I said, they become instant control freaks.

"I didn't bring a long black skirt and white blouse," I said. That's the de rigueur outfit worn by ladies of the chorus.

"Not to worry," said Celia. "We're the same size—you can wear mine."

"Then it's settled," said Edward happily as he arose from the piano. "I'll be off and you two can continue your interview. Celia will tell you the time and place details."

"Before you go, dear," said Celia, "would you be a

darling and bring in the coffee tray I set up in the kitchen?''

He kissed her and said, ''Of course.''

''How I hate being incapacitated,'' she said with a grimace after he left.

''I can tell,'' I said. ''You had the tentative tone of someone who's not used to asking for favors.''

She sighed. ''You're quite right. Edward's been a dear, but he's such a *kloz* as they say in Austria or, as you Americans call it, a klutz.''

We heard the sound of breaking china and she jumped. ''Oh dear, I do hope it's the saucer that matches the cup he broke this morning.''

When he came in a few minutes later, he said apologetically as he set the silver tray on the coffee table, ''I'm afraid one of the saucers slipped out of my hand.''

She looked at me and we smiled at each other.

''Not to worry, dear. It's only things, not people,'' she said like a good wife. She reminded me of my grandmother, who whenever anything was lost, stolen, or broken would always say reassuringly, ''At least no one's in the hospital.''

After he left, I said, ''I had a boyfriend like that once. By the time we broke up, he had broken so much of my china and glassware that my dinner parties had to be limited to five guests.''

She laughed. ''Luckily we don't throw broken people into the dustbin,'' and she tapped her leg cast.

Good. As cross-examining lawyers say, once she has opened the line of questioning, I can go into it. Now maybe I could clear up what had puzzled me.

''How do you suppose you were thrown? You're apparently an experienced rider and you were on your own horse in familiar territory.''

She was quiet for a moment. ''I didn't want to mention this while Edward was here—but my groom called just before to say that the girth had come apart.''

"You mean cut," I said. "The girth on a saddle doesn't usually wear out, does it?"

"Not as a rule," she said. "But it is possible. I usually check the entire saddle before I mount, but perhaps I forgot yesterday. I really don't remember," she said, rubbing her hand across her forehead.

Another anomaly to store in my brain bank for later consideration.

"How do you take your coffee?" she asked as she poured.

"Black, please."

She passed me the coffee and I winced as I looked at the exquisite cup and saucer. "Wedgwood?"

She nodded with a grimace as she handed me a silver tray with little *Buchterins*, those marvelous Austrian sweet rolls that literally melt in your mouth. So what if scarcely an hour ago I had consumed coffee mit schlag and two fruit kuchens. When would I be in Salzburg again, and Donna Karan clothes usually have a certain amount of give.

She filled her cup and put two pastries on her plate and then looked at me.

"Now that you've been forced to listen to a litany of my difficulties and we've inveigled you into filling in for me in the choir, why don't we do something for you? What would you like to know about my divorce?"

"For starters, why?"

She sighed. "Well, you've met Sidney, Andre tells me. So you know he's a dear man, has pots of money, and is the father of my children. And you're wondering why on earth a woman would leave a paragon like that. Of course, you're quite right in being puzzled."

I waited. As I've mentioned before, waiting is the interviewer's most effective weapon. Most people simply can't handle silence. Just keep quiet and they'll feel driven to fill the void.

"It was his terrible jealousy," she said.

The magic word.

"Of whom was he jealous?" I asked.

Aren't you impressed by my perfect syntax?

"Every man I so much as said 'good day' to. It was monstrous. It's not as though I had troops of lovers. I was completely faithful always. You may not be able to tell what I'm really like since my disposition has been somewhat soured by my little mishap, but I am generally a rather friendly sociable person. I was not able to be that when Sidney was around," she said emphatically. "If I smiled at the milkman, Sidney glowered. When we were on holiday, he went positively dotty when I struck up a conversation with the man at the next table—claimed I was leading him on. The most innocuous encounters with men would set him off." I noticed that Yorkshire crept into her language when she became agitated. " 'Twere constant aggro—seemed I could do owt right. No matter how I would tell him I loved only him, he would just not believe me."

The same pattern. He had driven away wife after wife, and hasn't learned yet. This is not schmuck behavior, it's sick behavior.

"I didn't want to break up our family, believe me. But unless you have lived through it, you cannot imagine how demeaning and destructive it is to live with a man who is monstrously possessive. He made life unbearable."

"Didn't you suggest marriage counseling? Or perhaps that wasn't available in England then. Your country lagged far behind the States in accepting the value of psychotherapy, which I'm not sure was to your national detriment. Sometimes I wonder if we in the U.S. hadn't abdicated personal responsibility for a policy of 'Why think—see a shrink.' But psychiatrists were certainly available in London, especially if money was no problem."

She started to shake her head and cried out in pain. I touched her arm in sympathy. "You're going to have to confine all your responses to the verbal rather than the physical until that neck brace comes off."

"He absolutely refused to go for any kind of help. He

scorned psychiatrists and psychologists and referred to them as self-appointed experts on how to live in the world which they had never entered.''

I laughed. "He's not too far off the mark, is he?''

"I was in despair until I met Edward."

"Where did you two meet?"

"Through Andre. His group was on the same program as one of Edward's chorale groups in Chichester. Isn't it wonderful about Andre performing with the Concertgebouw?'' she said with elation. "Edward and I are so proud of him.''

No mention of dear old Dad here.

"What made you move to Salzburg?'' I asked. I wanted to hear her version.

"I know it sounds mad, but when I told Sidney that I was leaving him for another man, he insisted on continuing to support me. I was willing to leave without a bean, I was that wretched. But as I said, he's a dear person and didn't want me to live in reduced circumstances. The children, of course, he would provide for, but when he heard Edward's profession, he immediately offered to provide for me as well. I must tell you I was truly flabbergasted. Sidney was always complaining about how poorly his enterprises were doing, and I didn't know how he would be able to afford it. Then I learned he had done a similar thing for his previous wife, of whom he never spoke.''

"Some people like to poor-mouth themselves,'' I said. "Either they believe in the virtue of humility and don't wish to call attention to their successes, or they believe in discretion and don't want to draw the attention of the Inland Revenue.''

"Perhaps,'' she said with a smile. "I never understood the legal details of Sidney's financial transactions, but the trust fund he established to support her and me is on the Isle of Sark with stipulation that we recipients of the income generated must live abroad.''

"How did he react when you told him you were leaving him?"

"As though I was telling him we're having grilled plaice for tea," she said with a wry grimace.

"No emotional outburst? No screaming abuse?"

"I was as surprised as you. I had dreaded the confrontation, fully expecting a bloody row. And then he takes it without so much as a blink of the eye. I was right stunned, I can tell you." She paused to think for a minute. "Funny, you know I recall getting the feeling that he seemed to be almost relieved."

Another aberrant tidbit to deposit in the brain bank.

"How did Sidney's parents take the breakup of your family?"

She shrugged. "I wouldn't know. I never met them."

My astonishment was apparent. "You were married for sixteen years and you never met his mother and father?"

"It was a religion thing. Sidney told me that they could not accept his marriage to a gentile. He said they actually went through their strange mourning ritual—it has a funny name."

"Shiva," I said. "They call it 'sitting shiva.' "

"Yes, that's it. He explained that to very pious Jews, a child who marries out of the religion is considered as good as dead. I thought that seemed like a rather excessive reaction, but I have long ago learned that religious practices are personal and inexplicable. It saddened me because I would have liked to have known them, and to give my children the pleasures of grandparents, but Sidney explained that was impossible."

Why, I wondered, would he go through such extreme machinations to keep his wives away from his family? What was he hiding?

Her eyes smiled. "I think my little story will make an unusual chapter in your book. I venture to guess there aren't many divorced wives whose ex-husbands voluntarily supply them with generous incomes for their lifetimes."

• • •

THE NEXT MORNING, I was one of the sixty-five tuxedoed men and black-skirt-white-bloused women who streamed across the square into St. Peter's Abbey, the most luxurious church in Salzburg. The bells were pealing, the sky was cloudless blue, and a light breeze was blowing. At that moment, I felt like one of the most privileged people in the world.

The square is rimmed by cotton-candy-pink two-story houses that look contemporary with the twelfth-century church. The abbey has a porch with beautiful Romanesque vaulted arches from the original structure. The lush interior has the stunning voluptuous quality of the late Baroque era when additions were made in the 1770's.

As we stood in the choir loft and the organist played his introduction, I got the sense of exhilarated anticipation I always experience when performing in a chorale. I enjoy the respectful attention of the audience, and the wonderful awareness of being part of a group that will bring pleasure to the listeners. By the time we reached the *Confitebor* movement, I knew I was a contributing member of a chorus that produced exquisite sound, and that's got to be one of the greatest feelings in the world. Edward conducted with a forceful firmness that one never dreamed could emerge from that wimpy exterior. When we raised our voices and the full-throated sounds of our final "amen" filled the church, I felt the up-and-down-the-spine chills I always experience. As we walked down the aisle acknowledging the applause of the audience, we were all on a high that's better than any recreational drug could possibly induce. I spotted Celia and stopped in front of her.

"You were wonderful, you were all wonderful. It was a superb performance," she said. "Thank you so much. Edward must be so pleased." She turned to the young woman at her side. "Emma, this is my daughter Alexandra."

Hello, Sidney's genes. She looked just like Daddy. Well, it's nice that he imparted some visible effect on one of his offspring because Andre was the image of his mother, red hair and all. Nice for Sidney but not too wonderful for Alexandra. That stolid build, somewhat wide flat nose, and bland blondness was O.K. on Sidney because his strong personality made the whole package appealing. Unfortunately, Alexandra had inherited the looks but not the charm. She had no effect and her face projected a disinterested detachment that made you feel she was repelling invaders. Blond can be pretty if you work on it. But Alexandra was one of those "this is me, take it or leave it" women who eschew outside help. Men have the option of adding a mustache and/or beard to give themselves more character. Our only choice is a paint job or cosmetic surgery.

After trying to engage Alexandra in something resembling conversation I almost gave up. I've gotten better responses from my gerbils. The usual technique when you meet someone new is to ask a leading question, which is called that because it is meant to lead somewhere, preferably to disclosure of some aspects of the person's vital statistics and lifestyle. For instance, a usual opening gambit is the weather. "Nice day today, isn't it?" This could get an answer like "Yes, thank goodness. We've had so much rain that the kids have been going stir-crazy." Fine. Now you know that she's a mother. She has brought you into her life, thus signifying she's interested in hearing about yours. The drill is that you then respond with some pertinent personal comment, and you're off. It's easy. That is, if the other person reacts correctly and you're not hit, as I was, with nods, head-shaking, and an occasional verbalized "yes" or "no." An interviewer's nightmare. To compound her sins, she was one of those rare people who can leave a conversational silence alone and is perfectly content to study her fingernails forever. I realized that a talk with her would require concentrated work to break down whatever barriers she had spent a lifetime building.

"Please come back to the house, Emma," said Celia. "We always have a small party for the choir after a performance. Alexandra, darling, you're coming, too, of course?''

Alexandra nodded her assent. She certainly was spare with words. Maybe she'd been watching too many Clint Eastwood movies.

When we got to the house, I watched for her to alight somewhere and then sat down next to her with my coffee and kuchen.

"Your father tells me you're a very busy architect," I said.

Her eyelids flickered. Aha, there's life there. This time I kept silent. Let her sweat this one out.

"You know my father?"

I thought you'd never ask, dearie.

"Yes, we had lunch together last week. He's very proud of you."

My God, she has teeth. She smiled!

"You must be a damned good architect to have won the commission to do the addition for the university."

She shrugged and looked embarrassed. "I was very lucky."

Now I understood her problem. She suffered from terminal shyness. I've often thought to suggest to SAG, the Screen Actors Guild, and AFTRA, the American Federation of TV and Radio Artists, that they issue bumper stickers to the children of members. "Growing up with an actor parent can be hazardous to your psyche." Unless they're cut from the same cloth, having an extroverted performer for a father can have a subduing effect on kids.

"What sort of structure are you planning?" I asked.

She looked at me with the pained look of an artist who is often forced to deal politely with people who are well-meaning but totally ignorant of her field of work. I could see her trying to figure how to handle such a question from someone whose knowledge of architecture was limited.

"I grew up in Ulrich Franzen's butterfly-roof house, which made me and my family architecture buffs," I said.

"Living in a designed space made us conscious of the elements involved, and of the great pleasure of living in a work of art rather than just a house."

Her eyes widened. "You mean the all glass house with what they call the steel-umbrella cantilevered roof?"

"Yes. My parents bought it from Mrs. Franzen."

I had her. Now that she had an understanding kindred soul, words poured out of her. She went into detail about her design ideas for the project, and her face became animated and vibrant. She was articulate, eloquent, and highly intelligent, and her concepts and ideas were fascinating. It was a delight to listen to her.

When she stopped to catch her breath, I smiled and said, "I'll bet your dad loves listening to your plans."

She laughed. "I'm afraid he doesn't have a clue about what I do. Nor, I might add, tremendous interest."

"But he's involved in real estate," I said. "That means buildings. And that means architecture."

"With Daddy all it means is money. The only art form he's truly interested in is theater. Not that I blame him," she said hastily. "Given his deprived childhood, having pots of money is very important to him."

"Was his family that badly off?" I asked. "Unless they go hungry, most kids aren't aware of being poor. As long as they get love, they're usually pretty happy."

"But he didn't have much of that either," she said sadly. "His mother died long before I was born, so I didn't know her, and his father, well, we never knew him either. Matter of fact, we never saw any of Daddy's family."

"Didn't you think that a bit strange?"

"Well, we had the impression that something was not quite right there. When you're children, you really don't think too much about family, do you, and you go wherever your parents take you. We used to visit Grandmum and Granddad Maitland often, they were Mummy's mom and dad, and there are scads of cousins so we never missed the other side of the family."

"But later, when you were grown up?"

"I asked Daddy once about his relatives, and he became terribly upset. I got the impression that he absolutely detested his father and he wouldn't speak of his mother. So I never mentioned it again."

"Do you get to see your dad often?" I asked.

She smiled. "Oh yes, he comes over fairly often. He visits Mum, too—they're still good friends. He knows I'm building my career, which means I can't get away readily. He's a wonderful dad—you won't find any better."

"The divorce must've been tough for you, then."

Her face clouded. "Yes and no. We used to hide our heads under the duvets when we'd hear them screaming at each other. I couldn't bear to see Mum so miserable, so it was almost a relief when they broke up. Of course, it was quite a wrench when we had to move, but she's so happy now and Edward is such a dear." She paused. "I don't know how well Daddy fared. Have you met Juliet?"

"Yes."

"Then you probably know she has left him." She made a moue. "That's number three. Perhaps there are some men who are just not made for marriage."

I smiled. "I think I've dated most of them."

She laughed. "I know what you mean. I'm thirty-two and until I met Franz two years ago, I thought being a wife would not be part of my future. He comes from a small town in Austria. His father was the highly respected village doctor, so he had a more traditional background, and marriage and family are all important to him. I think when we have children it will be difficult for him to accept a professional working wife and mother. But I'll worry about that situation when it comes. Right now, we're very happily married."

"Is he here?" I asked.

She looked around the room. "Yes, there he is." She pointed to a tall blond man who looked like he should be wearing lederhosen and drinking beer out of a huge stein instead of white wine out of a stemmed glass. He was deep in conversation with a portly gentleman dressed in a dark suit and white shirt with the kind of starched collar that was very handy for supporting the two chins above it.

She grinned. "He's talking to Herr Hildebrandt, the banker. Franz is trying to raise money for a development he designed." Her eyes danced with enthusiasm. "It's simply marvelous—he has this idea to build a virtually complete small city on the outskirts of Salzburg. The design is a brilliant concept. Getting financing is very difficult. But many people have shown interest and we have great hopes."

Lotsa luck. Any novice seeking backing for a dream is in for a rough ride. The first and hardest thing to accept is that, contrary to conventional beliefs, projects are not judged on their merits but on profit potential. Investors tend to be a steely-eyed unromantic group and they don't really give a damn what you're making, selling, or building—the only thing that turns them on is the bottom line. When you enter the world of high finance, you find that there are many other yardsticks used to evaluate the attractiveness of an offering, such as how it fits in with the potential investors' overall financial situations. Big money muck-a-mucks pay little attention to the rosy predictions of starry-eyed business starter-uppers. They usually have their own agendas and seek situations where the returns fit into their personal financial programs.

"Couldn't your father help?" I asked.

She shook her head. "He would if he could, he's very generous."

You ought to know, honey.

"Unfortunately, he has no available capital. All his money is tied up in property and trusts, you know."

Do I ever.

"I guess your mother doesn't have enough to help," I said.

"Actually, she's quite well off now," said Alexandra

happily. "She's always lived frugally, her only extravagance is her horse, who she loves dearly. With Daddy's advice, she's invested very well and by now has a lovely nest egg. But she needs that for her and Edward's old age. After all, she is getting on in years—she's sixty-two."

The last time I said something like that to my mother, I nearly got a faceful of creamed mushrooms. At dinner one evening, I had referred to some acquaintance as "an elderly woman of sixty-three," and my sixty-five-year-old tennis-playing, golfing, sailing, scuba-diving mother became livid. It was only my dad's deterring hand that stopped her from dumping the appetizer she was serving over my head rather than setting it on the table.

Franz came over to join us. I guessed he'd completed his briefing of Herr two-chins.

"Alexandra tells me you have a wonderful plan for building a new mini-city. It sounds fascinating," I said after we had been introduced.

His blond, blue-eyed Aryan face lit up, and he looked at her with fondness.

"Ah, yes, Alexandra is my most enthusiastic fan. I wish everyone could view the project with her eyes."

"Herr Hildebrand wasn't encouraging?" she asked.

He shook his head. "But not to worry, *Liebchen*," he said with the implacable confidence, strength, and emphasis of a true believer. "I will find a way."

She looked at him with adoration, and I looked at him with trepidation. Fanatics make me twitchy. I find them scary because they're unpredictable, amoral, and don't follow the rules. But maybe I'm being a bit harsh on Franz because the world hasn't fared well with Teutonic zealots.

"Where is your mother?" he asked, looking around. "How is she?"

"She's sitting over there near the window, talking to Edward. The doctor said she's doing fine."

"Wasn't it awful that someone cut her saddle girth?" I said.

Alexandra colored. "Mother didn't want anyone to know about that. It's only a suspicion."

"Oh, I am sorry," I said, displaying a remorse I didn't feel in the slightest.

She looked very upset and he looked pretty cool. "Her saddle was damaged?" he asked. "Why would anyone do that?"

Why, indeed? Cui bono?

"You would think," he said, "that for all the money she pays them to care for that darling horse of hers, those idiots would maintain her equipment properly."

It was hard to tell if his criticism was directed at the stable personnel for their inefficiency or his mother-in-law for her extravagance.

"Oh, darling—Mum doesn't spend all that much for her horse."

This was obviously a frequent sore point between them. I've always noticed most married couples have one or two hot buttons that set them off. He turned red with annoyance, not a flattering combination with his pale blond eyebrows and hair. "Ach, that animal lives in greater splendor than we do. There are far better things to do with money than waste it on a horse."

Like leave it for her heirs? I remember visiting my grandmother in Palm Beach and being amused when her octagenarian neighbor drove up with her new Mercedes and said triumphantly, "I bought it with my children's money."

"But it is her money to waste," said Alexandra tightly.

Good girl. I was glad to see she didn't allow him to goose-step all over her. The only Germans and Austrians with whom I'm uncomfortable are those in their sixties and over, the ones who piously claim to have been totally unaware of the ovens. But this fellow looked like a poster boy for the Hitler *Jugend*, the perfect Aryan, which set my antagonistic antennae quivering. So far, he'd done nothing to dispel that attitude. Suddenly, he looked over my shoulder and came to attention.

"Will you both excuse me?" he said. "I see someone I must talk to." He hurried in the direction of a short, pink-cheeked woman in a rather shabby-looking gray suit who had just come in.

"Frau Hauseknecht," she said. "He's been trying to interest her in the project for months."

I looked over at the woman. "She looks like she gets her clothes at Oxfam," I said. "Where would she get the money to invest in Franz?"

"From a husband who died last year, leaving her a huge mansion facing the Mirabell Gardens, a ski house in Kitz-bühel, a house overlooking the sea in Cannes, and a fortune of some billion Austrian marks."

"I gather she has resisted past pleas," I said, watching Franz fawn over her. He brought her a plate of food and a glass of champagne and looked as though he would happily hand-feed her if she would permit. I could see from Alexandra's reaction that she found the performance a little sickening. Suck-ups are always repellent. It was a perfect example of the old adage about Germanic peoples that they are either at your throat or at your feet. (I know I shouldn't repeat ethnic slurs, but always being Politically Correct can be a real drag.)

"I know he has to court people to get money, but I just can't bear it," she said bitterly. "Money was always more important to Franz than to me. But the financing for this project has made him into a driven man."

"Raising money is a very humbling experience," I said. "I've had friends who had to solicit funds for some reason or other, and it's not a pretty sight. The worst of it is they get to value people according to their cash potentials."

She nodded eagerly. "It's so good to talk to someone who understands. Mummy is such an innocent when it comes to money. It has never mattered to her, and she just cannot understand Franz's obsession with it."

"He knows about her trust fund?"

She looked slightly ashamed. "Oh, yes, indeed. I think he knows the terms better than she does."

"What are they?"

What the hell, she opened that line of testimony so don't I have the right to pursue it? I've found that asking outright personal questions works one of two ways: either the questionee is so taken aback by the unexpected chutzpah of the questioner that before she can think she answers with truth, or she has the quick presence of mind to say, "None of your business." So what do I have to lose?

Fortunately for me, Alexandra was from the first school.

"The monthly income from the fund is divided between the two wives in specified proportions of sixty/forty."

"What happens when one of them dies?"

"It all goes one hundred percent to the survivor."

Which means Celia will now be an even richer woman. Son-in-law Franz will be clicking his lederhosen in joy when he finds out. Or does he already know?

"He knows she gets all this money from Daddy every month. He believes so totally in his project that he cannot understand why anyone with money shouldn't willingly give it over to him." Her face clouded. "He was so wonderful and we were so happy before all this started," she said wistfully. "His plan is brilliant, but I wish he had never designed it."

"Mrs. Henry Ford probably wished the same thing. Mrs. Thomas Edison, too," I said consolingly. "Being the wife of a visionary is tough during the beginning, but think how happy he'll be when it comes to a reality."

Notice I omitted the word "if." You can't allow that word to even enter the subject's cognizance when you're in the encouragement mode.

She took my hand. "Thank you, Emma. You've really helped me. I am very appreciative. And I hope your work will be a smashing success."

For a minute, I didn't know what the devil she was talking about. The trouble with leading a double life is you can't always remember in which one you're living.

"And that the book sells trillions of copies," she said with a wide smile.

Oh, yes, that life.

"I'd better say good-bye to your mother," I said. "But before I do, can I take your picture?" I took out my trusty little Nikon. "I want one of everyone in the family. I'll catch Franz when he's finished with Madame Big Bucks."

She posed for me smilingly. "Is photography your hobby?" she asked.

"Not really," I answered, "I just like to keep mementoes of trips I've taken and people I've met."

I hated for her to think me one of those hordes of handbag-clutching polyester tourists who take thousands of pictures in order to torture the folks back home. But I thought she'd prefer that to the real explanation, which was that I was building a rogues' gallery for my casebook.

VII

―――――

WHEN I WALKED into my London flat, the answer phone was blinking red like a Christmas tree. Two messages. Every time I see this activity, I remember how my best friend in college refused to get a machine for fear she'd come home and find no messages. At eighteen, one is not yet socially secure, and her two main concerns in life at the time were popularity and her inadequate equipment for an impressive décolletage.

"I have some information about your current client. Ring me when you get back from wherever it is you have been. This is Caleb."

As if I couldn't recognize that deep, resonant, sexy voice.

"Hello, *ahuvati*, my sweet, give me a buzz when you return from the wonderful country that gave us Mozart and Hitler. I have news about the Lechwandowskis. Oh, yes, did your mama reach you? I hope you didn't mind my giving her your itinerary. But I figured why shouldn't you get loaded with the same guilt shit as we children of Jewish mothers who would track us down in the tundra if we forgot to call."

I called Abba first because I like to leave the best for last, like dessert.

"Emma—sweetheart. So what's the body count? Did you find wife number two in failing or fallen health?"

"Actually, Abba, you're uncannily accurate. She is in failing health right now because she had an accident and fell off her horse."

He roared with delight. "Now I can add 'Prescience' to the other credentials on my C.V. An accident, you say." He snorted in disbelief. "In my business accidents don't happen—they're created. The dictionary definition of 'accident' is an event that occurs unexpectedly or unintentionally. I'll buy the first, but not the second. What caused the fall? You said she fell off 'her' horse, not just 'a' horse—so she must be a seasoned rider if she owns her own nag—let alone rich. I understand that keeping up a horse is more expensive than paying off a Porsche."

"Right again, Sherlock," I said. "The girth on the saddle was almost cut through. I think it was meant to come apart earlier, at which time she'd have ended up at the bottom of a stone quarry. Fortunately she rode fast enough to have cleared the danger area when the thing separated, so she ended up on a gurney instead of a slab."

"I'm glad I'm not one of Sidney Bailey's ex-wives," he said. "On the other hand, I'd be loaded and I could quit this fucking job tomorrow."

"First place, you love your job, and secondly, somehow I don't think you'd qualify for the position as Mrs. Bailey."

"Why?" he shot back. "He doesn't like short people? We're of the same religion."

"It seems like a plot by someone who would like to remove both former Mrs. Baileys or it could be a coincidence. Both women happen to have relatives who would benefit from their deaths."

"Bullshit! I don't believe in coincidences. They're too convenient. There's gotta be one person who would get rich from knocking off the two women."

"The only one who fits that description is Sidney Bailey, and he's the one who, under no duress whatever, set up the trust fund in the first place. He wouldn't have to kill them to get his money back—all he'd have to do is close out the funds."

"Not if it's an irrevocable trust. Check it out. And while you're at it, why don't you look into Daddy Bigbucks' finances? These big hot-shit tycoons with their convoluted financial structures often get into a bind—they're so busy moving money from B corporation to shore up C corporation that they don't notice that A corporation is about to go down the toilet. He may be desperate for cash."

"So desperate that he'd murder the women he venerates? Somehow, it doesn't play, Abba."

"Any man who voluntarily supports ex-wives who fucked him over has either got to be the dumbest cocksucker in the western world or the sickest. Who knows what such a dickhead would do?"

"Abba, as always, your reasoning is aces. But it's your elegance of language that impresses me most."

"I was a star of the Brooklyn College Debating Society, you know," he said, "so kindly show a little respect. I never lost an argument."

"Yes, but did you win friends and influence people?" I asked.

"I don't view life as a popularity contest," he said. "When I have a mission, I take no prisoners."

But to help his friends and causes he believes in, he'd risk his life.

"Abba, you said something about the Lechwandowski will in your message. What's the story there?"

"I heard from Jan," he said. "The old bitch died intestate. Why does that always sound like someone who had their balls removed?"

That means Grace gets one half. Under Czech law, the surviving spouse gets one half. Rudy must be livid. He undoubtedly figured that Alicia would leave him everything.

What he didn't figure on was that she was one of those selfish vain women who can't bear to think or talk about death. They fancy themselves eternally young and immortal. What goes hand in hand with that attitude is a total lack of concern for anyone else's well-being. Like heirs. Which is why they never get around to making wills.

"Jan tells me that the fancy man husband has been filling the fuzz's ears with all sorts of nasty inferences about the daughter's undaughterly behavior," he continued.

"You mean like fancying fucking Dad?" I asked. "The son of a bitch is undoubtedly trying to set her up as the murderer so that he walks away with one hundred percent of the estate. She can't benefit from the death of her victim if she's convicted."

"According to Jan, he's doing a real number on Gracie," said Abba. "He's suggested to the police that she knew she'd be the big legatee. Another reason for killing Mom. The lawyers are holding off on probate until the case is resolved. Ludvik is still keeping the body on ice until he's got a candidate for the alleged perpetrator."

"I hate the idea of that slimebucket getting a single *heller* out of the whole thing," I said vehemently. Suddenly I got an idea.

"Abba, can you check into the background of the bereaved Mr. Sykes?"

"What kind of checking, *hamoodie*? What are we looking for?"

"Other Mrs. Sykeses."

"Aha—you think the *charah* piece of shit is a bigamist?"

"Let's say I wouldn't be surprised if he never bothered to go through the formalities of divorce. At his age, he's certainly been married before. He strikes me as a guy who wouldn't bother with legalities and would keep as far away as possible from lawyers and the courts."

"Emma, my love," he said with a sigh, "when are you going to stop wasting that sharp brain on the undeserving rich and famous and use it for deserving good people?''

"And when are you going to stop trying to recruit me
for the Mossad? I may have a strong mind, but I have a
weak character—I love luxury and hate danger. Besides,
Abba darling, I thought all people are created equal. Where
is it written in the Constitution or Bill of Rights that they
lose that entitlement when they get rich?''

He sighed. "Ach, what a waste. Golda Meir's brain and
Elizabeth Taylor's looks—you're probably the only living
human being who could win a landslide election in Israel.
But then, you're not Jewish, so why eat my heart out? O.K.,
I'll find out about Mr. Sykes. Wasn't he a Dickensian vil-
lain?''

"Bill Sykes in *Oliver Twist*. He was a bastard who used
women, too. Maybe that's why he took that name. He sure
as hell wasn't born with it.''

"I'll find that out, too. I'll call you as soon as I have
something. Now watch your *tuchis*, tootsie. You may be
getting too close to someone who doesn't want to be
reached.''

Then I called Caleb.

"Hi, Detective Chief Superintendent.''

I love saying that. Having been an avid fan of English
mysteries all my life, the words "Scotland Yard" carry a
mystique, an aura of skill, charm, and invincibility. I don't
consider myself an Anglophile, but somehow "N.Y.P.D.''
doesn't do it for me. The violent, profane rough-and-tumble
action and dialogue may roil the insides of some, but me,
I get turned on by the cerebral attitudes of opera-loving
Oxford man Inspector Morse and the elegant Roderick Al-
leyn.

"Emma! Is this an overseas phone call or have you returned to our United Kingdom?''

"I'm in residence again at the King's Road.''

"Does that mean Miss Rhodes is At Home receiving,
and I am invited to come by and drop my calling card in
the silver salver in the foyer?''

"By all means. But since my flat doesn't boast a foyer, and I pawned all the family silver salvers, why don't you just pop over and drop a bottle of chilled Veuve Cliquot on the first table you find—say at seven tonight."

"Ah," he said with great satisfaction. "That means we're dining in and I can look forward to one of those superb Emma Rhodes' culinary concoctions."

"Gee whiz," I said, "it sure is thrilling to date a detective. There's just no end to their marvelous deductive skills."

"You make mock of the constabulary, fair maiden, but that does not stop you from taking advantage of our facilities. Do you want me to deliver my report on your Mr. Sidney Bailey tonight or would you like to hear it now?"

"Now, please."

"He's in questionable repute with the financial community and being watched by the Yard's financial branch. He treads a fine line but is extremely shrewd and has never been found to break any law, although he along with many other offshore magnates is watched carefully. He doesn't operate in any arena that could harm the public, since he doesn't deal in shares that can be sold to unwary widows and orphans. He works alone and seems to have earned the begrudging admiration of our lads, who regard him as rather brilliant and fairly honorable in a field where that word is known only as a title, not an adjective. At the moment, it is rumored that he's in a bit of a cash bind, having recently purchased a large building on Canary Walk which is not doing too well. No one really knows how deeply he's in trouble because he's been known to pull rabbits out of his hat many times in similar situations."

"So the man is hurting for money at the moment."

"Yes, but I'm not sure how desperately. These sorts of chaps have their perennial ups and downs, it's a way of life with them, and it rarely causes them to alter their lifestyles. I'd say he still isn't glancing at the right side of the menu when he dines out."

"But I'll bet he does. Edsel Ford's greatest pleasure was going around his four-story Fifth Avenue mansion every night to check that all lights were out. And Jackie O wore fake pearls."

"The bizarre behavior of the obscenely wealthy has never caught my fancy. But you have."

"I gather Sergeant Parnell is not in the room with you."

"Quite right. Sergeant Parnell is downstairs in Records on a mission that should keep him busy for at least an hour. You see, I anticipated your call."

"And you wanted to be free to speak your mind and heart without the boys and girls taking a mickey out of you."

"They wouldn't dare—to my face, that is."

"I know, you're 'Gov.' See you at seven."

Thirty minutes later, the phone rang.

"Change of plan, love."

I felt a frisson of disappointment. I know the demands of a policeman's life require that all appointments are penciled in, never inked.

"If something's come up and you can't make it, that's O.K.," I said breezily. "I'll just freeze the bouillabaise."

He laughed. "I know you're a miracle woman, but even you couldn't make a bouillabaise in less than two hours. I'm not calling to cancel, though Lord knows I have to do that often enough in my business."

"I know. You just won the office pools and you want to take me to the Connaught for a wicked weekend."

"From what I hear they charge, that would only cover breakfast. Actually, the change has cultural rather than carnal overtones. One of my lads was given two free tickets to tonight's opening performance of the Royal Shakespearean Company's *Julius Caesar* starring John Wood at the National Theatre."

"Now there's a refreshing switch. I thought the usual make-nice freebie to your local bobby was a pie and a pint. This is payola with a touch of class."

My God, you would think I had accused the Queen of snorting coke. Caleb's voice took on a tone of controlled fury.

"I can assure you that not a single person under my command has or ever will take swag."

" 'Twas only a jest, Superintendent. I know all your lads and lassies are true-blue."

Of course, I wouldn't bet the farm on it. But I do believe that law enforcement officers are basically straight and it's only the few rotten apples here and there who can't resist the easy money.

"He was given the tickets by his sister who is an assistant manager," he said, sounding slightly mollified. "He offered them to me, saying that if he couldn't whistle a few of the show's tunes on his way out, he's not interested in theater. 'More your line of country than mine, Gov,' is the way he put it."

"That's wonderful, Caleb. I'd love to go."

"We'll go out for an after-theater dinner. Does that suit you?"

"Down to the ground, sir. I'll be ready at six-thirty."

I wore my wine-colored silk Ungaro suit with the very deep V neckline, silk crepe pumps from Christian Louboutin, and my Chanel bag. Nestled at the neck was a slim antique ruby-and-diamond choker I had been given by an extremely grateful client when I succeeded in sabotaging the imminent marriage of her daughter with the third son of the local butcher, a match her aristocrat mother had been trying to sever for months.

My method was straightforward and simple. Whereas the mother had been hammering away about the unsuitability of the alliance, which only stiffened the resolve of her modern egalitarian daughter, I worked on the groom's family. When I managed to convey to them the differences in morality as practiced by the upper classes, specifically their future in-laws' practice of sharing their beds with all and sundry, sometimes in tandem, and the future blushing bride

who had eagerly yielded her maidenhead to a visiting
cousin at twelve, and repeated the experience with many
others since, they were horrified. They convinced their son
to withdraw from any connection with this profligate clan
whose miscreant behavior defied the dictates of church and
God. As Hercule Poirot always said, it's all in using the
little gray cells.

When Caleb arrived, his reaction was perfect. His eyes
said WOW! but being English, his words were, "You look
lovely."

"You look pretty smashing yourself," I said as I looked
admiringly at his impeccably tailored charcoal-gray suit
with a thin white stripe, white shirt, and red Ferragamo tie.

I love London theater. Having tea served at your seat or
champagne in the lobby gives a delightful festive dimen-
sion to the evening. The performance was mesmerizing;
John Wood's superb Brutus had me riveted. Shakespeare is
like opera in that even though I know the plot, I still sit at
the edge of my seat in anticipation of the ultimate outcome.

I stood over to the side in the lobby while Caleb went
to fetch our champagne.

"Hello, Emma."

I turned. It was Mark Croft, Earl of Chelmsford, the man
who was to be my husband, which would have eventually
made me the Duchess of Sandringham—until I broke it off.

I shouldn't have been surprised. Although we had last
seen each other in Portugal, we were bound to meet again
eventually, since we frequented the same places and moved
in the same circles in London. But I felt a surge of mixed
emotions I hadn't expected. We had fallen madly in love,
and within two weeks had decided to marry after what the
gossip columnists refer to as a "whirlwind courtship." It
was a decision I had agonized over, since Mark's is one of
the oldest and most important dukedoms in England, carrying with it a responsibility for public visibility and social
activities that I didn't know that I wanted to assume. I was
also leery of the ingrained elite attitude of the high aristoc-

racy, which often translates into rudeness and total intolerance of whom they perceive as the lower orders. In fact, it was just such an episode that made me decide to terminate our relationship.

"Hello, Mark. I didn't know you were a Shakespearean devotee."

"My dear, every English schoolboy is brought up on the Bard." He tilted his head and said in a teasing voice, "Did you perhaps assume that my theatrical interest would run more to Andrew Lloyd Webber?"

He turned to the young blond woman who was standing at his side.

"Emma, this is Beatrice Carstairs. Beatrice, this is the Emma Rhodes you've heard about."

I recognized her, of course. She is a cousin of the Queen.

"When did you arrive back in London?" he asked.

"About a week ago," I answered.

"Why didn't you ring me up?"

I didn't register the surprise I felt. But then, I didn't know how much of this was for me and how much for his companion. Who knew what he told his friends of who dumped who? Was he taking the public pose of the kind, considerate chap who wants there to be no animosity between us and why not remain friends? Perhaps, but given the circumstances that would be difficult. Not that I haven't maintained friendships with some past lovers, but that only works when the breakup is mutual, when you may still like each other but the spark is gone. I understand that it's hard for a guy to want to have any sort of residual relationship with a woman who cast him aside and possibly broke his heart. However, after Mark's vituperative display of racism and anti-Semitism, I wasn't sure this was a person with whom any sort of friendship was possible for me.

At that moment, Caleb appeared carrying two glasses. Mark stiffened.

"Detective Chief Superintendent Franklin, we meet again."

Caleb handed me my drink and turned to Mark with a cool smile.

"Yes, we do."

Lady Beatrice looked wide-eyed.

"Are you then with Scotland Yard?" she asked. "I've never met a Detective Chief Superintendent of Scotland Yard."

"Well, now you shall," said Mark. "Superintendent, may I present Lady Beatrice Carstairs."

Notice he included her title in his introduction to Caleb, while to me she was just Beatrice Carstairs. Another instinctive seignorial response to distinguish between the classes.

Caleb nodded. "Lady Beatrice."

Her reaction, however, was quite different from Mark's. Caleb's profession intrigued her, his public school accent surprised her, and his stunning good looks set her juices flowing. Her sexual antennae were obviously fluttering. Even Mark noticed it as was apparent from the tightening of his lips and look of annoyance. It wasn't jealousy because their behavior and body language didn't indicate any sort of important relationship. But he had a residual antagonism to Caleb from that last encounter that was being reinforced now by seeing us together.

"Superintendent, I would love to hear some of your tales of derring-do," said Lady Beatrice, looking up at Caleb with an inviting smile. She was wearing Versace's rhinestone lace-edged miniskirt that came to about three inches below the pudenda and black top with a V neck that was cut down to about three inches above the skirt. She was very much aware that Caleb's 6'2" afforded him a splendid view of her offerings. "Why don't you join us for dinner after theater? It would be such fun."

Caleb's face remained remarkably impassive during the royal come-on. But Mark's didn't. I saved him the need to come up with an acceptable reason to cancel her invitation.

"That's very kind of you, Beatrice. But I have dinner awaiting us back in my flat."

It's only those years of British training to develop that stiff-upper-lip control that prevented Mark from exploding. The bell rang calling us back for the second act, so we all smiled and said our polite farewells.

"He's still very much in love with you," said Caleb as we sat down.

"Yes, I know."

"Will we really have dinner at your flat, or was that just to slip in the knife a bit deeper?"

"I guess we'll have to now, which means omelets all around," I said. "We can't go to a restaurant—we don't know which one they're going to."

"No problem," he said. "I know a place where his lord and her ladyship would never know or go. It's not tacky enough to be trendy, and it's not expensive enough to be stylish."

I LOOKED AROUND at the whitewashed walls and red-checked tablecloths.

"I haven't seen candles in Chianti bottles since college."

"The food is plain but good, and the service is great."

Everybody seemed to know him there, and the owner came over to fuss over us, especially me. He kept eyeing my décolletage as though it were a dish of gnocchi.

"Vincenzo apparently approves of my choice of companion," said Caleb with an amused smile.

"Had I known we were going to an Italian restaurant, I would've worn a turtleneck," I said resignedly.

He looked surprised. "Don't you find his interest flattering?" he asked. "I thought women liked admiration."

"Quiet admiration, yes—drooling lust, no. Flattering? Any Latin male who doesn't leer at every woman between eighteen and eighty is in big trouble. You see, they have to go for gender-checks periodically, like car inspections. I understand that in Rome, if you haven't groped at least

twelve asses and made at least twenty lewd comments a
month, you lose your machismo license. So why would I
find their interest flattering? It's nothing to do with my
ego—only theirs.''

He shook his head. ''You've really made a study of the
battle of the sexes, haven't you?''

''It's not a battle, Caleb, just jousting for position. It's
sort of a game, a pleasant competition, so it's best to understand the players and know the program.'' I looked
around the table. ''Speaking of programs, where's the
menu?''

''There isn't one,'' he said. ''Vincenzo just brings you
the specials of the day.''

The waiter came over and placed steaming bowls in front
of each of us.

''I can see I'm dressed all wrong for this establishment,''
I said. ''Had I known we were going to eat pasta, I would
have worn my paisley dress. I tell everybody it was originally white but years of marinara sauce have given it a
lovely pattern.''

''This is not a pasta restaurant—it's a spaghetti place.
That's the difference between dishes that cost three pounds
and those that cost ten. The food is the same, it's just the
prices and size of portions that differ.''

''I know. The smaller the portion, the bigger the price.
It's an inverse ratio situation.''

In response to Caleb's wave, a waiter came over with a
large white chef's apron, which he proceeded to drop over
my head and tie behind me. Caleb beamed broadly. ''It's
their version of the little lobster bib. Another example of
the inverse size ratio.''

The food was delicious, but this was southern, not north-
ern Italian cooking, which means you'd better love tomato
and garlic because red sauce goes on everything except the
salad. I think the only way to keep your figure in Calabria
is bulimia.

I sighed in a combination of contentment and discomfort.

"I'm stuffed. I'm dressed for nouvelle cuisine—there's no room for temporary expansion in this outfit."

"Perhaps you'd like to go somewhere where you can remove it until the condition subsides."

"And where would that be, sir?" I asked.

"I live just around the corner. Care to come up and see my grotty dray?"

He had the third floor in a small building block overlooking a verdant square. I was expecting an impersonal spare set of rooms that would reflect the unpredictable life of a policeman. You know, clothes strewn around where they were dropped after a forty-eight-hour on-duty siege. Dustbins overflowing with takeout cartons. Furnishings minimal due to a lack of time or interest to devote to purchasing and decorating.

Caleb watched my reaction with a smile of satisfaction.

I stood transfixed with surprise and delight. The front door opened into a large foyer that led into a huge living room with a bank of windows overlooking the tops of trees, which reflected the illumination from the garden lights below. You felt you were in an enchanted woods. Unlike most English floor plans where you enter a dark hall with doors that lead to other rooms, here you immediately stepped into spacious airy brightness. The foyer had a small refectory table with antique mirror over it. The living room had two deeply down-filled couches in creme cottons covered with colorful pillows. In front of the window, a pair of gold brocade club chairs faced each other across a mahogany butler's table. The short wall facing the windows had floor-to-ceiling, book-filled cherrywood shelves and a built-in stereo system, which he turned on immediately and the sound of the slaves' lament from *Nabucco* filled the flat. Hariz and Kerman rugs were scattered on the floors, and the walls were covered with a variety of art and artifacts that needed examination for identification.

"This can't be the flat of a policeman," I said. "It's the home of an intellectual house-proud collector with superb taste. Are you sure we didn't get off the lift on the wrong floor? Or are you house-sitting here for friends?''

He laughed. ''Did you envision me living in some squalid bed-sitter over a curry shop? I can see you've been reading too many English mysteries.''

''I didn't know that you liked opera,'' I said as I examined his C.D. collection.

''You think this is also antithetical to being a policeman?'' he asked with a grin. ''I've loved opera since my father took me to see Maria Callas in *Norma* when I was eight years old. I insisted he buy the record when we came home and played it so often that I think I wore out two needles.''

''Do you remember the scene in the film *Pretty Woman* when Richard Gere takes Julia Roberts to her first opera?'' I asked. ''He tells her that you either hate it at once or are transfixed immediately in which case you're hooked for life. My turn-on was Renata Tebaldi in *La Giaconda*. I see you have that recording.''

''Unfortunately,'' he said ruefully, ''the prices for opera tickets in London have become so astronomical that C.D.'s are my only choice. When Pavarotti performed in *La Boheme* last year, seats were going for one hundred pounds and over. Way out of reach of the ordinary copper like me.''

I walked over and put my arms around his neck. ''Caleb, there's nothing ordinary about you. Now how about showing me the rest of this gorgeous apartment?''

The kitchen was dazzling white—counters, appliances, fixtures.

''Good Lord, you continue to amaze me,'' I said as I looked around at the food processor, coffee grinder, Sabatier knives, and rack of Calphelon—all the appurtenances of the serious cook. ''I thought you said you didn't cook. I had the feeling you grew flowers in your oven.''

''I don't get the time to cook as much as I like to—but when I do, I like to have all the proper tools,'' he said proudly. ''I must invite you here for a proper meal.''

"Name the day and I'm yours," I said.

"Speaking of which, may I show you the bedroom?"

Two hours later, I looked at the magnificent sleeping body next to me, and sighed contentedly. There's no question that it's lovely to go to bed with a great-looking guy, but that's not what really does it for me. I won't deny the attractiveness of flat abs and trim torsos, but I always felt men were, if you'll pardon the expression, too hung up on the state and size of their equipment. For me, the act of making love is just that—the culmination of caring. It is not only sexual skills that matter, but the way he performs, which is in effect as personal a demonstration of character as handwriting. Caleb's concern for his partner's pleasure was apparently as important as for himself. Most men know the importance of foreplay, but they get no points for that because it's for their benefit as well. It's the really special few who realize the need for post-play. Besides being a powerful and satisfying lover, Caleb was a master in the fine art of cuddling.

I slipped out of bed and dressed quietly. I wouldn't sleep over because appearing at eight in the morning in evening finery is a telltale giveaway as to how one spent the night. Being a liberated woman, I shouldn't really give a damn. But somehow that smirk from cab drivers and concierges gets to me. I walked into the other room and phoned quietly for a cab, then I wrote a note that I put on his dresser.

"Aristotle was right—the three greatest things in the world do begin with S—Shakespeare, spaghetti, and sex."

VIII

~◆~

MY TERRACE IS a great place for mulling and musing. I sat out there in the bright morning sunlight sipping my coffee and putting my data-filled brain into PRINT.

This is Day Six in my assignment for Juliet Bishop, which leaves me today plus eight. At this point, I have accumulated sufficient intelligence to take the first and most important step in solving any situation—framing the right questions. Once that's accomplished, I then will know which direction to follow in order to resolve the entire matter. I now know that Sidney's corrosive jealousy of Juliet is not an isolated instance but part of a lifelong pattern. Why? What caused this obsession? His insistence on subsidizing his two ex-wives—is this part of the same psychodynamics? The death of Alicia and apparent attempt on the life of Celia—do these tie in with my investigation or could they be unconnected occurrences? Certainly Rudolf Sykes had good reason to rid himself of that harridan of a wife. And Alexandra's financially pressed husband could have been driven to collect the sizable chunk his wife would inherit. Like Abba, I don't trust coincidences. The question that really troubled me was, have I roiled the waters in some way that brought about the demise and potential demise of these two women?

The phone rang. I looked at my watch and wondered who would be calling at eight in the morning. I smiled as I picked up the phone—it's probably Caleb checking that I got home all right.

"Good morning, Emma."

It was Mark.

"I hope I didn't wake anyone, but I wanted to catch you before you started your day."

That's a crock. He's checking to find out if my date with Caleb had been a sleep-over. I could see last night that my young lordship was damaged by my dumping him, and that the fire is still burning in his bosom or wherever the conflagration of desire rests.

"No, Mark. I've been up for a while." I could have changed the pronoun to "we've" but what the hell—why torture the guy? It's not that this is "Be kind to old lovers week," but I have a policy of maintaining amicable relations with old flames. This comes under the heading of "don't throw out the baby with the bathwater" and other adages that point up the value of closing out just the relationship and not the person when your feelings toward them end. As my uncle Harry, whose principal conversation was confined to aphorisms, used to say, "Better to have a friend than an enemy," to which his wife Aunt Jane would always add with an enigmatic smile, "You never know!"

"You looked marvelous last night. Did you enjoy the play?"

I felt like Mrs. Lincoln.

"I've always been a big fan of John Wood," I said.

"Did your inspector enjoy it as well?"

Ah, the possessive pronoun—he's "my" inspector.

"Yes. I guess he learned to appreciate Shakespeare at Harrow just as you did at Eton."

"Oh, he's a Harrow man, is he? Beatrice will be interested to know that. She was quite smitten with him, you know. Both her brothers were at Harrow. Obviously the inspector is a man of many parts.''

And Beatrice covets every one of them.

Caleb had been a scholarship student at Harrow. As he told me, if he hadn't excelled at sports, he would've been made completely miserable by the other boys. Being the star of the soccer team enabled him to survive.

''I should tell you that when Beatrice wants something, she pursues it quite rigorously.''

I laughed. ''Then wish her tallyho.''

''Actually, Emma, I'm phoning to ask you to come up to the country tomorrow for the weekend. It's my birthday and the family insists on having a small do for me—just some dear friends.'' He paused for a second. ''That's a category I still presume to put you in, Emma—I hope you'll come.''

I had nothing on for the weekend. Why not?

''That depends,'' I said.

''On what?''

''Is there central heating?''

He roared. ''You spoiled Americans! Of course—Father had it installed years ago. We're not complete barbarians, you know.''

''It's usually not your level of civilization that determines such installations,'' I said. ''It's more the level of your exchequer. It must cost a bomb to heat those old manors.''

''Fortunately, that has never been one of the family problems. It's a subject we never discuss, however. Nanny always told us that it's vulgar to talk about money.''

''That's when you have it. It only becomes an issue when you don't. I have friends who are traumatized monthly by the arrival of their credit card bills.''

''So will you come?'' He sounded almost plaintive.

''I have a few more caveats,'' I said.

"You drive a hard bargain, my dear," he said sternly. "Go ahead. Name your terms."

"Will there be any blood sports like fox hunting or a pheasant shoot?"

"Why, are you vegetarian?" he asked.

"No, I eat meat that comes in those nice plastic-wrapped trays at the supermarket."

"Then why do you mind hunting animals?"

"Killing animals should only be done for survival, like Eskimos who do it for food and abbatoir workers who do it to make a living. People who kill for fun are a mystery to me. I can't understand what pleasure they could possibly get from ending the life of a living thing. I can't stop them, but I don't have to be around when they do it. I can't even bear those Richard Attenborough documentaries with lions ripping the guts out of zebras. I know it's all part of the natural order of things, but that doesn't mean I have to watch it."

"Well, you needn't worry. As it happens, my mother shares your point of view, so we do no hunting of any kind at home. Anything else?"

"Yes, will Princess Anne be there? As you may recall, when she and I met in Vila do Mar, the natives thought they were having an early frost in Portugal."

"There will be no royals present," he said firmly. "Remember I said only dear friends are invited. I spent a good deal of my childhood with members of the Royal Family and I am a faithful adherent to the monarchy. However, loyalty is not necessarily consanguineous with liking. Personally, except for the Queen, whom I adore, I think they're all a bunch of cretinous shits."

An Englishman willing to admit flaws in the Family? How delightful. I kept silent, hoping that would prompt him to continue in the same vein. It worked.

"Mother won't permit Fergie to the house anymore. Calls her a slut after her last visit when the servants found residual pieces of her undies in three of the male guests' rooms.''

"Somehow I didn't think marital fidelity was a major part of the Family ethic," I said. "From what I've gathered, Daddy Philip has been a rather poor role model."

Mark snorted in disgust. "Dear Prince Philip—the first consort since Victoria's Albert, who was a fine man who left a heritage of accomplishments for the nation. The only thing we English gentlemen have picked up from Philip is how to walk with our hands behind our backs. And that unforgettably instructive advice he gave to someone who asked him about the broadening potential of travel, to which he answered that the main thing he has learned on trips is never to pass up a toilet."

"Well, you've convinced me. I'll be delighted to come to celebrate your birthday."

When Caleb called and I told him why we couldn't spend any of the weekend together, his silence was deafening.

"I assumed we would see each other," he finally said.

That's a word that makes me bridle—assume. I am quite taken with Caleb, but I'm not in love with him, and we have no established relationship that gives him the right to assume my guaranteed presence anywhere, anytime.

"I thought you were finished with Mark. Why would you want to spend an entire weekend with him?" he went on.

Now I was annoyed. How can I tell him nicely that sleeping with me doesn't give him the right to demand an explanation for my activities? On the other hand, how would I feel if he told me he was going off with an old girlfriend? Pretty pissed off, I guess.

"It's not with him alone, Caleb—it's a country house weekend, which means swarms of people doing different things at different times. The only time everyone gets together is dinner—and then the table is usually so vast that you can talk only with the people on your left and right. I'll probably know many of the guests and that should be fun. Also, I understand the place has the most gorgeous gardens and topiary—even a famous maze. It should be an adventure, and you know I'm always up for that.''

There. Wasn't that nice of me? I didn't have to go into such an elaborate rationale for my accepting Mark's invitation.

"Will you call me when you get back?" He sounded mollified.

"Sure—if I can get through to you."

He sounded puzzled. "Why? Did you ever have a problem reaching me?"

"Not before—but I think I may now since the Lady Beatrice Carstairs has developed the hots for you."

"Who?"

I felt a stab of satisfaction. He doesn't remember her. Am I perverse or what? Here I talk about the need to be free of commitment to Caleb, yet I want him to be unaware of other women. Sure I'm being unfair—but where is it written that life is fair?

"You remember, the blonde who was with Mark last night. It seems she was quite taken with you, and I gather she's relentless in accomplishing her ends, if you'll pardon my choice of words."

"I've known such women, thank you very much," he said with annoyance. "To her, I'm a piece of captured exotica to titillate her vapid existence and arouse the envy of her equally idle friends."

"You may be right, Caleb, but don't overlook the career benefits of mingling with her and her crowd."

I may not be in love with Caleb, but I'm still very interested in having him as a lover and I don't look forward to competition from the voracious Lady B. However, he is a friend and a very admirable human being, and I want what's best for him. Police departments are very big on politics; who you know weighs heavily in your favor when it comes to moving up in the system. Caleb may be brilliant and personable, but he is black—a factor that would be greatly offset by the fact that he is a friend of the Queen's cousin.

"I'm ambitious, Emma—but I have to determine, at what price?"

For God's sake, Caleb, I thought. We're talking here about fucking a gorgeous nubile blonde and maybe being forced to attend some glitzy social functions. I don't see these as terribly distasteful chores. The only cost to you would probably be the purchase of some new evening clothes.

"Caleb, let me tell you a line I've heard from my mother all my life. 'Pride in the gutter.' Don't let a stiff neck prevent you from something that may bring you benefit."

"You sound like you want to get rid of me, Emma."

"If you saw the sad smile on my face now, Caleb, you wouldn't say that. I love what we have between us, but I'd be a rotten friend if I stood in the way of an opportunity for you."

He sighed. "All right. I'll keep an open mind. But who knows, she may have met some Pakistani bus conductor this morning who she finds equally alluring and I may never hear from her."

I heard voices at his end of the phone.

"Excuse me for a moment, Emma—Sergeant Parnell just popped in to tell me something. From the look on his face, it's important."

I heard an exchange of conversation but couldn't make out the words. Then he came back on the phone.

"The sergeant informs me there's an urgent call on his line for me from a Lady Beatrice Carstairs. She couldn't get through on my line so she demanded to speak to him."

"Well, Caleb, this is what the bullfighters call the *momento de verdad*—the moment of truth."

He hesitated. "Well, of course, I cannot be discourteous and refuse to speak with her. After all, she is the Queen's cousin. From the look on Sergeant Parnell's face, that would be a hanging offense."

"Of course, she may have a murder to report," I said.
"Right. The murder of my masculine ego."
We said good-bye and let the chase begin.

YOU MAY BE surprised and perhaps a bit disappointed
in me to see that I'm off for a weekend of pleasure in the
country when I have only about another week to complete
my case. To jeopardize $20,000 for a bit of slap and tickle
does seem like the irresponsible act of a dilettante who
regards her profession as a diverting hobby. Oh, ye of little
faith! By now, you ought to know me better than that. You
see, I have the matter pretty much worked out; it just needs
the filling in of details which I believe will be available
from a specific source. Right now, I could use a small res-
pite from my labors; two days with the landed gentry can
be incredibly boring, which means relaxing. This particular
visit also offers me the chance to see the life I turned down
when I refused to marry Mark. I've been in many stately
homes, but never one that could have been mine. And to
make a final point in defense of my professionalism, the
weekend also affords the opportunity to expand my acquaintance among the well-heeled set, who are the mainstay
of my client base. So like the executive who goes off on a
golfing trip with potential customers, I'm not not working,
I'm networking.

I drove along the A12 in my rented red MG and got off
as soon as I could so that I could enjoy my drive through
the gentle Essex countryside. It may take longer, but getting
there is half the fun. I passed through villages with the
marvelous names of Arkesdon, Finchingfield, Steeple
Bumpstead, and Paglesham. Now doesn't this sound like I
am a sensitive aesthete who seeks to derive the greatest
possible appreciation of her surroundings? Well, that's not
untrue, but let me confess that the major reason I get off
the motorways in England as fast as I can is because I'm
petrified of driving on the wrong side of the road, and their
murderous roundabouts terrify me. I think my record for

trying to enter one of those fiendish traffic circles was ten white-knuckled minutes when I couldn't get the nerve to pull into the proper lane until the ten-car line of angrily tooting motorists behind me forced me to take the plunge. You see, I'm not all Ms. Perfect Person—I do have my human weaknesses and areas of insecurity.

Mark had asked me to drive up with him, and perhaps that would have been a good way to see if he had in any way changed any of his abhorrent attitudes, and if I had softened in my ability to accept them. But I had to have the option of immediate escape should I find the weekend in any way trying. I detest being trapped anywhere, and my own car is the only way I could be totally independent.

When I arrived at Chelmsford, I followed his directions to Bowcroft House, the country seat of his father, the Duke of Sandringham. I drove through a massive carved stone triumphal arch into the park along a mile-long avenue, past Victorian gardens, ponds, and copses of trees, until I came upon the house. It was magnificent. Built in the sixteenth century by the first Duke of Sandringham, it has been home to the Croft family for over four hundred years. I find that awesome. Where I come from, the lord and lady of the split level usually abandon the old homestead for Florida as soon as the kids grow up. Which is probably just as well, since few houses built today are meant to stand up for more than three generations. As I drew up on the gravel sweep in front of the house, Mark emerged with a big welcoming smile, followed by two liveried footmen who opened the boot (trunk) of my car and took my luggage inside. He kissed me lightly on the cheek.

"Good trip?" he asked as he led me inside.

"Delightful," I said—and then just stood there in silent appreciation. The entry hall was a vast, magical space with a soaring, domed, coffered ceiling. Fluted Corinthian columns topped by Hellenic friezes rose from marble floors, and a series of niches displayed statuary and plinths that held huge vases of flowers. A balustraded gallery was built round halfway up so that the ancestral paintings could be hung on two levels.

"Come on, I'll take you up to your room. It's next to mine."

If it didn't have a locking door, I might have to do a little furniture moving. I've pushed many a chest of drawers against connecting doors in my stay-overs at country homes. Next to Scrabble, bed-hopping is one of the major indoor sports at these affairs. The host's obligation is to provide food, shelter, and some programmed activities. Guests are expected to bring suitable day and evening clothes, condoms, and a pleasant demeanor.

We walked up the carpeted grand staircase that rose from the center of the entry hall and along walls covered by paintings of ducal ancestors. When I came into my room, a maid was just finishing up unpacking my bag.

"I'll meet you in the library as soon as you've washed up," said Mark as he was about to walk out. "It's right downstairs along on the left."

"Hold on, sir," I said. "Last time I was told that at the Duke of Northumberland's house, I roamed around the seventy-six rooms for two hours. I'd like more specific directions or a road map, please."

I heard the maid giggle.

"Mary, could I ask you to please show Miss Rhodes the way?" asked Mark.

I swear she bobbed a curtsy. "Yessir." From the way she looked at him, I didn't think there was anything she wouldn't do for him if he asked. He's drop-dead handsome, he's stinking rich, and he's titled—what more could any woman want? I don't know at the moment, but can I get back to you on that?

There was no need to change, since I was wearing a beige Ralph Lauren jumpsuit with a violet and blue Hèrmes scarf and antique gold hoop earrings. Mary waited while I touched up my makeup and then led me down the stairs to a door and opened it for me. It was a large room with a handsomely decorated drop ceiling and eight tall windows with gold damask drapes pulled open to give a breathtaking view of a verdant landscape that looked like a Constable painting. Filled mahogany bookcases lined two walls from floor to ceiling. Another wall had one of the largest Gobelin tapestries I had ever seen, while the fourth wall was covered with paintings that were immediately recognizable as works by Gainsborough, Van Dyck, and Reynolds. A fire burned in the immense stone fireplace, over which hung an array of ancient sabers. The parquet floors were covered with Aubussons, and scattered around the room were leather wing chairs with the gleaming patina and softness that only age and authenticity can bestow. The overall effect was warm, inviting, and priceless.

"Mother and Father, may I present Miss Emma Rhodes? Emma, these are my parents, Lord William and Lady Catherine."

Oh, boy. The brother and sister-in-law of the man I had revealed as a murderer and drug lord. Here I am, the person who was responsible for besmirching their honorable ancient family name, and also, by the way, the woman their son would like to bring into that very family. I didn't know what to expect. A frosty tight-lipped greeting? A biting vindictive accusation? Or maybe just a rap in the mouth. What I certainly did not expect was broad smiles, extended hands, and a bright and friendly, "How nice to meet you at last. Mark has told us so much about you."

Carp and cavil as I may about the social behavior of the British upper class, I'll never cease to admire their breeding and civility. If this same situation had occurred in an Irish, Italian, or Jewish family, I'd probably be subjected to punching, garrotting, or terminal screaming. (If I've omitted any ethnic group in this insultingly outrageous statement, it was unintentional because I pride myself in being an equal opportunity offender.)

I didn't know how tense I'd been until I felt my body relaxing.

"It's lovely of you to have me here in your marvelous house," I said.

His lordship regarded me with a twinkle. "Were you expecting me to take down one of those sabers and challenge you to a duel, my dear?" I guess my apprehension had been apparent.

"Please don't feel in the slightest bit awkward here," said the duchess. "Dirk was always a bit of a wrong one and destined to end up in serious trouble."

What nice people. He was tall and burly with a dragoon mustache, and she was tall, beautiful, and regal with that manner of easy assurance that is bred into the aristocracy.

"Mark tells us you're a private detective. Isn't that sort of an unusual job for a woman?" her ladyship asked. She wasn't criticizing, just curious.

"Well, she's not really a detective, Mother," said Mark. "She's a resolver."

They looked puzzled. I didn't blame them—no one really understands what I do.

"I don't solve murders or spy on adulterous spouses," I said, "unless either of those occurrences happen along the way. People come to me with private problems and I resolve them, quickly, quietly, and expensively. It's that simple."

"Actually," said Mark proudly, "she's a lawyer."

They looked impressed, which was a welcome reaction in contrast to that which you get in the U.S. when you mention you're a member of that currently ill-thought-of profession.

"You must be quite clever, Miss Rhodes," said Lady Catherine. "I've heard of you from some friends who seem to feel you are a cross between Sherlock Holmes and Joan of Arc."

If she's just saying that to make me feel good, she's succeeding quite admirably.

"Lady Catherine," I said with a smile, "if you're running for office, you have my vote."

We all looked at each other happily. It was a true Hallmark moment. I thought I could see myself as part of this family.

"Excuse me, Milord." It was the butler.

"Yes, what is it, Palmer?"

"Lord Durwood and his daughter have arrived."

That's Juliet's father.

"Wonderful. Bring them in here, Palmer."

"Is that Juliet Bishop?" I asked.

"Why, yes," said Lady Catherine. "Do you know her?"

"Yes, we've met," I said.

What a kick. This was turning out better than I'd thought. I like to know more about my clients than I had managed to glean about Juliet.

A few minutes later, Palmer ushered in a short, fat man with a well-worn face that had the deep wrinkles and discolored blotching of the heavy smoker and the red-veined Ted Kennedy nose of the heavy drinker. Juliet was wearing a yellow suit—why on earth did she love a color that made her look jaundiced—and one of those vintage hats. It was a brown velour, crushed brim sort of thing with two amber-tipped hat pins threaded through the front and back. She looked slightly shocked to see me.

Lady Catherine moved forward with a welcoming smile. "Juliet, dear, how nice to see you. I understand you know Mark's friend, Emma Rhodes. Isn't that jolly? And Durwood, so happy you could come."

"Hello, Juliet," I said. "I'm so pleased you're here for the weekend. When Mark invited me, I thought I wouldn't know anyone."

I could see the struggle in her face of mixed feelings of not wanting anyone to know about her private problem, of wondering why was I here instead of out there working on it, and well-bred politeness that prevented her from showing either of the above concerns. I smiled, trying to convey to her that her worries were groundless, since total confidentiality was a given in my work. But frankly, Miss Juliet,

I don't give a damn. The reason I take no up-front payments or demand per diems or expenses is so that I can feel free to do what I want when I want and feel no obligation to clients whatever. I owed her no explanations, no excuses, not even results. That obligation I have only to myself.

"Why don't you both go upstairs to your rooms and freshen up? Lunch is in a half hour," said her ladyship.

They left and Lady Catherine shook her head. "Poor Juliet and those unfortunate hats."

"Why does she always wear those idiotic pot covers?" asked Mark.

"I'm afraid she believes they give her character," said her ladyship. "I think early on Juliet realized she would never be a beauty and decided to give herself a distinctive style."

"What I wonder is where on earth does she find those hats?" I asked.

"Jumble sales?" said her ladyship.

"Her char lady's rejects?" suggested Mark.

"Eliza Doolittle's hats from a *My Fair Lady* road company?" I said.

We all broke out laughing. "We really must not be unkind," said Lady Catherine, trying to keep a straight face. "Juliet has always been rather insecure since she was a little girl. Do you remember how she used to follow you around, Mark? Poor girl has always been unsure of herself."

"With good reason," said Mark. "She's a hopeless dog."

"Well, in spite of that," said Lord William, "she managed to marry herself to a very rich man, albeit an old Jew."

Mark colored and looked at me. So much for the Hallmark moment.

His mother caught the exchange and said quickly, "Why

don't you take Miss Rhodes on a small tour of the grounds before lunch, Mark?"

"Please call me Emma, your ladyship," I asked.

As we walked outside, I said to Mark, "Don't fret. You can't be responsible for your father's prejudices."

Of course, what I fretted about was the question of how much of those narrow points of view and biases the son had absorbed from the father. I stopped on the landing in front of the door and viewed the entire glorious park before us.

"Was this the work of Capability Brown?" I asked.

He looked delighted. "Yes. How did you know?"

"It has the romantic natural landscape look that's his hallmark," I said.

"Will we have time before lunch to see the dovecote?" I asked. "I spotted it on the way in."

"You're a bit of a marvel, Miss Rhodes. You don't miss a thing," he said admiringly.

I collect dovecotes—the images of them, that is. They're actually pigeon houses that you usually find snuggled up next to farm buildings and on country estates. In ancient times, they were living larders and were a major source for food, fertilizer, medicines, sport, not to mention feathers for stuffing pillows and mattresses which, according to ancient superstition, would guarantee the sleeper a longer life. Seventeenth-century England was said to have 26,000 dovecotes.

What I enjoy is the funky architecture of these sometimes bizarre little buildings. I've made special trips to estates or castles just to see their dovecotes. The Wichenford black-and-white half-timbered dovecote is a wonderful example of Worcestershire's Magpie design. The circular rubble-stone one at Garway in Herefordshire is probably the oldest in the country, bearing a Latin inscription over the door recording that it was built in 1326 by one Brother Richard.

"Oh, Mark, it's a beauty!" I said as we came upon a small stone tower with peaked roof and heavy red door.

The inscription read 1536, which testified to the exalted standing of Mark's ancestors, since the right to build a dovecote in medieval times was a feudal privilege allowed only to high aristocracy. We went inside and there were nesting alcoves for what looked like hundreds of birds. Mark pointed out that the potence was still functional—that's the rotating pole with ladders attached to its lateral arms for the columbarius (caretaker) to climb around.

I was loath to leave but it was time to get back for lunch and meet all the other guests.

"No need to rush," he said as he noticed my hurried pace. "Lunch is always a help-yourself buffet thing that runs from twelve to two in order to accommodate everyone. Those who slept in and missed breakfast are usually there at twelve chafing at the bit; the active ones and stragglers drift in later."

Mark led me to the family dining room, explaining that the more modest facility was used during the day while the state dining room was for dinner only. The room was just the right size for a family, if it includes four generations. My entire villa in Portugal would fit into one half of the area.

What must it be like to grow up in spaces like this? It seems outrageously luxurious until you consider the downside, like if you get hungry at night, the distance to the kitchen is so great you run the risk of fainting from starvation before you reach food. On the other hand, perhaps what accounts for the slenderness of the wealthy is that midnight noshing is not a viable option.

There were eight other people at the table: Lord William and Lady Catherine; Lord Durwood and Juliet, who was blessedly hatless; a blond, blue-eyed athletic-looking young woman who had to be the daughter of the house since she looked just like Lady Catherine; Alisdair Twombley, who I was delighted to learn was one of Mark's oldest friends; and a horsy-looking couple of about my age who were introduced as Giles and Cissy Rutherford, who lived in the

village, he being the local doctor. I was told that ten more
people would be arriving later in the day.

The sideboard gleamed with silver chafing dishes, which
the attendant servant uncovered to reveal mutton pie, beets,
and brussels sprouts. It's amazing how even the presenta-
tion in priceless heirloom silver pieces cannot improve the
visual appeal of limp sprouts. Cold stuff was a large sliced
ham, salad, and cheese. Obviously we were not going to
reach any Cordon Bleu pinnacles here. It has always
amazed me how wealthy British who are selectively gourmet when eating in restaurants are often willing to accept
an appalling less-than-pedestrian level of cooking at home.
I think it comes from their having been used to eating taste-
less pap in the nurseries with Nanny, which may make them
regard the stuff now as comfort food. Whenever I see a
food establishment that advertises "home cooking," my
question is always—whose home?

I piled salad on my plate and sat down. At first, the
conversation was about as thrilling as the food. I usually
eschew wine at lunch, since it tends to make me sleepy and
louses up the afternoon. But with the prospect of spending
it with this crew, maybe a little grogginess could be a plus.
I was just about to accept the footman's offer of wine in
my glass, when Lord William said to Juliet:

"Too bad your husband couldn't accompany you here,
Juliet. I was curious to meet him."

"Curious," like he was some rare specimen to be examined. Not "eager" or "looking forward to" meeting
him. I refused the wine. I might want my wits. How is she
going to handle Sidney's absence? Apparently they didn't
know of the estrangement.

"He's heavily involved in a business matter and couldn't
get away," said Juliet.

Good answer. No lie.

Lord William nodded. "Of course, those people always
put making money first."

''Those people?'' said Juliet. I felt Mark stiffening next to me. ''You mean Jews?''

''Well, my dear, some of them may be quite nice, but you know they're different than we are.''

''If by 'we' you mean the noble families, you're quite right, Lord William,'' said Juliet. ''Too bad for us. If our men had the brains and talent they have, perhaps so many of our great houses and estates wouldn't be in such a disastrous condition.''

I sat up straight in my chair in happy anticipation. I adore family fireworks, as a spectator, of course. This weekend might turn out to be more stimulating than I'd expected.

I saw her father shift in his chair.

''Sidney was born poor but ended up rich. I was born rich and ended up poor,'' she said contemptuously. ''I'm not sure who should be criticizing whom here.''

I felt like saying, ''Hip-hip, three cheers for Juliet''— not only courageous and frank but grammatical, too.

By now, her father's face was flushed and it wasn't just the wine.

''Now, now, my dear,'' he said, ''sometimes those things can't be helped. The times, the government—one can't always lay blame.''

She turned on her father bitterly. ''Oh, yes, that's something we're all very good at—blaming others for our failures.''

''Come off it, Juliet,'' said Alisdair in annoyance. ''You sound like you need a corner in Hyde Park.''

''I think that's quite enough,'' said Lady Catherine calmly. ''I have no objection to lively disagreements at the table, but perhaps you're forgetting this is my son's birthday and you were invited here to celebrate this happy occasion with us. I shouldn't like it to be marred by bitterness of any kind.''

''Here, here,'' said her husband.

Alisdair looked abashed and apologized instantly. Juliet was not instantly forthcoming; the discussion apparently cut too deep for her to kick it immediately. She sat quietly for a moment and then turned to Mark.

"I'm sorry, Mark. I didn't mean to spoil your birthday."

"Nonsense, Juliet," said Mark with a big smile. "Palmer, why don't we pour a bit more wine for everyone?"

"Better yet," said Lady Catherine, "make it champagne. Why don't we start toasting our guest of honor now instead of waiting for dinner? After all, his birthday is all day, is it not?"

We all cheered aloud, and I cheered inside for Juliet. The champagne was marvelous, and we all ended up in an aura of alcoholic goodwill which handled the temporary situation. How the rest of the weekend would go remained to be seen. That's why I insist on my own transportation. If things got too sticky and unpleasant, I could always find some reason to take off.

I followed Juliet out of the dining room while Mark chatted with his parents, and we walked silently together until we reached the Folly in the garden that had two benches. She looked at me expectantly.

"I knew Mark before I met you," I said. "And he doesn't know that you and I know each other or have any sort of arrangement. Now does that answer all the questions you were about to ask me?"

She nodded and her tension seemed to relax slightly. But her hand kept going to her hair in a nervous motion.

"I shouldn't have exploded in there," she said. "But I'm all nerves since this started with Sidney."

"I wouldn't be too bothered about it," I said. "They'll probably attribute it to P.M.S.; that's the way men deal with a woman whose opinions they find disagreeable. As for your home situation, let me worry about it."

She looked at me hopefully. "You really think you can solve it?"

"I wouldn't have undertaken the case if I didn't think I could. My time is too valuable to expend on any matter I can't resolve."

She looked dubious but happier.

"Now why don't we go back and mingle? Isn't that what we're expected to do?" I said.

After fifteen minutes of a brutally boring attempt at conversation with Cissy, the good doctor's wife, whose range of topics went from the antics of her toddler to the demanding skills required to make a proper gooseberry fool for the church supper, I took off for my room, complaining of lassitude brought on by the champagne. Afternoon napping is strictly a no-no for me. I once read that John F. Kennedy took five-minute snoozes on his plane in between campaign stops when he was running for president and they seem to revitalize him. Me, I just get wiped out. Napping makes me groggy and irritable. I intended just to throw some water on my face and return downstairs, maybe to search the library for an interesting volume. The bed looked surprisingly inviting, so I kicked off my shoes and lay down on it for a moment. When I awoke, I was stunned to see the clock read four-thirty. Cocktails were at six and dinner at seven. I'd better hop it.

I came downstairs at 5:45 wearing my red silk Armani strapless sheath with matching stole, of course. A blazon of bosom is expected, but a cover-up is required, since even with central heating these country houses tended to be a bit on the brisk side; the British idea of a comfortable thermostat reading is 65.

One of the problems about being a compulsive on-time person like me is you miss out on the rewarding effect of the grand entrance. I floated down the staircase looking pretty damned great, but unfortunately it was too early for an appreciative audience to have collected. I don't consider myself overly vain, but when you spend $4,000 on a gown, a small ripple of applause or at least a single wolf whistle would have been nice. This must be like the tree falling in the forest feels, I thought. I stood there trying to figure out whether to go north, south, east, or west when I heard music. I followed the sound of singing and piano until I came

to a closed door which I opened slowly. Lady Catherine
was seated at the keyboard and singing in a lovely soprano
voice. I walked closer and she saw me and stopped.

"Please don't stop," I implored her. "Mozart's *Regina
Coeli* is one of the most glorious pieces of music he ever
wrote, and you sing it wonderfully."

She smiled and returned to playing. I found myself humming it under my breath along with her.

"You know it?" she asked.

I nodded. "Yes, I've sung it."

"Wonderful," she said. "Please join me. I'll start from
the beginning. You can read the words over my shoulder."

"Not necessary," I said. "As I recall, the lyric is mostly
'alleluia.' "

She began to play and after the first few bars, we looked
at each other in smiling delight. She had a glorious voice
with the kind of purity that you heard in the young Julie
Andrews. I had nowhere near her talent, but it was one of
those marvelous musical moments when two voices blend
perfectly. It was exhilarating. After our last "alleluia" rang
out, we heard loud applause and turned in surprise to see
a veritable crowd standing just inside the door. His lordship
was wiping his eyes and Mark's face was shining. Two
maids and the butler Palmer were clapping enthusiastically,
and Alisdair said, "They should book you two in the Royal
Albert Hall."

"My dears, that was truly a treat," said his lordship, and
he came over and kissed both of us. Mark did the same and
took my arm, and we followed his parents into the lounge
and later, into the state dining room.

I'd been in rooms like this, but they never ceased to awe
me.

The table would seat thirty comfortably, which gives you
an idea of the proportions of the room. Looking down from
all sides were huge portraits of ancestors whose disapprov-
ing faces made me feel I'd better finish all my veggies.
From the highly polished wooden wainscoting up, the walls

were covered in pale blue damask silk. The table gleamed with crystal and silver, and was illuminated by four huge candelabras that cast flickering light on the flowers that lined the table. I counted six footmen standing against the wall ready to serve our needs. I was seated on the right of Lord William, and the doctor was on my other side. Mark was opposite. There were twenty of us altogether, many of whom had arrived just before dinner. Some were familiar acquaintances I had met at other stately homes. I recognized Bertie and Camilla, the Duke and Duchess of Norfolk. She was Camilla Fitz-Walton, heiress to a huge grocery fortune that had saved the duke from selling off half of his estates to developers. Then there was the Honorable Rupert "Nobby" Cavendish, a second son who had made quite a name racing at Le Mans. There were various family members, aunts, and cousins. We were a disparate mix of age levels, but except for me, the doctor and his wife, a very congruent congregation of social levels. This was just the kind of homogeneity that makes me loath to become part of Mark's life. These people live in a world of insular unreality that makes them unaware of and often unconcerned with what's really going on out there. Their interests, their opinions, their values are so far removed from the mainstream that they are only comfortable being with each other. How could I live such a life?

As so often happens in great English homes, the food was not memorable but the wine and service was. If you took two sips from your goblet, there was a footman behind you at once to refill it. That fact plus the general joy of the occasion made for a very lively dinner table. I was having a delightful time, and Mark's loving looks across the table plus Lord William's constant surreptitious glances at my décolletage made it more wonderful every minute. After all, a wildly expensive gown should have a reward ratio like two seconds of incurred admiration and lust per dollar or you're entitled to your money back.

"And what do you do?" I heard a voice say. It was the good doctor.

I turned to look at him. He was one of those rangy sandy-haired Brits with watery blue eyes who starts to bend like a reed at thirty, which was probably about ten years ago. That plus the dragoon mustache (which I always thought aptly named since it always seemed to drag in the soup and make you look like a bit of a goon) aged him about ten years, perhaps intentionally in order to seem more assuring to the elder population.

"What would you say if I said I pour tea, open jumble sales, and ride to the hounds?"

He smiled. "I'd say you're taking a mickey out of me."

"Why? Do I lack the gentility for such ladylike pursuits?"

"No, just the temperament. You strike me as a woman of action and achievement who could never be satisfied filling her days with such passive pursuits. So what do you do?"

Unfortunately, just as he uttered that last question, there was one of those conversational lulls that occur at tables in the midst of even the liveliest exchanges, and suddenly everyone turned to hear my answer.

"She is a Private Resolver," said Lady Catherine. There was a silence as everyone was either in shock or trying to figure it out.

"Is that like a Private Investigator, one of those lady P.I.'s who have become so popular in American literature?" asked Caroline, Mark's sister, with animated curiosity.

I sighed inwardly, as I always do when I have to explain my profession. I marvel at the tolerance of public figures who must be asked the same questions thousands of times. That's what I get and, believe me, it's a crashing bore. I didn't love being an attorney, but at least everyone knew what it was and I wasn't greeted with that blank stare followed up by a barrage of stupid, personal questions. Of course, given the public attitude to lawyers today, that statement generated a spate of scurrilous comments and venal lawyer jokes that didn't exactly make my day.

"It's something like a P.I., Caroline, but only partially. The main difference is that I don't just investigate a situation as P.I.'s are paid to do, I take it a step further. I resolve it."

"Do you peep into hotel keyholes and that sort of thing?" asked Cissy, who had a short upper lip and prematurely gray hair in tight curls all over her head so that she looked like a slightly intelligent sheep.

"Well, Cissy," I said, "since they started phasing out keyholes in favor of electronic cards for greater security, I've seriously considered giving up my profession."

"Isn't it dangerous?" asked Nobby excitedly.

"Sometimes, but on the whole far less dangerous than racing cars," I said with a smile.

"Do you run into many murders?" asked Lord Dunstan, a white-haired gentleman at the far end of the table.

"Not if I can help it," I answered, "but sometimes it's unavoidable."

I heard Lord William clear his throat loudly. Clearly the conversation was getting to areas that were sensitive to the family.

"I did some medical examiner work when I first started a practice in Leeds some years ago, before I came here," said the doctor, sort of wistfully. I imagined the work was a bit more challenging than tending to cases of arthritis, gout, and gallbladder, and the usual other complaints of a wealthy aging population.

"Oh, Giles," said his wife in disgust, "you're not going to bring up your ghastly cases at Lady Catherine's dinner table."

He looked sheepish. A few more and we'd have a flock. She turned her back on him dismissively.

"Lady Caroline, are you planning to take part in the equestrian show at Alderbury next week?" she asked.

The doctor slumped down a bit and pulled his head down into his neck like a turtle returning to its shell. His patients might regard him as a god, but his wife apparently treated him like cat litter. (I don't know what it is, but there's something about the English upper class that reminds me of livestock. Maybe their deep interest and love of animals has brought about the resemblance, or maybe it's the other way around.)

As a conversational gambit at an English dinner table, horses are a sure hit. Soon everyone was chatting away about the standings of various entrants and descriptions of their finer points. It's a subject that is said to be one of the only ones that can get the Queen really going. I have been told by many who know her that she's a lovely lady whose mind is not overburdened by complex intellect. She loves her dogs, horses, and children in that order. Given the cast of characters, who could blame her? Me, all I know about horses is what I read in Dick Francis. I was prepared to develop instant MEGO, but I was happy to be off the hook.

"I ran into some interesting cases," said the doctor quietly to me as the horsy conversation swirled around us. I could see he was eager to talk about days that he apparently found more stimulating than the present. But then living with an ovine woman with equine tastes couldn't make his current life too thrilling and didn't promise too exciting a future. I'll never understand what makes some men choose the women they do for life companions. Sometimes I think they give it less depth of analysis and consideration than in the selection of their ties.

I'm always interested in forensic medicine, so I turned a very receptive face toward him. I could see him open up like a flower under my attention. Poor bastard. I bet she makes him strip off his clinic clothing and bathe before being allowed downstairs for dinner. Maybe I'm being unfair to her. Here I am making up a whole punitive scenario when for all I know, she might be a millionaire's daughter who set him up in practice or maybe he has the sexual equipment of a chipmunk.

"There was one case where the police believed a young man had O.D.'d in his parents' home. The assumption was logical since there were needlemarks all over him and dozens of bruises from falling, which he did often. But what puzzled me was that the body had all the earmarks of suffocation. Then I noticed a needlemark that couldn't possibly have been self-inflicted."

"Where was that?" I said with interest.

"Bang on in the middle of the back of his neck," he said with great satisfaction.

"What did that tell you?" I asked.

"That someone who had some medical knowledge had killed him. I looked for and found evidence that a long needle had been inserted angled upward where it reached the cerebellum."

"What does that do?"

"It effectively suffocates the person by hitting the respiratory centers and other consciousness functions so that the person stops breathing. The police arrested his medical student brother. Poor chap couldn't bear to see the anguish his parents were being put through by the behavior of their addicted son, so he decided to end the wretch's life."

When he saw I was interested, he warmed to his subject. His eager enthusiasm indicated that he hadn't had a willing ear for quite some time, if ever. I've always believed there's a quid pro quo responsibility in relationships; I'll listen to his war stories and then he'll listen to mine. Maybe they had that going for them once, but he may have wearied of listening to her bemoaning the tuppence increase in the cost of cornflakes and the difficulties in dealing with her daily. Perhaps spilling his quid wasn't worth having to hear her quo.

"Then there was the case where the family doctor diagnosed a death as a heart attack. But I recognized it as anaphylactic shock, and the police found his wife had fed him lamb curry laced with pureed oysters to which he was violently allergic."

You may not find these stories too fascinating, but to me it's part of my professional education. I like amassing tid-bits of murder and mayhem; I file them in my head under the heading of "you never know."

Suddenly I heard the name of "Caleb Franklin" being mentioned on my left side. It may sound like I couldn't have been listening to the doctor too intently if I heard other conversations, but that's not true. I've always been able to hear multiple conversations simultaneously. If I was a shrink, I could probably make a fortune by listening to two couch occupants at the same time.

Apparently Alisdair had questioned the absence of Lady Beatrice Carstairs, to which Caroline had answered:

"Oh, haven't you heard? She's after a new prey. Some people like fox hunting—Beatrice prefers men. His name is Caleb Franklin, and I believe he's a poo-bah policeman."

"You don't mean the famous colored star of Scotland Yard?" asked Alisdair.

Caroline looked nervously down the other end of the table. "Please soft-pedal it, Alisdair. Her parents are right over there."

Alisdair snorted. "Come, come, Caroline. This is hardly her virgin conquest. If they haven't heard her sobriquet as the Piranha of Portman Square, then their heads must be stuffed with cotton wool."

"But, Alisdair—he's black!"

"Bollocks! I don't believe our Beatrice would care if he was magenta. In fact, that would probably increase his appeal. He's a Detective Chief Superintendent of Scotland Yard and, from what I hear, quite a hunk. She's already gone through ninety-eight percent of the socially acceptable male population; she's probably looking to branch out. Actually, he's Harrow and Cambridge, which means he's not right out of the trees."

Mark overheard the exchange and was looking at me. He

mouthed the words "I'm sorry," but his eyes weren't.

What a bunch. You've probably been thinking I'm some kind of idiot to turn down the chance to marry one of the most eligible titles in England. Maybe you could bear spending your life with people who value people based on bloodlines rather than brains. I could not.

Suddenly, the lovely pinging sound one gets only from tapping on a pure crystal glass rang out.

"May I offer a toast to my son on his birthday?" said Lord William, standing and raising his glass.

Palmer and the footmen were around the table instantly filling our crystal champagne flutes.

"To our son, who has given us only pleasure all his life, and who we hope will continue to produce further pleasures for us, and the future of the family."

"Hear, hear!" raised our glasses toward Mark, who was smiling broadly and looking pointedly at me.

Holy moly. What have I gotten myself into? His parents were looking at me with smiling approval as though this was Newmarket and I'm the prize mare who is expected to produce the thoroughbred heir. I've broken up with guys before, but never where my refusal jeopardized the continuity of a ducal family line. Help. How the hell do I get out of this?

At the end of the meal, Sir William arose and invited all the gentlemen into his study for brandy and cigars. I used to find that old-world ritual of postprandial sex-splitting insulting—now I find it amusing. Apparently Lord William still clung to the concept that only men are qualified to discuss serious events and affairs of state, matters in which we ladies of supposedly limited intellectual capacities would have no interest. I wonder what he would have done were Maggie Thatcher a guest? Mark caught my eye and shrugged with a smile. I smiled back at him to let him know that I was not offended. In fact, I enjoy sitting around with just us girls. Men like Lord William assume women talk only about child-rearing and needlepoint, when in fact we have some pretty heady and racy conversations that would proabably shock the hell out of those stiffs in the other room. Women talk about feelings and emotions—men talk only of things. As we streamed into Lady Catherine's sitting room, Caroline walked along next to me and said:

"Why don't we sit over in the corner? I would really love to talk to you, Emma."

This was unexpected but not unwelcome. We arranged ourselves in facing chairs near the window while the other women gathered around Lady Catherine in the center of the room. I waited.

"Are you and my brother going to get married?" she asked.

"It's certainly possible," I answered, "though not necessarily to each other."

She looked dumbstruck. She was in her mid-twenties, which is well past the age when one can get away with asking childishly blunt questions without being accused of poor manners. She had lovely blond hair, a beautiful figure, and shrewd eyes.

"I've seen him look at you. He's getting pretty old, and you're the first woman he's ever looked at like that."

Pretty old? The guy's in his thirties. What is with this twit?

"Do you like children?" she asked.

"Compared to what?" I asked.

Her face remained impassive. I wonder if anyone has done a study on the correlation between handsome men having humorless sisters.

"Mark should have a son," she said matter-of-factly. "I just wondered if you, er, well, if having children is a possibility for you—I mean, knowing your career and . . ." She broke off with a shrug.

"Are you listening for the ticking of my biological clock?" I asked sweetly.

She had the grace to look embarrassed.

"Look, Caroline, I don't think my fecundity should be a factor in our conversation."

She looked properly abashed.

"I'm terribly sorry—you're quite right," she said. "It's just that Mummy and Daddy go on so about the whole business that I'm afraid I just got caught up in it."

I decided to segue into a related topic of interest to me.

"Juliet seems hung up on money," I said.

"Is she ever," said Caroline, obviously grateful for the change of subject. "She always used to envy my clothes and our holiday trips. Often Daddy would take her with us on our *QE2* crossings. Poor girl hated being poor."

"Well, those poor days are over for her. She's married to a wealthy man now," I said.

"But I hear they're having a spot of trouble."

"It may pass," I said. "Most marriages go through a few bumps here and there."

"Anyway," she said cheerfully, "even if they divorce, he'll have to give her pots of money, won't he?"

Only if his pots are full, I thought.

Lord William walked in and announced, "To the ballroom, please, everyone."

We all trooped dutifully after him and were ushered into the Grand Ballroom, which was filled with people.

"Who are all these people?" I asked Mark.

"It's everyone from the village. Many of them live and farm on our land. It's the custom every year for them to attend my birthday party."

"Ah, the esnes," I said.

"The who?" he asked.

"Obviously you don't do crossword puzzles, Mark." (If you don't, esne is another name for a feudal-day serf.)

The Grand Ballroom was the size of Sherwood Forest. The room was suffused with glittering light, courtesy of a mass of crystal chandeliers—sixteen of them. I counted. The walls and ceiling were covered with murals like a mini Sistine Chapel. Along one short wall was a buffet ("short" being a comparative word, the table was about fifty feet long) filled with classic British fare like Scotch eggs (hardboiled eggs wrapped in sausage meat and breadcrumbs and deep-fried—yum-yum), Cornish pasties, pork pies, huge blocks of Stilton and other cheeses, sliced lamb and roast beef. At each end of the table was a silver punch bowl that was slightly smaller than Shea Stadium, filled with champagne punch being ladled out by smiling liveried footmen. Waiters were circulating with wine and soft drinks. At the far end was a platform that held a small orchestra. As we entered, we being Mark and I and his parents, they broke into "Happy Birthday" and everybody sang and applauded. Mark gave a short speech thanking them all for coming to share his birthday celebration, and then led me onto the dance floor as the orchestra played a Strauss waltz, which I gathered was the traditional opening number at these bashes since it enabled the lord and lady to join us. Then everyone followed and the music changed into pleasant ballroom dancing music.

Mark held me close and we were enjoying dancing. When they broke into rock and roll, we mutually decided to step outside for a breath of air.

"I'm sorry about Beatrice and Caleb Franklin. I feel somewhat responsible."

"It's not your fault," I said sadly, like the bereft lover, which was the position I instantly chose to take. As you know, I had encouraged Caleb to succumb to the royal succubus. As you may sense, I found him engaging, stimulating, sexually satisfying—but I was not madly in love. Why should I let Mark know that? Languishing was a good excuse for an indefinite put-off to his ardor. Notice I said putoff, not cutoff. No, I was not ready to close the door on his young lordship. I still had stronger feelings for him than I'd felt for any man in a long time. Maybe all I was waiting for was a sign that he could change. Voting Labour instead of Conservative could be a start.

"Miss Rhodes, I've been looking for you." It was Lord Durwood. "May I have this dance?"

Mark relinquished me graciously, and Juliet's father and I hit the dance floor. He was a good dancer, but I wished white gloves were still a mandatory accessory with a man's formal dress. His cold sweaty hand which should have been around my waist quickly crept up to my bare back.

"I'm sorry about that little scene with Juliet at the table," he said. "She hasn't forgiven me for some unfortunate financial episodes I was led into."

"Children can be very hard on their parents," I said.

"She's married to an excellent man," he said. "He's been most kind to me. Jewish people are so good at money, don't you think?"

Aha. Methinks dear old Lord Dad has been added to Sidney's list of private pensioners. Saint Sidney strikes again. I sure hope he's operating out of pure charity because you can't buy popularity.

As we danced I became surprisingly aware of a situation that made me realize I'd aroused his lordship's passion in a way that is unexpected in a man of his age. Fortunately, it was a short dance and I headed for Mark immediately after.

"I didn't think the old reprobate still had it in him," I said.

Mark laughed. "He used his old pipe-in-the-pants gambit, did he?"

He explained that Lord Durwood smoked a pipe for the sole reason that he could slip it deep into his trouser pocket as he pressed up against a young woman to enhance his reputation.

That cracked me up and I laughed until the tears flowed.

"Now you can see why Juliet had such a difficult childhood. Her father was this lascivious rascal who floated from woman to woman. Her mother couldn't tolerate his behavior and took off early on. Poor Juliet hated her home, there was always another stepmother. So she spent most of her time here. They live on adjoining lands,'' he added.

Don't get visions of their running next door to borrow a cup of sugar. It would require a twenty-minute jog or a five-minute ride from door to door. Adjoining in their parlance is like Brooklyn adjoins Manhattan, or Kentucky adjoins Ohio.

"She's obviously not too fond of her father. It's apparent that his ineptitude with finances bothers her a lot," I observed.

"Oh, yes, indeed. Lord Durwood inherited a large estate, both land and money, but he dissipated it on foolish investments and too many wives. My father paid for her schooling. Juliet despised being as she saw it a charity case. She was a most unhappy child."

"I'm not surprised. That unfortunate name couldn't make life easy either. I'll bet there were very few Romeos singing under her balcony."

"Quite right. She had a crush on me, but actually I was closer friends with her brother."

"Where is he?" I asked.

"Alfred is sheep-farming in Australia. I hope he's doing well, because when he returns to take over the title upon his father's death, the death duties and debts will cost a bomb."

She'd better not divorce Sidney. I foresaw a great need for his fine financial helping hand. I'd best get going to prevent her from making a serious mistake.

I left early Sunday morning, pleading the call of business. Mark was disappointed, but he accepted my reason. When I got back to London, I made a call and then phoned to reserve a seat on the noon flight to France.

IX

I FOLLOWED DENNIS Bailey's directions and managed to find my way out of Orly Airport in my rented Peugeot. I had phoned him from London, told him I was a friend of his brother and nephew who was deeply interested in pisciculture, would be in Paris this afternoon, and could I come out and see his collection which I understood to be superb?

I never doubted for a moment that he would be receptive to my visit, since serious hobbyists live to show off their collections, especially to one of like interests. Like me. Now what do I know of pisciculture which, as you may have assumed, is the breeding of fish under controlled conditions? One of the inevitable corollaries of doing the kind of work I do is the motley mass of information you pick up along the way. You run into all kinds of people doing all kinds of things, and if you have a photographic memory like I have, you remember what you've learned. Some years ago I had a client who raised rare fish, and my brain sopped up a rather exhaustive knowledge of his pursuit. You never know when these things might come in handy. Like now.

My trip from Paris took forty-five minutes; the drive through Plaisir took forty-five seconds. It was one of those hamlets whose entire center consists of a *boulangerie*, a *charcuterie*, and the inevitable bar and *tabac*. A long dirt road led to a sign that said "Bailey." After the sign was a neatly paved drive, bordered on both sides by those wonderful tall poplars that are ubiquitous throughout France and make roads seem like majestic verdant corridors. On a private road, they convey the impression of entering an estate. Well, not quite, but the house was no farmer's cottage. A mini-château would be more accurate. It was that lovely soft pink brick, with large floor-to-ceiling windows overlooking what seemed like acres of gardens. The entire aspect was *très* tranquil. Dennis must have heard the car and came out to greet me. At first glance, he looked like an inflated version of his brother. I'd put him at 195 pounds. Taller, larger, the same sandy hair and strong nose, but there's where the strength and similarity ended. The eyes did not have the bright, keen look that advertised Sidney's sharp mind, and the body language conveyed "sluggish." My instant reaction was that if Dennis didn't have a smart successful big brother, he'd be selling shoes in Selfridge's.

He held out his hand and smiled. "Welcome, Miss Rhodes. How good of you to come. It's rare that I have a knowledgable visitor who can enjoy my little hobby with me—and one who is so lovely." Another thing he was missing was Sidney's sonorous Shakespearian-trained voice and diction. Dennis was soft-spoken and his conversation bore traces of London.

"But you must be tired from the trip. Why don't we sit in the garden and have some refreshments before I show you my little collection?"

Whenever a collector disparages his collection, you can expect a lollapalooza. I hope I don't have to be here all day. I'd figured on heading back to London tonight.

"Something cold would be nice—and please call me Emma." I flashed one of my let's-be-friends smiles that usually goes over big with unattractive men. He positively beamed and led me to a stone table surrounded by elegant white metal chairs under a large tree on the side of the house. An aproned woman appeared.

"Would some chilled white wine be all right? We have a marvelous vineyard just down the road. I think you'll find it light and delicious. Or would you prefer something non-alcoholic?"

"Actually, I'd like both."

"Of course." He turned to the woman and told her in horrendously English-accented French to bring out *le vin, glace et l'eau minéral.* From what Andre had said, Dennis had been living in France for over ten years. You would think he would do better than that, but some people just don't have the ear for the music of a language no matter how long they hear it. It has nothing to do with intelligence—listen to Henry Kissinger.

I told him my prepared story of how I got interested in fish the summer between my junior and senior years at Sarah Lawrence when I interned at the famed Woods Hole Oceanographic Institution in Massachusetts. Actually it wasn't the fish that attracted me but the young bearded scientist there who had become a major challenge because he seemed more fascinated with the fish than me. I still count it as one of my life failures because it ended up with a score of Fish: ten and Emma: zip. My father always taught me that the truth is the best lie, so I always try to stick as close to fact as possible when I'm making up a whopper. In that way there's less to have to remember. I did graduate from Sarah Lawrence, and I did spend a summer at Martha's Vineyard, which is not too far from Woods Hole. Once my credentials were established, it was time to get to know brother rather than collector Dennis Bailey. And to further verify certain facts about Sidney.

"Do you get to see much of Sidney?" I asked.

He shook his head. "He's far too busy. Between the business and his new wife, he doesn't have much time, you ·

see.'' He wasn't resentful, just reporting. ''But he calls frequently.''

''He's quite a fellow,'' I said.

I find that statement to be valuably versatile because the listener puts his own spin on it. ''He's quite a fellow'' could mean he's an amazing achiever. It could also mean he's a major fuckup. It's all in the reading. I use it on fact-finding missions all the time—you just throw it out and see what comes back.

Dennis' face lit up. Score one for Sidney. ''He is indeed. He was a marvelous actor. You should have seen him do *Hamlet* with the Birmingham Repertory Theater years ago. And with all that artistic talent, he also has an incredible head for business. He's truly amazing.''

''Yes, he told me how he took over the family business.''

''Did he tell you there was almost no business to take over? Our father was one of those plunging businessmen who would put everything into a venture that he thought held promise. Sometimes the promise was fulfilled and we lived well. Other times things didn't work out and we were virtually penniless. Our life was one of extremes, which is very hard to explain to children. Why one year you can have new shoes every month and a holiday in Tenerife, and other years live on beans and toast. Unfortunately, our dad died when things were on the downside. If Sidney hadn't taken over we would have all ended up on our bums. My uncles were involved with our dad's business, too. Sidney made us all rich.''

No envy, no jealousy. With all the rotten vibes that run through so many families, it's nice to see a relationship that is uncomplicated love and gratitude. It's a testimonial to the fine characters of both brothers.

''What got you interested in fish, Dennis?'' We were Dennis and Emma now. ''Did it start when you were a little boy and your mother brought you some goldfish?''

''Oh, no. I never knew my mother.''

Confirmation of Andre's and Alexandra's statements.

Now to find out why Sidney told me she died five years ago.

"That's too bad. I suppose she died when you were a baby?"

"Actually, she ran off with a man to America shortly after I was born and we never heard from her again," he said without a trace of rancor or embarrassment.

The same story Sidney told me—only he said it was his grandmother.

I looked properly sympathetic. "That must've been hard on you, not having a mother when you were growing up."

He smiled. "But we had our grandmother, you see. She brought us up—she was a wonderful woman. No matter how bad things were, with almost nothing to eat, she'd manage. We would come home from school and she'd be there with some treat for tea. I don't know how she did it. And no matter how mean the place we lived in, she would keep it clean and cheerful."

Where had I heard those very words? From Sidney, but it was about his mother.

"I didn't miss having a mum, you see, because I never knew her. It was terrible for Sidney, though. He was only eight when she took off. From what I heard, he positively adored her. Never got along with our dad, though. Sidney came home from school one day and she just wasn't there. Gone. Just like that. No warning, no good-bye I don't remember any of it, of course, I was just a babe. But I know my father beat Sidney badly whenever he caught him crying about her. 'What's done is done and you have to learn to take it like a man,' he'd say. He was a hard, bitter man, our dad. I guess he held his own pain about the shame of it all. It couldn't have been easy to have been deserted by your wife and left with two little boys." His eyes glistened with tears. "I've often wondered why the two of them couldn't share their pain—they both loved her. Instead, Dad took out his own fury on poor Sidney. It was said in the family that Sidney went quiet for years, barely spoke a word. He never actually got over her leaving." He was silent for a moment. "I think he always hoped she'd come back someday. But we never heard from her again."

I was dying to take off at once so that I could quietly digest all this information. But, of course, I had to look at every one of his damned fish tanks. And react for an audience of one. Collectors who breed things are a breed unto themselves whose idea of ecstasy is watching other collectors burn with envy over their collections. I fulfilled my obligations and finally got out of there two hours later.

I sat in a window seat in the plane and could not shake the vision of that devastated little boy whose beloved mother suddenly abandoned him for no reason that any child could fathom. I tried to picture myself coming home one day when I was eight expecting my usual milk and cookies, looking forward to sharing my day with my mom, and instead finding the house dark and my mother gone. Forever.

"Are you all right, dear?" I looked over and the woman in the adjacent seat was regarding me with concern, and I realized that tears were running down my face.

"I'm O.K., thank you. Just having some sad thoughts."

She nodded sympathetically. "I guess we all have those moments."

A child whose parent has deserted them always feels guilty. "What did I do wrong? I must have been bad and that's why she left me." To compound the tragedy, Sidney had no one to explain it to him. All he had was an insensitive clod of a father who vented his own sense of guilt and rejection by brutalizing the child who reminded him of his own failure. Poor little Sidney.

Now that I understood what made him behave as he did with women, the question was how to change it. The method I have always used is the same as tribal sachems, village wise men, and Miss Marple. The job requires an eye for patterns and similarities. People do run to types. Experiences and stimuli that act as catalysts for one person will usually evoke similar responses from a similar individual. If you keep your antennae working at full power when it comes to the people you encounter throughout your life, you'll be able to predict reactions. Suddenly something about an individual's behavior strikes a familiar chord because you remember a comparable occurrence. It usually stands to reason that if A is like B, then chances are A will handle a problem very much like B did, and so you are guided as to how to resolve the situation. (You think I'm nuts for giving away my trade secrets here? If you believe that's all there is to it, just put out your own shingle and see how you do!)

X

I CALLED JULIET and arranged to come to her house. It was a lovely small building off Kensington High Street with a high flight of stairs leading to the front door. I hate stairs. I play tennis singles for two hours, I work out on nautilus machines for an hour—but I'd never live in a place with stairs because stairs make me huff and puff. Luckily, I remembered that she told me to ring the downstairs bell, which led to what would have been the servants' hall and kitchen in the good old days when Mrs. Bridges and Hudson and the rest of the staff lived in, and these days where the home owners spend their lives, since who wants to keep running upstairs downstairs.

Juliet answered the door herself. At first I thought it was the maid. She looked like an absolute frump. Her hair looked dank, and she was wearing a brown skirt of indeterminate length and a mustard-colored wool sweater that gave her skin a liverish pallor. Her only jewelry was a string of lovely pearls. No makeup, just dark tortoiseshell framed glasses. She looked nervous and unhappy as she led me through the dining room, which was slightly below

ground level. The walls were covered with paintings of ancestors, which made the room even darker. I think I might
find it difficult to eat with those somber censorious faces
staring down at me constantly with the same look I get from
my mother when I reach for a second piece of cake.

Through the dining room we came to the kitchen, which
was large and modernized and was obviously the living
room of choice. The far end had a floor-to-ceiling window
looking out into a lovely flower-filled garden. In the corner
was a long table with a phone answering machine, fax, C.D.
player, and a lineup of liquors—everything the modern
family needs to survive. In front of the window was a
round, heavy, old oak table surrounded by caned-back
chairs with bright red cushions. I was ready to settle down
into this inviting setup, since it looked like the place most
family business was transacted, located comfortably near
all mod cons which offered access to cold drinks and
snacks. However, Juliet apparently judged this an occasion
requiring more formality. So I followed her up the long
steep flight of stairs to the drawing room. I saw another
flight leading up to what I assumed were the bedrooms and
bathrooms.

We sat in the drawing room facing each other on an
uncomfortable, pale green, silk-covered couch loaded with
awkwardly large pastel pillows which felt like they were
filled with lima beans. The room was the full depth of the
house, and was overfurnished in dreary antiques. Just because something has been in your family or someone else's
for generations is not, to my mind, a valid reason for using
it. Juliet fingered her pearls nervously and looked at me
expectantly.

She knew of Alicia's death since I had phoned her, but
gasped when she heard about Celia's fall from her horse.

"Good heavens—if terrible accidents are happening to
both of Sidney's wives, could I be next?" She looked
frightened.

"Are you superstitious, Juliet?" I asked.

She looked slightly abashed. "A little. But one doesn't have to be to draw the conclusion that there's some evil karma afoot that affects those who marry Sidney."

"Perhaps they weren't accidents," I said.

She looked puzzled. "What else could they be?"

"How about murder and attempted murder?" I answered.

Her eyes widened in alarm. "Then I could be in worse danger."

"They may be only unrelated coincidences," I said, which I didn't believe for a second, but why allow her to be terrorized? "Besides, I assume you keep your doors locked and look up and down the street before crossing, so what can happen?" Let's see, how about a knife in the guts on a bus, being pushed in front of a lorry on Piccadilly, having someone drop a bit of cyanide in your tea at the Savoy? If she has an imagination like mine, she'll be shaking all the time.

"Now that you've heard about the wives, both of whom concurred on your complaint about his jealousy, by the way—let me tell you what I've learned about Sidney himself."

As I told her the story, her face crumpled and she began to sob softly.

"My poor, poor darling. How perfectly dreadful. To think I envied him when he would tell me about his wonderful mother, how kind and loving she was. My mother deserted us when I was eleven, but we knew where she was and she would take us out on holidays. When Sidney would talk about how abysmally poor they were at times when there was literally no food in the house whatever, I would scoff at that as unimportant compared to the warmth and reassurance of having a mother who was always there for you. My God, how my words must have pained him."

We discussed how this agonizing trauma seared him and its inevitable effect on his relationships with women. And then I told her what she must do to break the self-destructive pattern he had established. She was stunned, dubious, and needed convincing but ultimately agreed to give my idea a shot. She had nothing to lose.

WHEN I GOT back to my flat, I stretched out on a chaise lounge on my terrace. It was one of those glorious London late spring days when the sky is clear and the sun shines brightly. I'm not one for moods, but I felt sad. That image of eight-year-old Sidney haunted me. I've seen all sorts of harm that people inflict upon each other and I'm affected each time. But what I absolutely cannot bear is cruelty to a child or animal, because they are innocent and trusting, totally unprepared and unable to defend themselves. On top of that, my case was completed because I was quite certain that my recommended actions would be successful, and I was suffering from a bit of post-partum depression. So I called my cheerer-upper.

Abba listened sympathetically.

"Listen, *bubeleh*, shall I give you some cliché verbal mood elevators? Like '*Ala Bab Allah*' which is Arabic for '*qué sera sera*'—whatever will be will be. How about 'Things may seem terrible, but as long as you have your health'? I hate seeing kids victimized, but I see it all the time. Those pathetic Palestinian children who don't stand a chance because they were born into poverty, hate, and violence—who saw their brothers and parents killed and didn't know why. Kids coming into Israel now from the Balkans with legs missing who saw their mothers torn apart by guns and bombs. It's a stinking world, and if you want to really sink into a major depression, go visit Yad Va Shem or the Holocaust Museum in Washington, D.C., and find out to what depths human beings can sink."

"So how do you handle it, Abba?"

"By looking around at the beautiful things man has produced, like the Pietà, the gardens at Giverny, the stained glass at St. Chapelle. And by knowing and loving nice peo-

ple like you. And speaking of you, what's happening with
The Case of the Biased Baronet?''

I had told him I was going to Mark's for the weekend.
So I told him all that had happened there.

"Sounds like you liked his mama."

"Yes, very much. We got along wonderfully. Matter of
fact, I found a message on my machine inviting me to have
tea with her in London."

"You know, *tsotskele*, my love, people can change.
Maybe you should marry him and change him later. After
all, he's had his attitudes and beliefs bred into him for many
years so it won't take overnight to open his eyes to your
point of view. But he's nuts about you, anyone could see
that, and there's no end to what some men will do to please
the woman they love. Besides, you're a pretty smart, in-
sightful broad who's fuckin' damned good with people, and
if anyone can show his lordship the error of his ways, it's
you. So go for it, sweetheart—my money's on you."

"Ann Landers says it's a big mistake to think you can
change a man after you marry him."

"You would take the word of a loudmouthed bouffant
blonde yenta over my sage advice?" he said indignantly.

I laughed. "My dear Abba, you have lifted my spirits."

"I'll lift them even more. Seems our fancy Czech Rudolf
Sykes has done a Double Czech. We found a previous marriage and no record of a divorce or annulment. And by the
way, you were right. His real name is Rudolf Sychov."

"Do you have the name and address of the wife?"

He snorted. "Of course. Who do you think we are—the
Los Angeles D.A.'s office? When we do an investigation,
you can fuckin'-A bet your ass we'll come up with everything there is to know about the putz, right down to his
preferred brand of jockey shorts."

"I think I'll hop over to Prague one of these days. But
first I have a little mission in Amsterdam tomorrow."

"Taking the Schlong Special for some repeat action with
the red-bearded musician?"

I sighed. "Why is it that you always see sex as the prime motivation for all actions? You probably attribute the fall of the Soviet Union to a national shortage of condoms."

"Listen, *bubeleh*, it's a known fact that musicians have high testosterone."

"Really?" I asked. "And what research do you have that backs up that allegation, Doctor?"

"All right, I'll give you research. A recent study in the *New York Times* said that exercise increases testosterone levels. So it goes to reason that schlepping those heavy instruments makes musicians horny, if you'll pardon the play on words. Look at Pablo Casals—just from lugging that cello around, he fathered a child in his eighties. And Artie Shaw—he was known for shtupping all the gorgeous women in Hollywood and he married I think four times."

"And this I'm supposed to accept as scientific proof, Abba? It's good you majored in psychology at Brooklyn College and not premed. If you were a doctor, you'd probably tell all your patients to eat chicken soup because your grandmother ate it every day and lived till one hundred."

"And what's so crazy? Look at all those guys in Russia who ate yogurt and lived till one hundred twenty?"

"Abba, that was only a commercial, not a news bulletin."

"O.K.—so why are you going to Amsterdam?"

"Well, my dear friend, I don't mean to burst your *bubbemayseh*, but my mission has a serious basis and is important to the resolution of my case."

"Right. If you say so."

"I say so."

DISCRETION IS A major principle in my business, and I deal with all facts as privileged information. However, the advantage of my methods over that of priests and lawyers is I am not bound by canons since I alone created and monitor them, which means I can bend them when the situation dictates. I decided to tell Andre the real truth about

Sidney's childhood because I felt it would help him better understand his father's attitudes and behavior and ultimately improve their relationship.

I met him in that same restaurant along the canal where we had originally met. As he came toward me with his tall, red-bearded, imposingly handsome looks, I thought how nice it was to see him again. When I caught my breath after a full minute's kiss, which the sophisticated Hollanders around us totally ignored, I realized happily that apparently he shared my feelings.

We chatted and kind of caught up on each other's activities.

"My mother and sister really liked you," he said.

"And I them," I said. "Your mother's quite a lady. She handles her handicap in the way I admire."

"You mean she ignores it," he said with a grimace. "Mum will never make a fuss about herself. I just don't understand how that accident could happen. You should see her ride—the horse and she become one."

"Even the most skilled horsewoman can't stay on when the saddle gives way."

"That's another thing I don't understand," he said, looking troubled. "She and the groom keep the equipment in tip-top shape always. Well, humans being the fallible beings we are, I guess error is always a possibility."

"Your sister was a bit of a surprise," I said.

"You mean because she's such a humorless prig?"

"Well, you and both your parents are so open and outgoing, I guess I expected more of the same."

He sighed. "She's always been dead serious since she was little. She's really a good old girl, it's just that she takes everything so big. And basically, she's very shy. But she took to you immediately, which is really unusual for her."

He was silent for a moment. "It's that Teutonic twit she's married to who keeps her down."

I smiled. "He did seem sort of dedicated."

"Dedicated! The man's obsessed with himself."

"Perhaps because he cares so much about this project of his."

Andre exploded. "I care deeply about my music, but I don't spend my days and nights preaching and proselytizing about it. The man's a fanatic." Then he shrugged. "But then, he's Austrian."

"Alexandra seems quite happy with him. Maybe that's what she needs."

He shook his head. "I'll never in a million years figure out what makes some people marry who they do. My father is a case in point. I never met his first wife, but I gather that she was a virago. And his current spouse, she's just an upper-class bird who acts like she doesn't have all her buttons done up."

"You're wrong about Juliet."

Another of my rules of discretion is to never reveal the name of the person who engaged my services. This was time for another exception. To resolve Juliet's problems fully, it was necessary for all parties involved to understand and know each other. With all their excessive mannerisms and "dahlings," Juliet's crowd tends to sound like the parody of a Noel Coward play. It was hard to believe they had a serious thought in their heads. But I knew if Juliet and Sidney were to be happy, it would be necessary for Andre to respect his father's wife. When I told him of the depth and caring Juliet had displayed for his father as evidenced by her hiring me, he was stunned, doubly so when I was forced to explain what I do.

He put his head in his hands. "This is just too much for me to absorb at once. You're a kind of private investigator?" He looked up at me. "I can't believe it. I went to bed with a detective!"

"Would that have affected your performance had you known?" I asked.

He laughed. "Can I get back to you later on that after I've put it to the test?" Then he shook his head. "But

Juliet—that's unbelievable. I can't get over the fact that she who holds tight to every tuppence is willing to pay you to help their marriage. Good Lord, and I thought all she worried about was the seating plan of her next dinner party."

He looked thoughtful for a moment. "Is that really why you went to visit my mum? Not to do some research but to check into Mum and Dad's marriage?"

"Yes. I had to find out how many of Juliet's allegations about her and Sidney's marriage had any validity."

He looked surprised. "You mean clients lie to you?"

"Frequently."

"Why? How can you help them if you don't have all the facts?"

"I tell them that all the time, but often pride and wavering self-esteem prevents them from telling the truth, not only to me but to themselves."

"And did my mother substantiate Juliet's version?"

"Yes."

"Then I guess you'll be visiting the first Mrs. Sidney Bailey."

"I already have."

"And did she back up Juliet and Mum?"

"Yes—but we had a short visit." I paused for a moment. "She died."

His eyes flew open. "She's dead? When? How?"

"Just a few days ago, and the police aren't quite sure how."

"The police? You mean they think she may have been murdered?"

I nodded and I waited. It took him five seconds.

"And my mother was almost killed a few days ago. Is there some sort of conspiracy to rid the world of Mrs. Sidney Baileys? If so, shouldn't my mother and Juliet have some sort of bodyguards?"

"Perhaps. I intend to find out. In the interim, it wouldn't hurt for both of them to be extra careful."

He shook his head in consternation. "What is it about

my father and marriage that seems to bring about so much aggro?''

''That's a question I believe I can answer,'' I said.

I told him the facts as related to me by his uncle. He listened avidly. When I told him about his grandfather's harsh treatment of the sensitive, vulnerable child, the anguish on his face was so unbearable I had to look away. The tears streamed down his cheeks as he kept murmuring, ''I didn't know, I didn't know.''

Parents usually know and understand their children, but children rarely have the same advantage with their parents. The adults have been involved in their offsprings' growth and development since birth, but kids get their parents fully formed. Perhaps that's why, although parents frequently impose high expectations on their children, children impose impossible ones on parents. Usually unaware of the parents' earlier traumas, difficulties, and inner pains, the children rarely allow them the weaknesses of people but demand nothing short of perfection and guidance, advice, even financial responsibility for life.

Andre knew his father as a strong, demanding man from whom he heard only criticism. There's nothing more useless than upbraiding children for not appreciating the easy life and wealth to which you have accustomed them. How can they be expected to know what it would be like to be without when they never were? All his life, Andre had heard of his father's financial deprivation, but never about the emotional. It thoroughly threw him to realize that his seemingly self-sufficient, always in control father was vulnerable. Andre was a very caring sensitive man, and he ached for his father's pain and his own mistake of never trying to see past the bluster and recognize a cry for love.

''I thought I knew Juliet. I thought I knew my father, too.'' He shook his head sadly. ''I've been a prize idiot, haven't I?''

XI

———————

I MET LADY Catherine for tea at the Dorchester the next day after I returned from Amsterdam. I love having high tea in one of London's five-star hotels. To me it's one of the most sybaritic self-indulgent experiences that money can buy. From the moment you are guided to your table by the white-gloved attendant, you feel special and utterly pampered. Of course, being with a duchess insures a level of fawning, respectful treatment that we mere mortals can never command. It was delightful.

After we had made our selections from the tray of sandwiches, we began to chat. The range of subjects was endless; she was knowledgeable about art, music, politics, and altogether a stimulating conversationalist. It wasn't until we got to the little jelly cakes that she hit upon the reason for the meeting.

"You know, Emma, Pamela Churchill Harriman and I were girlhood chums. Our friendship was based on our similar backgrounds: both of us were daughters of minor barons, she of Lord Digby, who dairy farmed in Dorchester, and I of Lord Rittendon, who raised sheep in Kent. We had a lot in common because we were both young and ambitious and unhappy with what we regarded as our lowly state. We both longed to marry into the houses of major aristocracy and we both succeeded. She married Randolph Churchill, Winston's son and the great grandson of the seventh Duke of Marlborough, and I married Lord William, sixth Duke of Sandringham. The only difference between us was that I would only marry a man with whom I was in love, and I did. She did not. Most women are too jealous of her to see what a terrible price she has paid for only allying herself to men who could give her money or status. I have had the happiness of marriage to a man with whom I am still in love, in spite of the shortcomings of which you are aware, I'm sure, and also two lovely children. But both Pamela and I paid another price—that of being forced to give up ourselves and the chance to develop our abilities and become the best of whatever we could be. I think I could have had a place in the world of music or politics, but that would have been impossible. Pamela has always been a superbly talented diplomat and politician. But only toward the end of her life was she able to pursue a career in her own right rather than as a behind-the-scenes helpmeet. I'm happy for her that she was finally able to realize her own ambition.'' She smiled sadly. ''Unfortunately, I have not. Thus all my drive has gone into ambitions for my son.''

I wondered where this was all leading.

She smiled intuitively and I knew she was reading my mind. ''You may be thinking this is merely the rambling of an old woman but there is a point. My son loves you, and I believe you reciprocate his feelings. I also believe that two things are holding you back from marrying him—which I should very much like to see happen.'' She stopped. ''My dear, you look surprised.''

Was I ever. ''I thought you wanted a very different kind of wife for him than me.''

"You mean one who pours tea, opens bazaars, and rides to the hounds?"

I must've turned pink.

"My dear, I overheard your little exchange with Dr. Giles."

"But, Lady Catherine, I'm not the kind who will assume the responsibilities of a baronet's wife if it interferes with my own career."

"Precisely the kind of woman Mark needs. Times have changed, and no wife should be forced to accept the very unrewarding secondary position as assistant to her husband. I assure you the ducal estates can survive quite well without the lady of the manor running the Girl Guide meetings. This is the nineties, and in today's era, you would make an excellent wife for my son."

"I'm stunned, Lady Catherine. But what's the thing that you see as my second reason for resisting marriage to Mark?"

She sighed. "I have always detested the smug bigotry that seems to permeate the noble families. The sense of eliteness is bred in their bones. I tried to avoid instilling those feelings in my children, but unfortunately I failed. Perhaps because our class stupidly and blindly turns over our children to others to raise—nannies when they're babes and schools when they reach the ripe age of eight years old. We abdicate parental responsibility and give our children to those who perpetuate the worst as well as the best in us."

"That only explains it, Lady Catherine, it doesn't excuse it."

She nodded. "Quite right."

"Then how do you propose I live with that? I was brought up to accept everyone on the basis of what kind of person they were and what they themselves achieved. How can I fit in, in a world where people are judged solely on who their ancestors were? Most of my friends can trace their dog's lineage back further than they can their own, and no one really cares."

"But he can change, my dear. You can change him, I feel sure."

I sighed. "You sound like my friend Abba. I don't say that's not possible, but it is improbable given all the years those miserable values have been drummed into his head."

"Do you love my son, Emma?"

I was silent for a moment. "Yes."

"Then as I've heard you Americans say—isn't it worth a shot?"

"I honestly don't know, Lady Catherine. Believe me, I've agonized over it."

She put her hand on mine. "Please, my dear—don't jump to any hasty conclusions. All I ask is that you think about it and remember that I'm very much on your side and will do all I can to help."

As we stood outside in front of her waiting limousine, she said, "My son is an unusual and wonderful young man, and you are a unique and marvelous young woman. I think you would make an ideal team." And she drove off.

An ideal *team*?

"OF COURSE SHE thinks of you as a team," said Caleb when I told him the whole story at dinner. "Didn't you know the good lady has political aspirations for her son? The rumor has it that he's being put up for the slot of M.P. in Suffolk, an area that's filled with new posh estate developments filled with yuppies. Methinks she sees you as a sort of Hillary and Bill, the perfect team to appeal to the enlightened career wives of the area."

"We're not talking the Labour party here, of course," I said. "Does she seriously think I would marry her son and help him win a *Conservative* seat in Parliament? I don't know if I ought to be flattered or pissed," I said.

Caleb and I were relaxing on the couch, enjoying a post-prandial espresso after a magnificent home-cooked dinner. This was his home, which meant he cooked the dinner— rack of lamb with rosemary and garlic, flageolets and asparagus, followed by lemon sorbet with *gaufrette* biscuits.

"That was the most delicious lamb I ever tasted. What did you do to it?" I asked.

"An old family recipe—you slash the lamb all over and insert slivers of garlic and anchovy."

"Anchovy? I didn't detect them at all."

"Right. It's not an assertive element and just kills the lamby taste and gives it a rich flavor, as you saw."

I sighed. "How I envy people with culinary heritages. The first M word of little American WASP baby girls isn't mama, it's Miracle Whip. I grew up thinking tuna casseroles and Jell-O molds were gourmet fare. When I moved into my first apartment, I invited friends for dinner and decided to bake a ham. I bought this giant piece of meat and before putting it into the pan, I cut off the end as I had always seen my mother do. Then I thought, Why did she do that? So I called Mom and asked. She said, 'I don't know, dear. My mother always did that. Why don't you call Grandma and ask her?' So I did. 'Why did I cut the end off the ham? Well, dear, my pan was too small.' That's when I learned never to accept givens without learning the origin."

He laughed and stroked my head. "Poor deprived Emma. But think of it, you wouldn't have to concern yourself with such mundane chores; you'll have cooks and housekeepers when you become the Duchess of Sandringham and the wife of the Prime Minister."

I nearly choked on a sip of coffee. "You mean they're planning to groom him for P.M.?"

He shrugged. "Why not? He's the perfect candidate for the 2,000s. Handsome, well-born, educated, married to not one of those two-steps-behind-him toadies, but a complete equal who is a beautiful, highly intelligent solicitor. The ideal chap to beat Tony and Cherie Blair."

I eyed him narrowly. "Are you telling me this to suggest that it's not true love that drives Mark to pursue me, but true ambition?"

"My dear, I am merely laying out the facts. You may draw your own conclusions."

No, I'm absolutely certain that Mark is in love with me. I've seen the vital signs too often not to recognize the genuine article. The rest of this baggage may be purely his mother's dream, although politics has a seductive pull that has lured men for centuries. It's difficult to resist the flattering importuning of important men who offer you a position of supreme power. But if he's counting on me to help fulfill his aspirations, boy, does he ever have the wrong number.

"How are you making out with the lovely Lady Beatrice?" I asked. "I assume if you've seen her you've made out."

"Crudeness from you, Emma?" he said in mock horror. "I forgive you only because I know you did it to bring about a rapid change of subject."

"You do admit that we seem to spend an inordinate amount of time discussing my love life—I think it only fair that we hit on yours once in a while," I said as I held up my empty cup.

He walked into the kitchen and came back with more coffee.

"You know I would really prefer that those two topics would become one. That we would both only be involved in *our* love life. But somehow I suspect that is not to be a viable possibility."

He's right. I'm very attracted to Caleb, but I think I'm in love with Mark. At this precise moment, however, I'm not certain of anything except that I don't want to be a part of anyone's life but my own.

"To answer your question about the Lady Beatrice, she certainly is what you Americans call a piece of work. I seem to be her project of the month," he said wryly.

"Has it gotten you any brownie points yet?"

He looked puzzled. "What are brownie points?"

"It translates as commendations that have usually evolved from ass-kissing."

"Well, I did meet the Commissioner at a dinner in her home on Eaton Place." He smiled contentedly. "He did not seem best pleased to see me there at first. However, ultimately he had to be impressed with Beatrice's shall we say somewhat active approval of me."

"What did she do? Zip open your pants during cock-tails?"

"Not quite. Let us say she was all over my person—sat on my lap after dinner, and insisted that I stay after every-one left. It's funny, behavior that would be considered rude by the middle classes is totally acceptable by the upper."

"I know," I said. "The slinging food at each other and walking on the tables that's considered a de rigueur lark in Oxford and at upper-class children's parties would get them tossed out of any home or establishment of a so-called lower social level. That's part of the sense of entitlement that I find so obnoxious. They regard it as their exclusive right to indulge in the most outrageous behavior. Yet when they're on the magistrate's bench judging some working-class wretch who's overdone it at the pub a bit, they toss him in the clink. "

"Which is why you're at sixes and sevens about his lord-ship," he said contentedly.

"How did this get back to me? We were talking about you," I said indignantly. "Beatrice's antics notwithstand-ing, the association with her ought to give a major boost to your career, Caleb. Now that the Commissioner sees that you're apparently shall we say on intimate terms with the aristocracy, he'll look upon you as one of theirs. You've entered the exclusive hallowed circles that will make him regard you as part of his upper stratosphere. Maybe even his replacement when he comes to retiring."

"I admire your enthusiasm, Emma—but somehow I can-not envision a day when a black man will become head of the Metropolitan Police."

I smiled. "Ten years ago, no one would have dreamed there'd be a black governor of Virginia. Times they are a'changin', Caleb. And I think you are the ideal person to break through long entrenched barriers."

He put his arms around me. "There's a delightful expression I learned from Abba," he said. " 'From your lips to God's ear.' Emma, you're a wonderful ego-booster and supporter. I fully understand Lady Catherine's point of view. Anyone who has you in his corner is a lucky man."

Flattery will get you everywhere. Fifteen minutes later we were in bed. Tomorrow would be time enough to wrap up my case.

XII

I DIDN'T HEAR from Juliet the next day but five days later, but that's not unusual in my business. My job is to devise the solution within two weeks. The client's job is to implement my plan, put it into work, and wait to get the desired results.

"Can you come over at twelve today to have lunch with us?"

"I'd be delighted," I answered. "Who's 'us'?"

Notice I accepted her invitation before I queried her guest list. Don't you hate people who withhold the yes or no until they've ascertained who else will be there? What they're saying is (1) the pleasure of my company alone would not be sufficient, or (2) my friends must be subjected to their evaluation before determining if it's worth accepting my invitation. When anyone does that to me, I immediately supply them with a phony guest list consisting of the most obnoxious people they know. This insures their refusal of my invitation—and also the fact that this will be the last one they'll ever get from me.

"It will be just Sidney, you, and me."

I arrived promptly at twelve and couldn't believe it was the same Juliet. She looked ten years younger and absolutely radiant. Her entire demeanor and carriage had changed—she fairly bounced out of the door to greet me and threw her arms around me and kissed me. From the stiff undemonstrative upper class, that's like getting the D.S.O. Everything about her looked sparkling and new. Her hair was shiny, she was wearing a pink sweater that gave her face a soft rosy look. She actually looked—dare I use the word—pretty. Have you ever wondered why all brides are beautiful? It's because all the makeup and creams in the world can't bring a woman the loveliness that happiness does.

"Sidney just got back from a trip and has some work to catch up on. Why don't we go upstairs to my sitting room for a bit until he's done?"

Was I good or what? This meant Sidney had moved back in and all was hotsy-totsy between them.

There were billowing yellow curtains on the windows and gold carpeting on the floor. A large antique French desk stood against one wall, and two pale yellow brocade love seats were in front of the window flanking an English butler's table. Four pull-up chairs were placed around the room, two upholstered in white silk and two in pale blue. Small tables were scattered about, each covered with silver framed photos and crystal vases filled with fresh flowers.

"What a charming room!" I exclaimed.

"I love it here," she said as we settled ourselves on the love seats. "I spend a lot of time in this room." Then she began to talk animatedly in a nonstop gush.

"It worked—just as you said it would," she said triumphantly. "I told Sidney I had been very attracted to Geoffrey Fraser and was sorely tempted to have an affair with him. He looked smug and self-satisfied, as though things had gone as he had expected. Then when I told Sidney I couldn't do it because I realized how deeply I loved him, how much more wonderful and exciting I found him

than any other man I knew, how I adored and missed him
and would he please, please come back home to me—well,
he was over the moon with joy. He's been a changed man
ever since. Of course, now that I understand his jealousy
and fear of rejection and abandonment, I'm very careful to
give him absolutely no hint of a cause. And I don't mind
at all because I love him and he's suffered so much, and I
want to make his life happy to make up for what that dreadful mother of his did.''

What I had told Juliet to do was to confess to her husband of an almost affair that never was. In actuality, she
couldn't stand Geoffrey. She was never unfaithful with anyone. I decided that what Sidney needed was a repenting
sinner, a woman he dearly loved who, like his mother,
would abandon him—but would fulfill a little boy's lifetime dream by coming back home to him.

Sidney expected women to leave him just like his mother
did. To create a self-fulfilling prophecy with all wives, he
would bedevil them with unfounded accusations of adultery
until he drove them away, as he must have felt he did with
his mother. It was a pattern to create the punishment he felt
he deserved. When a mother leaves a young child, either
by departing or committing suicide, the child feels he must
be in some way responsible. He was so bad that she had
to go away. If he were better, if he truly loved him, she
would have stayed. What Sidney needed to expiate his guilt
was to have a woman he loved and lost to reconsider, decide she had made a terrible mistake, that he was too lov-
able and wonderful to lose, and return to him for always.
As he forever and ever wished his mother would do.

''Oh, yes, something else wonderful happened. Sidney's
son Andre is *famous*. Last night he and his group performed
his music with the Amsterdam Concertgebouw at the Barbican. Sidney was positively bursting with pride. He kept
turning to perfect strangers in the audience saying, 'That's
my son!' ''

I felt like telling her that if Andre had performed at the

Barbican even half as well as he'd performed last night in my bedroom, he must've gotten a standing ovation.

"Not only that," she went on, "Andre has changed toward his father and me. When he arrived at our house, I saw the usual stiffening in Sidney that I cannot bear. It's as though he's preparing to be hurt. Usually Andre gives his father a perfunctory hello and barely glances at me, which inevitably leads to a tirade from Sidney about manners, which ends with Andre storming out of the room." She smiled. "This time, Andre came in, walked right over to Sidney, and gave him a big hug and kiss, then came over and kissed me. I looked at Sidney and there were tears in his eyes." Her eyes misted at the memory. "Andre and Sidney talked endlessly after that, as though they were catching up on years of lost time—and not a cross word. I know you met with Andre. I don't know what you did with him but it was wonderful."

I'll say.

She arose and walked over to her desk and picked up an envelope which she handed to me. "Sidney gave me this as what he called a 'welcome home present' and told me to spend it on anything that makes me happy. I cannot think of anything that would make me happier than giving it to you. What you achieved for me and our family is priceless. I thank God I took the train that day instead of driving down to Tunbridge Wells. I'm going downstairs now to check with Marie about lunch. Come down whenever you're ready. Take your time. The loo is right through my bedroom." She pointed to the next room and left.

I opened the envelope and drew out a check for twenty thousand pounds which is about thirty-three thousand dollars. Pretty nice for less than two weeks' work. Gnash your teeth, Kinsey and Ms. Warshawski.

I walked into Juliet's bedroom and stopped at the dresser mirror to check my makeup and hair. The dresser top was covered with expensive perfumes, some of the bottles not even opened, probably gifts from Sidney. Then I noticed a pincushion with all her hat pins—there were dozens, tipped with gold, silver, pearl, and various stones. Suddenly my heart seemed to stop. In the middle, as though it were the newest addition, was the garnet-topped pin with the replica of the saint's head from St. George's Church that I had seen in Prague.

XIII

MY MIND WAS churning, but I sat at the lunch table chatting away so lightheartedly that I think I'm entitled to an Oscar for outstanding performance in a miserable life situation. Luckily they were so lovey-dovey that I don't think they would have noticed if I had lapsed into Tibetan.

The service was beautiful. Villeroy & Boch Botanica dishes on a gleaming Chippendale table with a centerpiece consisting of a single branch of stephanotis. We started with prosciutto and melon and champagne, followed with the most delicious shepherd's pie I've ever had, and salad, and ended with cheese and coffee.

When we finished, I took out my camera. As you've seen, it's a snap to get people to pose for you. I find everyone is immensely flattered when you evince interest in photographing them or their home. It's amazing the kind of untoward things that can come out when the photos are developed. Like the dinner party when I caught the background image of the stodgy banker Sir Everett Pickering's hand on the rump of a startled but evidently not displeased Dame Maggie Smith.

I took pictures of Sidney alone, then the two of them, and then Juliet alone. After Sidney went back upstairs to his work, I asked Juliet if she would pose for me in the hat she was wearing when we met on the train.

"I'd like to have a client photo for my casebook, preferably the way you looked when we first met."

Great idea. I'll have to start doing that.

As she was posing, I asked her how she explained me to Sidney. Since he and I had met earlier, didn't he wonder about how she and I knew each other?

"That was easy—I told him the truth—that we met at Mark's party. He didn't question it for a moment. When you move in certain circles, you're bound to run into the same people." She smiled impishly. "Of course, I didn't tell him that this wasn't the first time. He has no idea of our professional connection—and never shall."

"Before I leave, Juliet, I have a favor to ask. Could I please have the recipe for that delicious shepherd's pie?"

Her face was suffused with pleasure.

"Of course. It's from Mrs. Tuck, our family cook."

I groaned. "Oh, no, then it probably has twenty-seven ingredients and takes three days to make."

"It's really quite simple, Emma."

I looked around at her huge kitchen that took up almost half the entire first floor.

"Right. Remember, I don't have a kitchen the size of Westminster Abbey and someone to do K.P. I have just me and an eight by ten kitchen. Also I'm new at this cooking stuff. I've just recently started only because I couldn't stand facing another load of last night's take-out containers when I came in for breakfast. But I'm not ready yet to compete with the brothers Troisgros. My culinary abilities are minimal and so are my prerequisites for recipes: the list of ingredients must be no more than one inch long, instructions one and a half inches, and preparation time no more than an hour."

She laughed. "I think this will suit your needs, Emma.

The recipe is for six people but it freezes well.''

"The ingredients are one and a half pounds of chopped beef, three onions, two leeks, four carrots, a small package of mushrooms, one aubergine (eggplant), a large can of tomato sauce, eight potatoes, and cheddar cheese.''

I wrote it all down quickly. Easy so far.

"Then you chunk the vegetables and sauté them together with the meat until brown. Pile it all into a covered casserole together with the can of tomato sauce in a 350-degree oven for two hours. Then cool in the fridge overnight. In the morning, skim off the fat, add cornstarch to thicken a bit, then put it back in the oven for a half hour. In the meantime, cut up and boil the potatoes and mash together with shredded cheddar cheese. Pile and spread the potato mixture over the casserole, put it back in the oven for twenty minutes, or whatever it takes to melt the cheese and get the topping all beautifully brown, and that's it.''

Great. I had taken it all down in my pocket pad and it took up less than a page handwritten.

I thanked her for everything and left. Her farewell was less effusive than her initial greeting, but that's usual with clients who are grateful for my efforts but now want to get on with their lives and really forget that anyone else but themselves was responsible for the successful resolution of their problems.

When I got home, I phoned Prague. I sat on my terrace awaiting the callback. I tried to read but found it difficult to concentrate. When the phone rang an hour later, I listened to the confirmation I expected but dreaded. After hanging up, I sat quietly for a few minutes and then called Grace Lechwandowski.

"Hello, Grace. How are you doing?''

"Emma! How nice to hear from you.''

Her voice sounded "up" and happy, which puzzled me when she said that she was back home in her mother's house, as was Rudolf Sykes.

"Is that a good idea?'' I asked.

"Leif is living here, too," she said.

That accounted for the cheerful voice.

"I couldn't do it without him. I had to come back. After all, it is still my home. Actually, Jan instructed me to move back. Something about the legality of possession if Rudy took the place over for himself. You see, until the estate is settled, we don't know who gets what. Mother left no will, you know."

"I'll bet Rudy is plenty pissed off about that."

She laughed. "Oh, yes. Apparently Mum promised him she would leave him everything, but her lawyer said she just kept procrastinating about making a will. Rudy insists there must be what I guess you call a holographic will somewhere in the house. He's been taking the place apart looking and so far nothing has turned up, of course. I'm not surprised. Mum hated dealing with unpleasant things. He claims he saw her writing one, but knowing my mother, she was probably writing a shopping list and told him it was her will just to keep him quiet and happy. Thinking or talking about dying was something she would never do. Without any will, I understand I get half and Rudy gets half."

Then her tone changed. "But I'm afraid they still think I killed Mum," she said with fear and worry in her voice. "I wish they'd decide one way or another—the suspense is wearing me down. It's like living with a bomb ticking away under you."

"Grace, you may know by now that I'm not a writer."

"Yes, Jan told me you are an attorney and a sort of private investigator."

"I believe I can prove that you didn't kill your mother, and also insure that you are the sole heiress to your mother's estate."

"You can?" she said, her voice raised in excitement. "Truly?"

"My terms are very simple, Grace." And I told her my no-up-front-but-whopping-big-after fee if I was successful.

"It sounds marvelous, but where will I get such money?" she said sadly.

"That's easy. Have Jan draw up a paper to guarantee that the first money you pay when you inhererit your mother's estate will be my fee."

I heard her hesitate. "Can you hold on just a moment, Emma? Leif just came in. I would like to talk it over with him."

She came back on the line in a few minutes, her voice breathy with excitement.

"Leif says I have nothing to lose. If I don't do anything I could lose half the estate, and possibly my freedom as well. Please—go ahead. I will speak to Jan and he will send you the letter immediately."

I gave her my fax number and told her I'd be back to her probably within days.

O.K., you may be thinking I'm a bit of a shit. Charge the poor girl for solving a problem when you derived most of your substantive data from another case? First place, she's not a poor girl. If she was the penniless student I met originally, I wouldn't charge her a crown. I'm not heartless, you know. However, how and where I got my information should not matter. It takes perception, analysis, and judgment to put it all together and that's what I charge for. Besides, there was still work to be done to clinch the case. We weren't there yet.

JAN MALECEK MET me at the airport in Prague the next morning. As we drove along the highway from the airport, he looked at me out of the corner of his eye.

"You're sure you want me to take you to the Palace Praha? As I've mentioned before, I have plenty of room at my place."

Isn't that just the way of it? Months can go by when I'm so manless that I'd welcome an obscene phone call and now I'm suffering from an oversupply. He's attractive, he's intelligent, and he's here. I've already broken my monogamous rule with Caleb and Andre (no, I didn't sleep with Mark during his birthday weekend). It was tempting but would have bordered on promiscuity. And that I don't do.

"Thanks for the invitation, Jan, but Abba would be scandalized."

He laughed so hard he nearly lost control of the wheel. I had to giggle, too. Abba has done almost everything with almost everybody, and what he hasn't done himself, he has seen others do. I think the only thing that might get a ripple of surprise from him would be if he found the Pope and the Grand Rabbi in flagrante delicto. And even then I'm not sure. When we arrived at my hotel, I asked Jan to wait.

"I'll just drop my stuff in my room and be right down. I'd like to get started."

We zipped along the motorway in his BMW at a speed that made me feel we were on one of Germany's unlimited autobahns. I guess when you're the president's nephew, you don't need a radar detector. From the exuberant look on his face, I could see he was one of those driving buffs who become one with the machine and revel in the challenge of maneuvering cars at high speeds. This is not one of the pleasures I share. I adore challenges—cerebral ones. Physical ones leave me cold—with abject fear. I know there must have been some lovely scenery along the way, but my eyes were frozen facing forward and my right foot was on the nonexistent brake. When we saw the signpost BARDEJOV, our destination, my heart went back down from my throat to its normal position. As he slowed down in town, he said, looking at me sideways:

"Does my driving bother you?"

"Terrify would be a better word," I answered. "I trust your obviously superb ability to control the car—it's the other drivers who worry me. Having to deal with some stupid jerk's sudden turn when you're doing one hundred kilometers an hour is hairy but doable—but at 150, the odds are against even the winner of the Grand Prix."

"I promise to do no more than one hundred on our return. All right?"

"Jan—stop. Look at those houses."

We had come upon a scene out of the fifteenth century, a street that was so ancient that our car was a total anachronism. In front of us was a row of connected buildings, each peaked with a beautifully carved rounded top, and each having three arcades on the street level. They were so perfect, with flat fronts, that it looked like a stage set for *The Student Prince*.

Jan was delighted with my reaction. Like every Czech I had met, he was proud of the timeless beauty of his country.

"Bardejov has the best-preserved medieval town in Slovakia," he explained. "In this country, we have great respect for our antiquities. We have established historical town reserves that give national protection to the preservation of buildings and even environments. This is the original Gothic village as it was in the fourteenth century, and it will always sit as it is in the center of town. Notice it has an unusual right-angled ground plan. We're now in the town center, but around us are fortifications from the fourteenth and fifteenth centuries."

I was enchanted. The oblong square was surrounded by Gothic and Renaissance houses. "What's that imposing edifice over there?" I asked.

"The Old Town Hall, built in 1505. It's now a museum that has the largest collection of icons in Slovakia."

We pulled over to the side to give Jan the chance to examine a street map.

"It's just a few blocks from here."

We came to a huge block of obviously Communist-built housing. The complex consisted of six buildings of what were once white stone but were now streaked with mildew and dirt. They had the impersonal, uninviting ugliness of all totalitarian government structures that look like they were built without the benefit of an architect and with no concern for aesthetics. Fortunately there was a small forest behind the buildings, which at least gave a touch of soft green to the neighborhood. We parked next to a playground that was filled with small children and mothers pushing carriages. Signs were nonexistent, so Jan asked one of the women, who pointed to the building we were looking for. We crossed a small concrete square and walked into a lobby with walls painted institutional brown and took the small slow elevator up to the sixth floor. There were no signs indicating which flats were right or left, so we guessed and wended our way around a series of long halls that smelled of cabbage until we reached Flat 7 and rang the bell. After a few minutes, someone peered through the peephole and opened the door.

"*Dobrý den, Paní Sychov. Jmenuji se Pane Dr. Jan Malecek.*"

I knew enough Czech to know he was saying, "Good day, Mrs. Sychov. My name is Dr. Jan Malecek."

She was a small dumpling of a woman with curly brown hair touched with gray and a lovely smile. Her dark green dress was surprisingly stylish and well-made, which indicated a higher income than the surroundings suggested, or a woman who was very talented at the sewing machine. We followed her into a large and appealing room that overlooked the forest. There was much of the usual heavy dark Slovakian furniture, but the effect had been lightened by a glass-topped coffee table and a few black leather sling chairs. It looked like either someone got stuck with a pile of inherited furniture and tried to mitigate the effect, or someone started to furnish the home and changed taste midstream. The room was dominated by a piano. I walked over to look at the framed photographs that covered the silk-shawl-covered top, and saw a familiar face.

We sat down on a heavily stuffed couch and Jan reiterated the explanation for our presence that he had given her on the phone when he made the appointment. I'd brought him with me because I speak no Czech, and I imagine you don't either. So in the interests of clarity rather than authenticity. I'll report our conversation in English.

"Miss Rhodes has been hired by the government to do a study of women who have chosen to be housewives and bring up their children themselves. We need to contrast that to the effect of the new generation who are going to work and leaving their children in day care. We want to compare their feelings, and their children. It's a very large and long-term study, and you have been chosen as one of the women to participate."

Do I get points for imagination? Jan had wanted to know how I could possibly hope to secure entrée to the home of Mrs. Sychov and get her to reveal the intimate details of her life, and I came up with this gambit. He thought it was brilliant. It is because it pushes all the right buttons. To a person who has lived in a Communist state, government requests for information of the most private nature are commonplace. The pride in being selected for the study and thus given the chance to show off her home and children are factors that must undoubtedly charm any woman. And to top it off, being visited by the president's nephew not only gave authenticity to my project but was sure to make her the star of the housing development.

I took out my tape recorder and notebook and began by asking her how long she had been married.

"Sixteen years come June."

"How many children do you have?"

"Two, a daughter of fourteen and a son of twelve."

"What is your husband's name?"

"Rudolf Sychov."

Also known as Rudy Sykes. He didn't even have to change the initials on his cuff links.

"What does your husband do?"

"He is a salesman. He sells techincal equipment."

I think the equipment he makes his living from is more personal than technical.

"He travels all over the world," she said proudly.

"Then he is not home too much."

"True, but he calls us very often."

"That would mean that, in a sense, you have had to bring up your children alone."

"Yes, but he is a very loving and good father and husband." And she pointed to the things he had brought home as gifts. The glass coffee table and the modern chairs. Apparently the exposure to the Bauhaus pieces he saw in Alicia's home had had its effect. The door from the other room opened and a lovely girl and boy entered, both looking very shy.

"These are my children," she said with obvious love and pride. "This is Nadia," who did a little curtsy, "she is fourteen, and this is Josef, he is twelve."

The children sat down next to their mother.

"That's a very pretty dress, Nadia," I commented.

She blushed and said, "Papa brought it for me."

"Whenever he returns from a trip, he always brings presents for us," said Mrs. Sychov. "Come, let me show you."

We went into the bedroom. It was a small boxlike room furnished sparsely with a double bed and a chest of drawers. She opened the closet and pushed back clothes to show me a lineup of about six expensive dresses that did not look new.

"These are from the wife of the director of Rudy's company. They think so highly of my Rudy that I am the wife she has chosen to send them to," she said proudly. "You see, she is a very rich lady and wears things just a few times and then she tires of them. Look at this material and workmanship. I just have to adjust them a bit here and there—we are almost the same size but I am a bit bigger in certain places," and she smiled.

Alicia's castoffs. I felt like telling her that she looked much lovelier in the clothes than her benefactor did. Grace had mentioned that her mother was a big spender on things for herself. I enjoyed the irony of the fact that her selfish extravagance provided a luxurious wardrobe for a woman she would have hated. Rudy dressed his wife with Alicia's clothes, he supported his family with Alicia's money. A regular Robin Hood.

We went back into the other room and I stopped at the piano to look at the framed family photographs.

"This is our wedding picture. Isn't my Rudy handsome?"

"Yes, and you, too, are very lovely," I said.

I heard Jan talking to Nadia about her schooling.

"She is number one in her class," said Mrs. Sychov proudly. "She will go to university someday."

"And what do you want to be?" asked Jan.

Nadia answered immediately. "A lawyer."

Jan smiled broadly. "Good for you. We can always use intelligent members of the bar. What makes you want to study law?"

She looked very serious. "Daddy says the law is the only way to protect the citizenry. Under the Communists, we had much injustice. The only way to have a free social system is to have open courts that operate fairly. I want to be part of that system," she said simply.

I looked at Jan and saw that he, too, was both stunned and moved. How could such wisdom come from the mouth of that charlatan? Could one person be two people?

"I wish to be an engineer," said Josef firmly.

We smiled. He, too, was dead serious.

"Why?" I asked.

"Daddy says I am good with machines and things," he said softly but with apparent pride. "He says I should design industrial technical equipment. He says that will not only help the people who use it, but give jobs to the ones who make it."

Ye gods, I couldn't believe what I was hearing. Could a man who was a vain, lecherous opportunist in one house turn into an altruistic sage in another? The respect and love with which his wife and children held him was wonderful to see. If I didn't know him, from their description, I would have been anxious to meet this paragon of parenting.

I could see from Jan's expression that he was as thunderstruck as I. There was no question that Rudy Sykes and Rudolf Sychov were the same person—but how could he have such disparate personas?

I had all the information I needed and signaled to Jan that we should leave. Our hostess saw the signal and said something quickly to Nadia, who left the room and returned a few minutes later with a silver tray with coffee and homemade cookies.

"Please, you cannot leave without having some food with us."

I looked at Jan, who smiled and nodded, and we sat down again. It would be rude to refuse her hospitality. After we had finished, I took out my camera and asked if I might take a picture of the family. Mrs. Sychov looked flustered for a moment and began patting her hair.

"Not to worry," I said with a smile. "You look lovely."

I sat the three of them on the couch and snapped them together—the perfect family.

JAN AND I were silent for a while in the car as we drove.

"You wonder how such a bastard could produce such a lovely family," he said.

"Do you remember an old Alec Guinness movie called *The Captain's Paradise*?" I asked.

"Isn't that the one where he had a wife in one port with whom he lived a sedentary homebody life, and a wife in another port where he insisted on going out and partying every night?"

"That's the one. That's our Rudy. He lives a totally bifurcated life, and the way he probably sees it is that he's making two women happy instead of one."

"The difference," said Jan, "is that the captain supported both wives. Rudy used one wife to support the other."

"You know, I can almost understand and sympathize with his morality," I said.

"You can't mean that," protested Jan. "The man's a lying bigamist. He's not only broken the law, but probably the heart of that good woman back there when she learns the truth."

"I don't know. Women like Alicia who are shallow and totally self-indulgent are fairly repellent. They devote their lives solely to their own pleasure using money they themselves didn't earn. If you're poor and struggling to support a family you love, it's easy to convince yourself that such women don't deserve their riches and there's nothing wrong with balancing the inequity of cruel fate. I can see where you can easily justify your actions. It's the have-nots trying to even the score with the haves."

"I can see where you must be an excellent lawyer. You make a very convincing case, Emma. But I am not a jury to be swayed by the emotional factors involved. You know that I must report him to the police. He has committed a crime. I am a lawyer, an officer of the court. It is my duty."

"I know," I said. "Well, for one thing, it will make Grace happy because now she'll inherit everything. But what will it do to that lovely innocent mother and children back there?"

We both thought quietly for a number of miles. By the time we had reached the outskirts of Prague, I had worked out an idea. We stopped at Jan's office, and I waited for him to draw up some papers. Then we proceeded to Grace's home.

When she opened the door, she looked at us in total surprise, then her face broke out in a large smile.

"Emma, Jan—how wonderful to see you." And she threw her arms around Jan's neck and hugged him. "Leif," she shouted, "look who is here."

We went into the main salon and Rudy entered. He looked different than when I saw him last. He was haggard and harassed. Now that he no longer had to play the dashing Beau Brummell, his collar was slightly soiled and his trousers could have used a pressing. I guess he couldn't totally relinquish the fop role because he still sported an ascot, but it was carelessly askew.

"I thought I heard a car," he said morosely.

"Please join us, Pane Sykes," said Jan cordially. "What we have to say concerns you as well as Grace."

A spark of fear flashed in his eyes and then disappeared. He sat on one of the black leather chairs, and we all grouped ourselves accordingly.

"Mr. Sykes," I said, "or should I say Sychov? May I show you a picture?"

Grace and Leif sat up. "Sychov? His name is not Sykes?"

"No," I said.

Rudy looked at me silently for a moment, then reached for the photo. His face turned white.

"No, I didn't tell them," I said gently.

He sighed and his shoulders dropped. "Thank you," he said almost inaudibly.

"What is this all about?" asked Grace.

"Rudy has another wife whom he never divorced. He was never legally married to your mother," I said.

She was stunned. Then the full realization of the meaning of my words hit her and she jumped up in excitement. "Then he can't inherit half of Mum's things. It will now all be mine—the house, the money, everything!"

Jan opened his briefcase and withdrew some papers.

"Pane Sychov, please give me five crowns."

Rudy looked stunned. "Why? What for?"

"You will please sign these papers appointing me your legal representative upon payment of a fee of five crowns."

He still looked totally puzzled.

"Then he won't have to report you for bigamy because if you are his client, he cannot breach the rule of client confidentiality," I explained.

The color began to come back into his face as he realized the meaning of the procedure.

"You mean, you won't have to turn me over to the

police?'' he asked. Then he looked at me. ''But you know, and they know.''

''We don't have the obligation to report you as Jan does. He's an officer of the court. However, Grace, Leif, and I are not bound by such rules, only by our consciences.'' I looked at them. ''We will have no reason to report you once you've signed these papers that stipulate you're giving up all claim to Alicia Sykes' estate, is that not so?''

Grace nodded.

''But why does he have to sign such papers?'' asked Leif. ''If he has another wife, he automatically loses rights to the estate.''

Jan smiled. ''Smart boy. You're right. But Alicia's lawyer, who will arrange for the disbursement of the estate, does not know of the other wife. If he did, not being bound by the client-lawyer privilege with Rudy, he would be forced to report the matter to the police. Since he will not have that information, he will expect to turn over half of the estate to Rudy unless he has Rudy's legally drawn up disavowal.''

''But won't he think it suspicious?'' asked Leif.

Jan shrugged. ''Perhaps. But suspicion is not fact. And in such a situation, most lawyers are concerned only with the facts and do not look for trouble. Especially lawyers who deal only in civil matters—they try to avoid involvement in criminal affairs. It's out of their bailiwick and they usually resist having anything to do with the police and the prosecutors.''

Jan handed the papers to Rudy, who signed them immediately.

Leif jumped up, his fair skin a blazing red under his blond hair. ''But why should he get off so easy? The man is an evil monster.''

''Look,'' I said placatingly, ''I wouldn't put him up for the Citizen of the Year award, but let's look at what he actually did. He married Alicia and treated her like a china doll and made her very happy. True, he misled Grace and broke her heart, and for that I do not excuse or forgive him. But Grace is twenty years old, this was not exactly child abuse. And fortunately, she has you to love and care for her. She suffered for a while, but can you compare that to the suffering these children will go through for the rest of their lives if their father is convicted?''

I showed Grace and Leif the photograph and described the mother and children and their loving trusting relationship with Rudy. I told them about Nadia's excellent school record, and her and Josef's goals. I also told them what Rudy had told the children to guide them into their future professions. Their eyes widened and they looked incredulously at Rudy, who was sobbing quietly.

"I know what I did was wrong," he said. "But was I not a good husband to Alicia? Did I not make her happy? My children are my life," he said. "You see how bright they are, how much they have to give to the world. They deserve the kind of education and future that I could not afford to give them. I didn't want them to grow up to be a nothing like me. The only talent I ever had was to make women like me. So I used that. Believe me, I worked hard for my money," he said bitterly.

Then he turned to look directly at Grace.

"Grace, I am terribly, terribly sorry for what I did to you," and he looked at her sadly. "But truly I could not help myself. I was so lonely here, your mother made me feel so little and worthless—and you were so lovely and soft and caring, so unlike the hardness of your mother. I was not lying when I told you I loved you—I did. I knew what I was doing was wrong, but I was desperate and you were the only ray of light in this house." He looked at her pleadingly. "I ask for your forgiveness, although I know I do not deserve it."

She looked at him sympathetically and then took Leif's hand.

"There have been enough victims in this—let's not have

any more. We will say nothing.'' She looked up at Leif, who nodded.

Rudy sat up slowly, a look of joy suffusing his face. *''Děkuji!''*—thank you—he kept saying over and over again.

I got up and excused myself. I walked into the kitchen to look for Alena.

''Dobrý den, Alena,'' I said as I saw her sitting and shelling peas. I sat down at the table and pulled out a photograph to show her.

When I returned to the salon, Rudy had gone upstairs to pack.

''Well, Emma,'' said Grace. ''You've done what you promised.''

''Not all of it, Grace,'' said Leif.

I smiled with total assurance. ''I have two weeks, remember?''

XIV

WHEN I GOT back to my hotel room that evening, I fell into bed exhausted. It had been quite a day. I picked up the phone to call into my answering machine in London. There was one message—I heard the agitated voice of Andre.

"Emma, someone has tried again to kill my mother. Please call me as soon as you can. I am in my mother's house in Salzburg. I need you."

Whoever was after Celia was either very inept or having damned bad luck, fortunately for Celia. I phoned Andre. I didn't ask for details, just about Celia's condition. He told me she was badly battered but not critically.

"I planned to come to Salzburg tomorrow anyway—I have reservations on the eight a.m. flight."

"I'll be there to pick you up."

"No need," I said. "I've already booked a car. I'll meet you at the house."

HE HUGGED ME tightly when he opened the door. He looked distraught.

"You were right—once may be an accident or sloppiness, but twice? This cannot be just coincidence.''

He told me that Celia was going from the Old Town to the New Town, which involves crossing the river. There's an underwater tunnel that Celia was using, going down the access steps carefully on her crutches when suddenly she went flying. She said she didn't know why, but she'd just suddenly lost her balance.

''Could someone have pushed or jostled her?'' I asked Andre.

''We asked her that, but she doesn't remember. Unfortunately it was noontime and the steps were jammed with people going to lunch.''

As I recalled, those steps are steep and they're stone. It was amazing that she wasn't hurt badly or killed. Apparently she'd been swathed in some sort of hooded cape that softened the fall and avoided any breakage of bones. Fortunately she didn't land on her head.

As we walked into the sunny front room, we were greeted by Alexandra, who had just arrived with Franz. Edward was sitting next to Celia, holding her hand solicitously. No one questioned my presence; it was obvious they assumed I was here to visit Andre.

''Emma, dear—you always seem to arrive when I'm in extremis. You must think me some sort of accident-prone klutz.''

''Darling, you're taking this too lightly,'' said Edward.

''Oh, Edward, you see plots against my life everywhere. You've seen too many operas. Who would ever want to kill me?''

I had a couple of candidates in mind, but I wasn't about to tell her or anyone of my suspicions until I had more credible evidence. But actually, I did have my favorite.

''Why don't we do what Perry Mason would do?'' I said with a smile.

They all looked at me. ''And what would that be, Emma?'' asked Alexandra.

"Ask everyone where they were at the time of the accident."

Guess who got all huffy and indignant. Right—son-in-law Franz, the Aryan asshole.

"Are you accusing one of us? What utter nonsense," he said, turning pink with anger. "How dare you even suggest it."

"If you called in the police, which I assume you didn't, that's probably the first thing they'd do." So maybe they wouldn't. What did these people know about police procedure anyway?

"I was at rehearsal at the church with my chorale group," said Edward quickly. He looked at me with a small knowing smile and then looked expectantly around the room.

"I was working at my atelier with my assistant Elsa," said Alexandra.

"I was having lunch at St. Peter's Stiftskeller with Eric Muller," said Andre.

They all looked expectantly at Franz, who sat silent.

"How about you, dear?" said Alexandra.

Celia, seeing Franz's stubborn fury, said, "Oh, let's not fuss. Perhaps I fancied the whole thing and it was just someone who bumped into me quite accidentally. I was feeling slightly nackered and I might just have been unsteady on those infernal crutches."

Then she turned to me with a social smile. "I do hope you're having lunch with us, Emma."

The rapid change of subject was accepted but did not go unnoticed. Andre looked at Franz quizzically, and Alexandra's face was stone. Edward hadn't turned off that small knowing smile.

"No, I'm afraid I have a few stops to make, Celia, and then I'm back to the airport for home. I just stopped by to see how you were."

I got up and started for the door when something struck me.

"Celia, did you happen to feel anything before the push? Like around your head or neck?" I'm beginning to really understand Columbo. You really do get sudden ideas just as you're at the door.

She thought for a moment. "Yes," she said hesitantly. "Now that you mention it, I felt sort of a sticking in the back of my neck. In fact, I think that's what made me pull forward and fall."

"Could I please see the cape you were wearing?" I asked.

Franz made a derogatory snort. "Oh, for God's sake. Do you think you're that Fletcher woman on that inane television show that I never watch because the plots and resolutions are so stupid?"

"If you never watch it, Franz, how do you know the plots are stupid?" I asked sweetly.

Edward smiled broadly. Obviously Franz was not on his list of favorite people. He went over to the hall closet and brought over a long, brown, wool, hooded cape. I looked carefully at the back of the hood. There was an almost imperceptible hole at the center of the neckline.

They all looked at me curiously. Andre regarded me especially quizzically, since he was the only one in the room who knew my true profession.

"I think, Celia, you were extremely lucky. This garment saved you from what could've been serious injury."

She brightened. "There, you see? Why is everybody sitting around with such long faces. My cape cushioned the fall—I shall call it my lucky cape from now on."

Andre saw me to the door. "Can I come along with you, Emma?" he asked with a pleading look that was flattering but inconvenient.

Sorry, fella. This mission is strictly solo.

I shook my head. "I'll phone you and maybe we can have a drink before I fly back."

•   •   •

I DROVE THROUGH the lovely countryside. This was *Sound of Music* country with green hills, alpine chalets, and a horizon of snowcapped Alps, and I should have been able to enjoy the scenery but I couldn't. The car was going at 100 kilometers per hour and my mind was racing along at 200.

I headed south of Salzburg toward Lustschloss Hellbrunn, which was the pleasure palace of the prince-archbishops. It was built in the early seventeenth century and has some fascinating features like octagonal rooms and trompe l'oeil ceilings. Best of all are the trick fountains called the Wasserspielen that spurt water out of the most unexpected orifices at unpredictable times. The Monatsschlosschen, which is the old hunting lodge, now contains a lovely folklore museum. The palace deer park has a somewhat weird zoo that has free-flying vultures and alpine creatures that roam freely contained only by moats. I had enjoyed visiting here a few years ago, but right now my head wasn't on sight-seeing. I passed blue mountain lakes that were breathtaking, where ordinarily I would have stopped to savor the stunning vistas, but I just kept right on going.

I finally arrived at the small country road that led to the stables where Celia Ramsay boarded her horse. No one seemed to be around—which meant anyone could come and go as he or she pleased.

"Can I help you?" a man's voice said.

I spun around to see a man in jeans and a heavy sweater carrying a saddle.

"How did you know I needed English?" I asked.

He smiled, showing a display of irregular yellowed teeth. "I guessed. Somehow you do not have the look of a fräulein."

"I don't think I want to ask if that's a compliment or not."

He looked at me in surprise. "But for someone who looks like you, it can only be that."

He didn't speak in a flirtatious way, just merely stating a fact. I found that refreshing.

"Actually, yes, you can help me."

I told him I was a friend of Celia Ramsay and just wanted to ask him a few questions.

"Ach, Frau Ramsay has many friends who are interested in horses, I see. One of them was here just a few days ago."

I took out a picture. "Is that person in this photograph?"

He carefully took out glasses from his pocket and examined the picture.

"Ya—this one."

We chatted a bit, then I thanked him and asked if he had a phone I could use. He led me to a little office that smelled of coffee, tobacco, and manure, and pushed aside papers on an old scarred desk in the corner to reveal a telephone. Then he pointed to a small box where he instructed me to deposit the required amount of shillings. One gets nothing for nothing in Austria. He walked out and I phoned Andre to ask him to meet me tomorrow morning in London.

XV

I THOUGHT THIS visit warranted coming in through the front entrance. I rang the bell and a few minutes later—it takes time to run up from the kitchen—Marie opened the door.

"Good morning, Marie. I believe madam is expecting me."

She nodded and led us into the drawing room. Sidney and Juliet were seated on the couch, and Andre was in the large chair next to the window. They all arose as we entered. Sidney walked over and kissed me with a smile.

"What's all this cloak-and-dagger mystery, Emma? Juliet said you had something urgent to discuss with us." He looked behind me. "My, my, it must be of major proportions if you've brought your bodyguards," he said jovially.

"This is Detective Chief Superintendent Caleb Franklin and Inspector Ludvik of the Prague police. Gentlemen, may I introduce you to Mr. Sidney Bailey, Mrs. Juliet Bailey, and Mr. Andre Bailey."

Everybody nodded to each other, Inspector Ludvik made a small, stiff Eastern European bow. I quickly scanned the room for reactions and noted that Juliet looked frightened, Andre looked concerned, and Sidney looked cool and urbane. Don't bother trying to read anything into those responses because most people become nervous when police appear on the scene. Even the most law-abiding citizens worry that they might have, however inadvertently, done something wrong. Who of us hasn't committed some minor infraction sufficient to evoke a feeling of guilt? Of course, it's highly unlikely that a Detective Chief Superintendent of Scotland Yard would come to your home to present you with a ticket for spitting on the sidewalk. But in England where authority treads lightly when the aristocracy is involved, anything is possible; we mustn't forget that Juliet is the daughter of a duke. Then there's the fear that something may have happened to someone you love and the police are bearers of tragic tidings. So it's not unnatural for people to look slightly apprehensive when the police arrive at their homes. As for Sidney's insouciant reaction, remember that he's an actor who was trained to display any emotion he chose rather than felt.

"To what do we owe the honor of a visit from such distinguished officers of the law?" asked Sidney with a smile. "But first, can we offer you some coffee or tea?"

Deucedly civilized, what? He was playing the role of the charming host, and doing it handsomely. It's not easy to appear totally unconcerned when heavy-duty fuzz arrive on your doorstep at ten in the morning. We would have been there at nine, but when I phoned the evening before to make the appointment, Sidney advised me they were late-night-outers and thus late risers. I had heard from mutual friends that he was working seriously at developing a reputation as a bon vivant man about town in London, which means being seen every evening at the hottest hostelries of the moment. Since such dining requires vintage wines, haute cuisine, brandies, and a minimum check of two hundred pounds, if the Baileys made it home by two a.m., they probably considered it an early night.

"Coffee would be fine for me," said Caleb.

The inspector and I took our cue from Caleb and asked for the same. Sidney nodded to Marie, who immediately went down to the kitchen. This opening move is highly significant to any observer of police methodology. If there is a strong case of almost certain guilt, refreshments are not on the agenda; it's all strictly business. If it's a fact-finding mission, then the amenities may be observed to lead smoothly and subtly into extracting needed information. I've used the same technique myself because I've found that the social routine causes people to relax their guards. The exchange of pleasantries serves to convince them that the situation is not threatening and the visitors appear benign. After all, who would sit there chatting amiably over a cup of tea or coffee if they plan to clap you in irons?

Marie brought up the tray, and Juliet was the hostess.

"Cream or sugar?" she asked, now thoroughly poised.

"All right, Detective Superintendent," said Sidney. "We're delighted to have such an illustrious member of Scotland Yard," and he turned to Inspector Ludvik, "and the constabulary of Prague here in our home, but what's this all about?"

"It's about the murder of your ex-wife Alicia Lechwandowski, in Prague," said Caleb easily.

Juliet turned pale, Andre's eyes widened, and again Sidney seemed totally unmoved.

"Murdered? I thought she fell and hit her head."

"Who told you that, Mr. Bailey?"

He looked nonplussed for a moment, then his face cleared and he turned to me.

"I believe Emma told Juliet who told me."

"No, Sidney. I told Juliet about Alicia's death, but I did not mention the circumstances. She never asked."

He looked at Juliet, who just sat there saying nothing. He recouped quickly.

"Of course, it was Grace, Alicia's daughter. I phoned her after I heard about her mother. She must have told me."

That's easy enough to check.

"I understand you had been supporting your ex-wife through an offshore irrevocable trust which you set up," Caleb said.

"That's no secret, nothing illegal I assure you."

Caleb smiled. "I'm certain of that, Mr. Bailey. Now that she's dead, where does her income go?"

Sidney's face darkened. "It goes to my second wife, but I'm not sure why this should concern Scotland Yard or why I should answer your questions."

"I understand your hesitation, Mr. Bailey. But all I'm asking is for you to help the police in their inquiries concerning a murder. You may wish to refuse to answer my questions, sir, but I cannot imagine why you would," he said with a winning smile. "Especially since the victim is someone who must have meant something to you at some time."

Sidney shrugged. "Oh, very well."

"And if your second ex-wife dies, what happens to the trust?"

"The trust is dissolved and all the moneys revert to me. But what's all this in aid of? Fortunately, Celia is still very much alive."

"Fortunately is the right word, Dad," said Andre. "There have been two attempts on her life that she was lucky to survive."

Sidney looked thunderstruck. Act III, Scene IV, Macbeth is confronted by Banquo's ghost. That's the trouble with dealing with actors; they have reactions to suit all occasions.

"Good heavens! Nobody told me. Is she all right?"

"Not really. She's on crutches, in a brace, and under doctor's care," I said.

Sidney looked at me as if realizing for the first time that I was there.

"How did you know that, Emma? In fact, what are you doing here? What part do you play in all this?"

I looked over at Juliet, who shook her head imperceptibly. The myth must continue.

"I happened to be visiting Alicia a short time before she died, and Celia shortly after her first mishap. I was interviewing them for a book I'm writing on expatriate divorced women. Let's say I'm an involved observer who is helping the police with their inquiries—much as you are, Sidney. It may seem strangely coincidental that I met them both, but certainly no more so than you having been married to them both."

"It seems to me to be more of a conspiracy rather than a coincidence," said Inspector Ludvik.

He hadn't uttered a word until now. We all turned to look at him in surprise and he smiled shyly. "I hope my English is correct."

"Indeed it is, Inspector," said Caleb.

I got up and looked at Juliet. "Upstairs and to the right?"

She nodded and I headed for the loo. I walked into Juliet's bedroom and went right over to the dresser. The garnet-topped hat pin was still in the pincushion. I slipped it into a plastic bag I had brought with me and put it carefully into my pocket. Then I walked into Juliet's sitting room and rummaged through the top drawer of her magnificent French desk until I found the envelope I sought. I looked through it, extracted the pieces of paper I needed, which I also slipped into my pocket, and returned the envelope to the drawer.

When I came back down to the drawing room, Sidney was in a flushed fury.

"I know what 'cui bono' means, Superintendent—who benefits. You're assuming that because I will be the beneficiary of the fund when both women die, I killed Alicia and attempted to kill Celia."

There was a cry from Juliet, and she had her hand to her mouth. Sidney ran over to her at once. "Now don't worry, darling. This is all utter nonsense." Then he turned to

Caleb. "Why would I do such things? I don't need the money. Sure, I'm short a few thousand quid here and there from time to time, but that's the nature of my business. Right now, I'm in fine financial fettle. In fact, better than fine. Yesterday my corporation sold our Canary Walk property that we bought less than a month ago at a price that was one million pounds more than we paid for it."

There was an audible gasp. We all looked around. Juliet was white.

"What is it, darling?" Sidney said with deep concern.

"But I thought you were in terrible financial trouble," she said softly.

He looked puzzled. "Why ever would you think that?"

"Why? Because that's what you always tell me."

Andre sighed. "You know, Dad, you always moan and groan about how terrible business is. When I was a child, I used to ask Mum all the time if we were rich or poor this week. As long as I remember, it seems to me you've complained about being on the verge of pauperism."

Sidney shrugged and laughed. "Oh, that's just my way. It's how I was brought up. If you spoke of your success, you might get a *kineahora*, which in Yiddish means the evil eye. If you spoke only of difficulties and poverty, the wicked evil eye would pass you by. Also, I sort of got in the habit of talking poor with my first wife, who was a dreadful spendthrift. If she ever knew how much money I really had, she'd be out there buying out four floors of Harrod's."

Juliet looked stunned. "So you were really never going bankrupt? You mean it was just talk?"

"Yes, love—I'm sorry if I frightened you. I won't do it again, I promise."

I looked at Juliet. Too late, Sidney. The damage is done.

"And that, Juliet, is why you killed Alicia and tried to kill Celia, isn't it?" I said.

Sidney stood stock-still with a look of shocked incredulity, and Andre jumped up to his side.

"What the hell are you talking about?" said Sidney.

I pulled the bag with the hat pin out of my pocket. When she saw it, Juliet shrunk back into the couch. Sidney looked from her to the pin.

"What is she talking about, Juliet? What's that hat pin got to do with anything?"

"I'll bet tests will show this pin has Alicia's blood and brains on it." I handed it to Caleb.

"You got there right after Grace and I left, didn't you? She left the front door open because she was so upset after the terrible fight with her mother. You probably walked right in. Why did you come—to ask Alicia to relinquish her share in the trust for Sidney's sake? How long did it take for you to realize what a mistake that was? You reckoned without her self-centered psyche. She probably laughed in your face and told you to bug off.

"And that," I said softly, "is when you took the new pin you had just bought from your hat and stabbed her in the back of the neck and she fell, smashing her head against the fireplace fender."

Everyone stared at the long pin with fascination and horror. It was no longer an ornament, it was a weapon. Sidney leaped forward and Andre moved forward quickly to restrain him.

"What are you saying?" he said. He stood in front of his wife, who was curled up in a ball on the couch. His face reflected disbelief.

"Juliet, is this true?"

She sat up straight and turned on me with a look of vicious hatred. "How could you do this, Emma? You were such a wonderful, supportive friend. How could you become a Judas?"

I felt as though my heart were breaking and my soul had left my body. I truly despised what I was doing. I had just gone through tremendous efforts to bring a family back together. It had given me great pleasure to have been able to bring to them a level of happiness they had never before enjoyed. Now I was tearing the whole thing apart. And it was tearing me apart.

Caleb looked at me and I saw the empathy in his eyes.

"Mrs. Bailey, Ms. Rhodes had no choice. She did what is the responsibility of any honorable person. If we could not depend upon the cooperation of our citizens, our efforts to fight crime would be severely handicapped."

"Juliet," said Sidney pleadingly, "did you kill Alicia?" Gone was the dramatic sonorous diction. Gone was the poised performer. What we had before us now was a simple, terribly anguished man.

"She was a horrible woman," said Juliet. "After all those years of you supporting her, giving her all that money—she lived like a queen—she wouldn't do a thing to help you. So I had to."

She turned to us and began to speak in a calm rational tone that is sadly familiar to me. It's the voice of reason I have heard from many murderers who want to convey the righteousness of their actions in which they deeply and sincerely believe.

"She was hateful. She said she didn't give a tinker's damn if Sidney went flat broke. He had given her the trust fund because she deserved it and as far as she was concerned, that was that. She had the supreme gall to say he set it up for her because he still loved her and I was just a pathetic piece of goods he took up with because I'm the daughter of a duke. Imagine the nerve of that cheap-looking tart."

Then she turned to her husband and seemed totally unaware of the agonized look on his face.

"Sidney, I'll never understand how you could have ever married such a dreadful woman. Then she laughed at me, told me to bugger off, and just got up and started to leave the room as though I were a servant. I was furious, I can tell you. I had taken my hat off when I came in, of course, and had started to put it back on; the new hat pin was in my hand. Then I suddenly realized if she died, and the other wife died, I wouldn't have to demean myself pleading with these wretched women, and all that money would be Sidney's again and everything would be all right.''

Juliet was so intent on her recital that she was totally unaware of the effect her words were having on her husband and stepson.

''So when she rudely turned her back on me, I saw that vulnerable point in the middle of her ugly neck, and plunged the pin in. You see, having worked in the neurosurgeon's operating theater, I knew that a long needle thrust upward into a specific spot in the middle of the neck will reach the cerebellum and cause instant death.''

I'll be damned if she didn't look around proudly expecting commendation for her knowledge and skill.

The room went totally silent for a moment as everyone looked at Juliet with looks ranging from horror to sorrow. Sidney jumped up suddenly and went to her side.

''Don't say another word, Juliet,'' he said. ''We'll get a lawyer. They can't use the hat pin in evidence, the police had no right to come into my home and take it without a warrant.''

''The police didn't, Sidney,'' I said calmly. ''I did. As well as these receipts from the restaurant in which she had lunch in Prague and bus ticket receipts and the airline flight receipt all dated the day of Alicia's murder.''

''How dare you come in here and take my wife's personal possessions? I'll have you arrested for thievery!''

Caleb took out a piece of paper from his pocket. ''No need. I have a warrant to search the premises. So you can just give those things to me, Emma. Thank you for saving us the time to search for them.''

In response to the quizzical look I noted on Caleb's face, I explained how I knew where to look and what to look for.

''Knowing Juliet's reputation for frugality, I was sure she'd save all her receipts. Such people always do.''

Caleb turned to Sidney, who was glaring at me.

"Actually, Mr. Bailey, you should be very grateful to Ms. Rhodes for having forestalled having your home taken apart by my men. They're very thorough, you see. They do try to put everything back as they found it, but I know it's a terrible violation of privacy to have someone pawing through your personal possessions."

"We also have an eyewitness," said Inspector Ludvik.

"Alena, the maid, saw you leave, Juliet," I said. "She thought it was the new seamstress—but I showed her your picture and she identified you immediately," I said. "That hat."

Sidney was distraught. "Those hats—those foolish hats," he kept repeating. "I always thought they were an adorable affectation. Now look what they've done."

Then he jumped up and looked at Inspector Ludvik.

"You have no jurisdiction here, Inspector." And then he turned to Caleb. "And you have no jurisdiction there, Superintendent. The murder occurred in Prague. So what is this all about? You can't take Juliet," he said triumphantly.

"I have an International Provisional Arrest Warrant from the Ministry of Justice in Prague which was obtained through Interpol," said Inspector Ludvik.

"The Ministry of Justice here in England is aware of the warrant," said Caleb, "and will evaluate the evidence for extradition."

I was waiting for the eruption from Andre when the full impact of Juliet's actions sank in, when he realized this wasn't just another family fracas that he could tune out.

"Juliet—you tried to kill my mother!"

"But, Andre, I had to, didn't I?" she said. "What would have been the good of getting rid of one wife if the trust remained intact for the second wife? Don't you see?"

Incredible. I never fail to be amazed at the twisted reasoning of people who commit grievous crimes. Once you start with the premise that your cause is absolutely just, then any deed performed in its name is acceptable, and you create your own moral code. It's the philosophy of Islamic terrorists, the IRA, the American militant right-wing groups—fanatics everywhere.

"I spoke to the hostler who takes care of Celia's horse," I said. "He remembered a woman who came around asking about buying a horse. She told him she had been recommended by Frau Ramsay and she was interested in seeing her horse. He said she was very knowledgeable about horses, so he felt perfectly free to leave her alone to wander about the stables. He mentioned she spoke German fairly well—and she wore this funny hat. Then I showed him the picture and he positively identified it."

Sidney had his head in his hands. Andre looked like he wanted to comfort him, but was torn with mixed emotions.

"And that hole through the back of Mum's hood," said Andre.

I held up two more airline ticket receipts.

"Juliet made trips to Austria on the two dates of your mother's assaults. So we know she was there. The stairs were crowded, but I imagine if we asked the newspapers to print Juliet's photo, someone would come forward who saw her there. She's fairly distinctive, you know."

Sidney groaned. "Those infernal hats again. I should have burned them long ago." And then a gleam came into his eye.

"Don't even think it, Mr. Bailey," said Caleb sternly. "We'll be taking Mrs. Bailey's hat collection with us today as evidence."

Sidney turned to Juliet and cried out, "But why, darling—why?"

"I thought you were in desperate need of money," she said. "It sounded like everything was crumbling about you. I was so frightened for you. I just couldn't sit back and watch that happen. I know how important your wealth and financial empire are to you, my darling," and she reached out to take his hand.

And to you, too, honey. It wasn't Sidney you were saving—it was you. The fear of being poor again had to be the major impetus for your activities. But I'm sure as hell not going to mention this to Sidney and undermine his hard-won new belief in his lovability. The anguish about Juliet would be somewhat mitigated by the fact that he'd view her actions as proof of her intense devotion to him. And at this moment, the poor guy needed all the emotional help he could get.

Sidney took his wife in his arms. "My poor darling. I'm so sorry. It's just my way. Some people complain about the weather, I complain about cash flow. But it meant nothing. My God, it was just talk."

"Words can be as lethal as bullets, Sidney. Irresponsible talk can affect impressionable people in dangerous ways," I said.

"My darling, my darling," he said, putting his arms around her. "It's all my fault. Don't worry—I won't let them hurt you. We'll get the best Q.C. in England."

"Dad," said Andre in a white fury. "She tried twice to kill my mother."

"But, Son," said Sidney, "she did it for me!"

XVI

SOME WOMEN GO out and buy furs and jewelry when they've gone through an emotional blockbuster. Me, I eat. I went to the Hyde Park Hotel to have a full English breakfast late the next morning. I ate a full bowl of porridge, scrambled eggs with bacon, grilled tomatoes and mushrooms, and drank two cups of coffee. Fortunately I don't go through these upheavals too often or I'd resemble the Fuji blimp. What I desperately needed besides comfort food was the luxury of being pampered and served. Yesterday had been, to put it delicately, a real pisser.

When I returned to my flat, as I put the key in the door, I heard the full sounds of Beethoven's Ninth. I smiled and hurried in.

"Abba!" I threw my arms around the 250 pounds of hair, muscle, fat, brains, and heart who was stretched out on the couch. "You came, you darling man. God, am I glad to see you!"

He hugged me and smiled broadly. "How could I refuse? When the *shtarker* of the year, the strong independent Emma Rhodes who can handle everything and never needs anybody, calls to ask me to please come, I classify that as a serious S.O.S."

He looked at me sharply. "So what gives, *bubeleh*? You look as succulent and gorgeous as ever, but my keen trained eye detects a note of sadness. What happened? Did they revoke your American Express card?"

"Would you like some coffee or a drink?" I asked.

"It's that bad, eh?" he asked. "No, thanks, nothing now. Talk first—we'll get to the social stuff later."

I plopped down on the couch next to him. "It's my latest case. I'm sure I did the right thing—so why do I feel like such a shit?"

Abba Levitar is to me what my father always calls a "foxhole buddy." I would trust my life to Abba because I know he would act courageously, honorably, and with total consideration for my welfare before his own. Also, we share the same sense of right and wrong, and I know that from him I will always get absolute truth. Which is why I phoned him yesterday asking him to come. I knew that his job demanded that he live on the edge with a totally unpredictable timetable, but I took the chance that he might be able to get away for a day or so. I got lucky.

He listened intently as I told him the entire story.

"So you feel like the person who saved a man's life and then found he had escaped from prison where he was about to be executed and you were loath to turn him in. It wasn't the right and wrong of it, just your own ego."

I looked a bit puzzled.

"Look, you're proud of the great job you did in converting a dysfunctional family into Ozzie and Harriet. Makes you feel a little like God. And then you find you yourself have to cock it all up. It hurts to have to undo all that good work, but there's no choice."

"I know—it's my civic duty to report a crime."

He tossed his head disdainfully. "*Shtuyot*—bullshit! That's the kind of fucking righteous talk your Scotland Yard lover boy might spout. Listen, *motek*, my darling,

there are bad people in this world to whom bad things
should happen and there are good people whose misdeeds
should not always be punished. The law does not always
produce justice. There are times when wise people have to
intercede.''

''Abba, that's vigilantism, which carried to its inevitable
end leads to anarchy. And if you believe in your personal
code method of handling lawbreakers, why did I have no
choice in reporting Juliet to the authorities?''

''Because she didn't just murder one miserable bitch, a
little bagatelle that might have been overlooked. Tell me
honestly, would you have felt compelled to turn her in if
that were it?''

I thought for a moment. ''I might have hesitated.''

''Why, Ms. Law-and-Order?'' he asked.

''Because Alicia was an evil woman who was feeding
off people and destroying her daughter, and the world was
better off without her.''

''So suddenly when it involves real people and not just
theory, your fuckin' sense of civic duty takes a backseat to
your sense of right and wrong. That's exactly how we work
in my business.''

''Now you've really got me confused, Abba. Then why
did you say I had no choice but to turn Juliet in?''

''Because she may be educated, elegant, and of noble
blood, but to me she's just a twisted, self-involved *chatichah charah*, a piece of shit, who is a threat to society. She
didn't kill out of anger, or self-defense, or justice—she did
it strictly for venal reasons . . . money. And she tried to kill
another woman for the same reason. Once she got the taste
of blood and learned how easy it was to get rid of her
problems, who's next? When her husband gets a few years
older and starts to pee in his pants and fart when he walks,
she's liable to decide it's time to abridge his golden years.''

My spirits began to lift. ''So I should feel no guilt or
remorse for turning her in?''

''Absolutely not,'' he said firmly.

Then I got sad again.

"Now what?" he asked.

"In a sense I'm responsible for the death of Alicia and the two attempts on Celia's life."

"How do you figure that one out? Don't turn martyr on me—soon you'll be blaming yourself for the fall of Saigon."

"If it were not for that chance meeting with me on the train, Juliet would have gone through with the divorce, contented to come out of it with her own little trust fund, not to mention that not too shabby homestead on Allen Street. I gave her the idea about the fund reverting to Sidney upon the death of the two former wives. She had to figure that getting rid of them would work well for her no matter which way her marriage went. If the divorce went through, there would be more money for the generous Mr. Bailey to award her. And if I succeeded in getting them back together, she would remain the one and only very wealthy Mrs. Sidney Bailey and live happily ever after."

Abba shook his head. "Don't flatter yourself, *hamoodie*. She's a sick broad. With some people it's sex, with her it's money. It's just a matter of time before she'd start eating herself with wanting more. Remember, all that gorgeous cash comes from one source—Sidney—and the thinner he has to spread his largess, the less she gets. You can bet that at some point, she'd figure the trust was cutting into her income and she'd pop those ladies or, as I just said, maybe Mr. Big Bucks himself."

"Or Andre and Alexandra."

"Right. Now do you feel better and can we have coffee?"

I got up and went into the kitchen. He followed me. "By the way, I hope you got paid," he said as he opened the fridge looking for goodies.

"Of course," I said as I ground the coffee beans.

"When?" he asked.

"Just before I discovered the telltale hat pin in her bedroom."

"When did you turn her in?"

"Two days later."

"Was that wise?" he asked. "Couldn't she have stopped the check?"

"No," I said as I poured the water into the coffeemaker.

"How come?"

"Because I went to her bank and had the check certified ten minutes after leaving her house. After seeing that hat pin, I had a sneaking suspicion that she might not be too happy with me in the near future."

He roared with laughter and I joined in. We were laughing so hard I almost didn't hear the doorbell. It was Caleb and Inspector Ludvik.

"What on earth is so funny?" Caleb asked.

"I regained my full faith in Ms. Rhodes, my precious P.P.R.—Pragmatic Private Resolver. For a minute back there I thought I might be losing her to the Salvation Army."

Caleb looked slightly bewildered.

"Don't bother trying to figure him out, Caleb. It loses something in the translation," I said happily. Then I introduced Inspector Ludvik and Abba. As always, the inspector's eyes widened with a bit of awe and respect when he heard that Abba was in the Mossad.

"So what's the latest skinny on the actor and the baronet's daughter?" asked Abba.

Both Caleb and Inspector Ludvik stared at him. "Skinny?"

I explained the American slang word for "news," and they both were delighted the way people always feel when they feel they have picked up a new "in" word.

"Why don't you gentlemen go out on the terrace? It's a gorgeous day and I'm taking drink orders because no one is on duty as of this minute."

Caleb looked at his watch. "It's not quite noon, Emma. Isn't it a wee bit early for cocktails?"

"You mean there's a correct time for drinking in this country?" said Abba in mock dismay. "Me, I drink by the need, not by the clock. And methinks our friend Emma here could stand a few belts. Besides, if I talk long enough, it'll be lunchtime and, Superintendent, even you must often have a tipple or two with your bangers."

I went into the kitchen to prepare drinks and peered into my freezer for hors d'oeuvres. Lucky guys—I found the foil-wrapped gravlax I had made last month. All it required was a quick zap in the microwave, plus the mustard dill sauce and pumpernickel, also in the freezer. This is one of the haute cuisine delicacies that makes everyone look at you like you're Andre Soltner and is actually not only easy to make, but extremely satisfying because it has to be ministered to in some very gratifying procedures that go to the Mother Earth in me. Don't feel shocked and betrayed; one can be a feminist and still enjoy being a nurturer, you know. Since the pressure is off and my guests are enjoying the sunshine, I have a minute to give you the recipe.

Basically, it's lox (as in lox and bagels) Scandinavian style. Don't be put off by the fact that the dish takes three days to complete. Actual work time falls within my one-hour prep time stipulation for Emma Rhodes' recipes.

Ingredients are two salmon filets, about 1-1/2 pounds each, one bunch fresh dill, 1/4 cup kosher salt, 1/4 cup sugar, 2 tablespoons crushed peppercorns. Place one filet skin-side down in a deep glass, enamel, or stainless steel baking dish or loaf pan. Spread all the dill (except for a handful) over filet. Combine sugar, salt, and crushed peppercorns (I put them in a dish towel and hammer them). Sprinkle mix over dill, and place other salmon filet (skin-side up) on top. In effect, you've made a dill sandwich. Cover with plastic wrap and aluminum foil. Then cover with weights like cans of food or a brick. Refrigerate for three days. But every twelve hours, turn the fish and *baste it* (that's the fun part) with the juices that have accumulated. Baste between the filets, too. I don't know about you, but I find there's something very satisfying about basting. After two and a half or three days, you're done. Scrape off the dill mixture. Slice each half, skin-side down, on the bias *very thin*. Serve on black bread with mustard sauce: whisk together 3-1/2 tablespoons Dijon mustard, 1 teaspoon powdered mustard, 3 tablespoons of honey, 1-1/2 tablespoons white vinegar, 1/3 cup vegetable oil, 3 tablespoons fresh dill. Decorate your serving platter with fresh dill (but I probably didn't have to tell you that).

When I set down the tray, they all attacked the gravlax.

"Mmm, this is delicious. Marks and Spencer or Fortnum and Mason?" Caleb asked.

"Emma and Rhodes," I answered.

The three stared at me incredulously.

"*You* made it?"

Abba put his arm around me. "Emma, you break my heart. If only you weren't a shiksa—I'd ask you to marry me in a shot. A woman who's smart, fuckin' gorgeous, makes enough money so I can quit work, and can cook yet. What a tragic loss!"

I looked over at the inspector, who looked slightly embarrassed. Abba causes that kind of reaction from people who don't know him and don't understand his need to let off steam with foul language. Time to change the subject.

"Why don't we talk over the details of the case that we're all here for before the inspector has to catch his plane back to Prague? Caleb, how do you think the Ministry of Justice will rule on Juliet's extradition?" I asked.

"It's too soon to tell. Sidney Bailey has some powerful friends. And even more important, she's the daughter of a duke, albeit a minor one; he's still of the nobility, which will probably bring the Home Office into it. They're not going to jump readily into turning her over to the Czech courts."

"Even though it was another British citizen she murdered, not some unimportant foreigner?'' asked Inspector Ludvik with a bit of irony in his voice.

"Sadly, your point is well taken, given the chauvinistic bias often shown by some judges," said Caleb.

"What about the fact that she twice attempted to murder another British citizen?" I asked.

"If we can get that into the record, we may have a good chance," said Caleb. "Actually, I believe eventually she will be sent to your country to stand trial, Inspector. The Royal Family has fallen from grace to such a degree these days that being an aristocrat may backfire. The people are getting pretty fed up with special treatment of the increasingly perceived as undeserving nobility."

"Maybe it's time to bring back the guillotine," said Abba. "I'll form the first chapter of the Madame DeFarge Knitting Club."

"That's another of the things that endear you to me, Abba," I said. "Your solutions are so direct and absolute."

"Now I have a question or two for you, Emma," began Caleb. "How did you come up with this idea about the hat pin being the murder weapon?"

"Well, I knew that garnet pin was a one-of-a-kind antique, which meant the purchaser had to be in Prague soon after me to have bought it. For a time, I thought it might be Sidney. But then I saw Juliet's receipts showing she had been to Prague on the same day. I remembered a similar murder being described to me by a doctor at Mark's party. And I also remembered Juliet had sufficient medical knowledge and know-how to commit such a murder. So I called Prague to have the medical examiner look for a pinhole at the back of the neck."

"Fortunately we had not yet released the body for burial," said the inspector, "because the *Patalog* was not satisfied with the cause of death. She said it could have been caused by the head injury, but there were other conditions that puzzled her, like the fact that the body exhibited signs of suffocation."

"As Juliet so clearly explained," I continued, "when the needle hits the cerebellum, which is the respiratory center for the body, the victim stops breathing immediately and in effect suffocates."

"Of course," said Abba. In his job, there was no kind of swift and almost undetectable means of killing with which he wasn't familiar.

Caleb looked at his watch. "Inspector, I think it's time for me to take you to the airport."

"Please, Superintendent, it is not necessary for you to drive me yourself."

"You are my guest in this country and I am the one who must see that you get off comfortably and safely," said Caleb firmly with a smile.

The inspector looked extremely pleased, and we wished him a safe journey.

After they left, Abba said, "What a man, that Franklin. One of nature's noblemen. He's got the innate kindness of a really good guy and the sharp instincts of a politician, a winning combination. He could have sent Ludvik off in a police car, but how much shrewder to flatter him with the personal attention of a high ranking officer. Who ever knows when Franklin will need an important friend in the Czech Republic? I tell you, the guy's going far."

Then he turned to look at me with one of those piercing Abba looks. "So how far has he gone with you?"

"No home runs," I said. "I like him very much, but that's all."

"But the ball game isn't over yet," said Abba.

The phone rang. It was Jan Malecek calling to tell me that Alicia Sykes' will had been probated and my check was in the mail.

"How is Grace?" I asked.

"She's right here," he said, "and wants to talk to you."

"Emma! Thank you so much—I'm so happy."

If I hadn't known it was Grace Lechwandowski, I would

not have recognized her. The voice, the tone, the cadence
was filled with élan and spirit.

"It's as though a tremendous load was lifted from my
soul," she said.

The fear of being indicted for your mother's death or the
relief of being freed from her pervasive persecution? I'd
guess a bit of both.

"What are your plans now, Grace? Are you staying in
that big house?"

"Oh, yes, but I've made it into a student residence. I've
rented rooms to Keith and three other people from my
school. It helps pay the upkeep and makes the place so
much jollier."

"And what of Leif? I assume he's one of your tenants."

"Oh, no, he lives in my rooms," she said, and I could
hear her smile through the wires.

We said our good-byes and then Abba asked to speak to
Jan. They chatted in Hebrew, and I walked out to the terrace and sat down on one of the chaise lounges to enjoy
the lovely day and my sense of inner peace.

"Well, you certainly effected a *mitzvah* there," said
Abba as he plopped down on an adjacent chaise. "That's
one happy young woman."

"The aspect of my strange profession that I love best,
Abba, is that I get to actually do some good in this world.
I know that sounds a bit ingenuous, but what I hated about
being a corporate lawyer was that your total concern is
money and greed. Look, I know I'm not Jonas Salk or
Mother Teresa, but in my small way I help people, and I'm
fortunate enough to enjoy seeing the immediate results of
my labors. That's why I was so upset about Juliet. Here I
completed my mission and then I have to be the whistle-
blower who destroys everything I achieved for her."

"What sage was it who said no good deed goes unpun-
ished?" said Abba, as he sat back and sipped his Scotch.

I looked to my left at the beautiful eighteenth-century
clock steeple on St. Andrew's Church that stood out against

the cloudless blue sky and to my right at my wonderful friend Abba, and I felt fortunate. I sighed deeply.

"Was that an '*oy veh*' sigh or a sigh of joy and contentment?" he asked.

"Strictly the latter, my good friend. I did good, Abba, didn't I?"

He nodded. "In the broad picture, I'd say so. You gave a future to that good woman and took it away from a bad one. That's a pretty fair score."

I looked at him fondly. "What would I do without you, Abba?"

He leaned over to give me a friendly kiss. "Oh, you'd manage to live." Then he smiled impishly. "But, of course, you wouldn't enjoy it."

The phone rang again. I picked up the cordless instrument. "Hello, Mark." Abba's eyebrows went up.

"Dinner tonight?" I looked at Abba. "Hold it a minute, Mark, let me check."

Abba shook his head. "Don't worry about me, *tstoskele*, I've got a date. I won't be home until tomorrow morning, I expect."

"Fine, Mark. Seven will be fine."

I looked at Abba. "You've been here less than three hours, and already you have a date?"

He smiled. "Her name is Brigette. We met on the plane coming over here."

I groaned. "Another one of your six-foot Scandinavian Amazons?"

He looked smug. "What can I tell you? These luscious statuesque blondes are turned on by short hairy Jewish men. I think they believe there's a correlation between the size of the man's schlong and the density of his body hair."

He went inside to refill his drink and get more pumpernickel, which he loaded with gravlax when he returned.

"So you're back to seeing his lordship, *hamoodie*, my love. You still have feelings for him? He obviously still has the hots for you."

I told him about my lunch with Lady Catherine and her ambitions for her son and me.

"Hmm, that's very interesting. But you said these are Mama's ambitions. What about sonny boy?"

"I haven't spoken about it to him yet. Maybe this evening."

He looked very thoughtful. "You know, *ahuvati*, this merits serious consideration. Being married to a rich duke, that's nice. But being the wife of a powerful politician can be highly significant. You said you enjoy helping people, even though it's limited to one-on-one stuff. Think of what someone with your talents could achieve for the good of the country and perhaps the world if you were in a position of power."

"First place, Abba, I don't know how good a politician he is. He may just end up a back bencher with no power at all."

"So you'll just have to spend your days living in a castle with homes in Cannes and London and having to take out the family jewels to wear to royal receptions. *Nebbish*, poor thing."

"Secondly, he's Conservative, not Labour. How can I marry that?"

Abba snorted. "Labour, schmabor it's all the same shit. They're just labels. Look at history—and the big surprises from people we thought were paralyzed by political affiliations. Nixon opened China. A southern-born president, Johnson, created the Great Society that improved life for black people. Just get the power, no matter how, and then do your stuff for mankind."

THAT EVENING AT seven, when I opened the door, I looked at Mark with new eyes.

Of course, he looked me over with the same old eyes.

"Emma, darling—you look fantastic."

I had dressed for the occasion in a Dana Buchman shaped, pale blue, sueded silk jacket with a very short, silk chiffon skirt in a black print with pale blue morning glories. My favorite black pearl necklace nested demurely in the décolletage.

We had dinner at Ménage à Trois on Beauchamp Place, the old hangout for Sloan Rangers, the upper-class airhead group whose most prominent member had been Princess Di. As Mark talked, I found myself looking and listening for signs of the kind of powerful character that moves men and drives events. Probably a dumb thing to do. Did I expect him to dash off the equivalent of the Gettysburg Address on a napkin? Should he exhibit the kind of charisma that would have people fawning over us? True, we were given a superbly attentive welcome by the maître d', but I attributed that to his title rather than his personality. It certainly didn't come from heavy tipping, because I've noticed that the peerage is notoriously prone to keeping their hands in their pockets. They don't have to, darling. It's only the rest of us peasants who have to bribe our way into favored seating.

We got onto the subject of politics and I told him about my lunch with his mother. He twirled the stem of his wineglass and looked down as I mentioned her political plans for him. I didn't tell him how she fitted me into the picture.

"Actually, she is the one in the family with political drive and interests. When she was young, she and her friend Pamela Digby used to talk and dream politics. Unfortunately, Pamela made it and Mother did not. Pamela married Winston Churchill's son and went on from there to end up the American ambassador to France. And poor Mum seethed with envy, though she never mentions it. I think she believes I can propel her into the political limelight."

"Is being the mother of a prime minister equivalent to an ambassadorship?" I asked with a smile.

"Perhaps so in her mind."

"Those are her ambitions," I said. "Are they yours?"

He didn't answer for a moment. "I'm not sure. They have asked me to run for a specific seat where they seem to feel I would have a good chance of being elected. It does sound exciting, and certainly far more challenging than managing the family properties. But am I suited to the rough and tumble of politics? Dealing with rumbustious countrymen bred in beef and beer—I just don't know how much I would enjoy that, and how well I would do at it.''

Notice no mention of the great opportunity to help these countrymen, to improve the positions and lives of people who are less fortunate than he. Not that I'm some starry-eyed naif who expects pure altruism. I'm fully aware that most people in politics are drawn to it by the lust for power. That's O.K., it must be pretty heady stuff—as long as you have some ideals and ideas about how to use that power for the common good and not entirely your own. But this guy doesn't seem to have a clue about the purpose of power. He just seems to see the whole thing as a fun job. But he sure as hell is attractive. He still looks like a Ralph Lauren model but the real thing—not one of Mr. Lauren's Anglophiliac fantasies.

"Emma darling, I may not be sure about how I feel about politics, but I do know how I feel about you. I love you. And more than anything, I want you to be my wife—to spend my life with you.''

That's what scares the hell out of me. I don't know how I'll feel about you next month, fella, let alone twenty years down the road. I sat silent.

"I know you're not ready for such a commitment—that I've been a perfect idiot about many things. But I promise you, I want to change—but I need your help to do so.''

He looked into my eyes with such intensity that I couldn't look away. I have such mixed feelings—I think I do love him, I'm wildly attracted to him, more than to any other man I've ever met. But there are so many things about him that bother me. But that goes for all men, and is total perfection a reasonable reality?

He reached into his pocket and drew out a small box and

handed it across the table to me. "Please open it," he asked.

It was an exquisite antique ring with a ruby center surrounded by diamonds in platinum filigree.

"It belonged to my great-great-grandmother, and is mine. Please, I want you to have it. It would give me the greatest pleasure to see you wear it."

"But I can't take this, Mark. I don't know if I want to marry you—though I admit I do have strong feelings for you."

His face lit up. "You mean there's a chance?"

I smiled. "There's always a chance."

"Then why won't you take the ring?"

"Because I can't feel tied by any strings when I'm making up my mind."

He reached out to hold my hand. "Then will you take it if it involves no strings?"

I looked down at the ring, and then at him. "No strings—absolutely?"

"No strings—positively," he said firmly.

I slipped the ring on and he rose, came around to my side of the table, lifted me from my chair and kissed me. When I came up for breath I gasped the words:

"Remember—no strings."

GLOSSARY

As I'm sure you've noticed, Abba cannot control his trilingual tendencies (English, Hebrew and Yiddish) but he usually accompanies foreign words with English hints of their meaning. After a while, you usually get the drift by his usage. However, why struggle? Here are translations.

Hebrew

Ahuvati - sweetheart
Ahuva - love
Charah - shit
Chatichah Charah - piece of shit
Hamoodie - my love
Motek - my darling
Shtuyot - bullshit

Yiddish

Bubeleh - a term of endearment
Gonif - thief
Mitzvah - good deed
Nebbish - wimp
Oy vey - alas!
Shidach - an arranged match between two people
Shiksa - gentile girl
Shlemileon - play on words schlemiel (fool) and chameleon (a lizard that can change its color)

Shmatte - a rag
Shtarker - a strong person
Shtupping - fucking
Tstotskele - a term of endearment